THE LAST HOUR

What would you tell someone
who was about to die?

by Andy Lovenduski

CONTENTS

PREFACE

Tyrone Frazier, or Ty as his friends would call him, sat alone at his dining room table. The giant oak table was a bit too big for his modest-sized home, but it had been in his family for generations, so there was no way he could get rid of it. The intricate wood carvings lined the edges and curled themselves around the memories that echoed the untold hours of family conversations this piece of furniture had heard. Quietly, he stared at the familiar marks along the edge near the head of the table. His fingers traced the grooves he put in the wood when he was just a kid. He did it on a dare from his older brother, and they both got a good beating from their father for it too.

Now he was seated at the very same table. Forty-nine years old with two kids of his own. As if on cue, the gentle roar of his two sons came tumbling down the stairs like two boulders bouncing down a mountainside, crushing everything in their path. He just smiled at the sight of his boys quickly becoming young men. The older one, Alex, was looking more and more like his mother, while Jackson was Ty's spitting image. "OK, bring it down a notch, will ya, boys?" Tyrone said as he smiled, remembering the days when he would wrestle with them. Now at the ages of thirteen and sixteen, they had grown up to be taller and stronger than he ever remembered being when he was that age.

He had always been the kind of dad that most boys would have loved to have while growing up. Tyrone didn't have much of a father figure in his life, so he vowed to give his boys everything he never had. He took the boys camping, hunting, fishing, and to countless sporting events. All that was until his diabetes set in a few years ago. Now, he struggled to get around at all, let alone wrestle with them.

"Tyrone Fitzgerald Frazier! Why do you look like someone just kicked your dog?" Janice asked as she entered the room, holding a small cake covered in burning candles.

"You better straighten up, or I'm not going to let you have any of your own birthday cake."

Ty broke out of his thought when he saw his wife's face. After all these years, she still took his breath away. He loved her from the first time he set eyes on her. This woman was indeed his joy and his whole world.

"Yes dear," he sighed with an even bigger grin on his face. The boys pushed and shoved one another as they took their seats on each side of the table.

"Doesn't that cake look great, boys?" he asked in mouth-watering anticipation.

"Yeah, Dad, but remember your sugar levels," Jackson advised with the caring tone of a drill sergeant.

"Jacks, you be nice!" his mother scolded. "He can have a little. It is not every day that your father turns 50." She set the cake down in front of him and lit the candles, one for every decade. The candles' soft glow reflected off the tiny beads of sweat forming on his brow. As bright as the candles were that lit his round face, the pride he had for his family illuminated his face even more.

"Happy Birthday to you ..." his family began to sing in a unified chorus of mismatched voices.

The song faded in Tyrone's ears like someone turning down the volume on a stereo. His eyes went from person to person as he looked around the table. When he got to his wife, he noticed something that startled him. A strange man was now seated at the far end of the long wooden table. Ty didn't recognize the guy, and where in the world did he come from in the first place. The man was too old to be one of the boys' friends. The figure was dressed all in black and wearing a leather jacket. His face had a strangely relaxed, casual look to it, while his glacial blue eyes stared back at Tyrone with such ferocity that it left him stunned. Glancing back at his wife and sons, he wondered why no one was doing anything about this stranger in their house.

It was then that Tyrone felt the first tingle of pain down his arm. Then a tightness pressed against his chest as if an iron fist had just clenched around his lungs. Try as he wanted, Tyrone couldn't make his mouth move. He silently shouted into the wall of echoed birthday wishes as the pain forced its way down his arm. His eyes returned to the man at the end of the table. The stranger's blank stare melted Tyrone's resolve.

"Happy Birthday, dear daddy ..." the song came back to Tyrone's ears, but he could still do nothing to stop them. He desperately tried to do anything to get their attention. His breathing came in short gulps as his hand reached to loosen the top button on his polo shirt. The pain in his chest pressed harder against his ribcage. It was like an unseen hand was squeezing the breath out of his lungs.

Suddenly, the stranger in black stood up and leaned over the edge of the table. Despite the vast length of the wooden table, the man's cold, dead eyes grew closer and closer to Tyrone. The man's lips parted, and Tyrone heard a voice in his head as clear as a bell. "It is time," said the dry, monotone voice.

As he fell back into the chair, the last thing Tyrone saw was the look on his wife's face. The pain in her eyes reflected his own, radiating in crushing waves from his chest. Helpless, she watched as his hands waved aimlessly for anything he could use to stop himself from falling.

Flashes of light came to his eyes as memories washed over his mind. The blackness covered him like a comforting blanket that was being pulled over his head. For a few short seconds, he heard his family screaming at him to wake up. Then there was silence and then he was gone.

Sarah sat alone in the dark room, staring at the same spot on the floor as if she could somehow will it to help her. She could not even force her own mind to help her, what could she expect from anything else in this God forsaken world? Not showered in days, holding her knees against her chest, she was lost in her Darkness. A self-inflicted captive inside her own prison. As much as her apartment was washed with the blackness of night, it served as a metaphor for her life. Her apartment, once filled with sunshine just a short time ago, now mirrored the shadows of her mind. In a time before her dim memories started creeping in, light ruled her world. Then like tiny waves that slowly eroded a shoreline, the taunts of her Darkness slowly pulled away the mental walls she had erected to stop her demons from hurting her. As the memories turned from light to dark, she sat motionless while the night crept in and stole the brightness of the Sun. Even after hours and countless memories, only one singular tear fell from her cheek.

The two voices screamed inside her psyche. Fighting against each other as opposing soldiers on the battlefield. The victor would have the right to plant their flag and lay claim to her thoughts and mind. One side that would help her to heal and grow, while the other would desire to see her wallow in the never-ending darkness of her own sadness. But she knew that she didn't have the strength to pick a side. Sometimes it was just easier to give in, and not feel anything. She knew she needed help, but there was no one to help her. That thought itself was just another win for the Darkness. Her Darkness.

CHAPTER ONE

Present day.

Sarah's body jerked slightly as she awoke. She was more tired than she realized. Disoriented, she looked around to gather herself. Thankfully, she was still on the bus heading home. Straightening herself, she tried to close her eyes again to clear her mind. Sarah had been tired from a long shift at work, but she didn't think she could be so exhausted that she'd possibly fall asleep on the bus. She remembered getting on and pouring herself into a seat near the back. She preferred to stay away from the other passengers. It's not that she disliked people; she truly loved people. That's why she liked being a waitress. However, after a long day of serving food and making idle chitchat, she longed for some peace and quiet.

With shoulder-length brown hair that framed her face and hazel eyes reflecting a blend of determination and curiosity, she possessed a slender, semi-athletic build. However, her beauty wasn't just skin deep; it was a reflection of the strength and resilience that defined her character. Beyond her physical attributes, Sarah's beauty was complemented by a kind and compassionate soul. Her pretty face lit up with warmth when she interacted with others, and her hazel eyes revealed a depth of empathy that drew people towards her. Despite the challenges she faced, there was a resilience in her gaze that hinted at a history of overcoming obstacles.

If she had to admit it, it wasn't even the people that frustrated her. The more she thought about it, she just wanted to be alone, especially now. Her birthday was coming up soon, and not just any birthday – her thirtieth birthday. She had been trying to forget about it since she turned twenty-nine. Birthdays were not one of the days she genuinely enjoyed anymore. She'd almost forgotten how close it was until her boss stopped her as she left the café today. He wanted to know if she was going to take her birthday off next week. She actually hadn't even thought about it until he said something. She didn't even notice it was approaching, let alone it being her "*milestone birthday*," as he put it. The big 3-0. Since her parents died nearly five years ago, she never looked forward to celebrating anything in general, let alone birthdays. Turning thirty was going to be even worse. She knew that she would have to suffer through it one way or the other, but the thought of spending the day at work was probably more than she could bear.

Her hair was a mess from pulling it out of the ponytail she had it locked into all day. Straightening up in the bus seat took more effort than it should have after working all day. Sarah smiled for a moment. *Maybe she was getting old*, she thought ruefully to herself. Her body was still tone, and everything was where it should be. She wouldn't call herself petite, but she certainly felt like she could be in better shape. Along with her approachable personality, the way she looked scored well with some customers when it came to getting tips.

Over the last few years, she tried to force herself to have a positive attitude about things. But the happiness did not always come easy. She knew she had to stay optimistic. If she looked at it right, maybe turning thirty wouldn't be so bad, she tried unconvincingly to tell herself over and over again. Then she remembered a magazine article she read a while back: *thirty was the new twenty*. She nearly snorted as she laughed to herself. That article was full of crap. It was probably written by a woman that was closer to forty than thirty and trying to recapture her youth. Or maybe the author used the article so she could lie to herself about growing old. Sarah's mood became serious again when she thought about everything people do to lie to themselves.

Regardless, Sarah's birthday was fast approaching, and she certainly didn't feel much better about getting any older. The decade of her twenties held nothing but pain, bad memories, and heartache. Even though she should've been happy that those years were coming to a close, she wasn't ready to dash off into her thirties with any sort of hope or enthusiasm. Things really couldn't get any worse, but she also knew better than to challenge fate. As her father always told her, "As *bad as things might seem, they could always get a little worse*." She knew well enough from past experiences, never challenge the word, *worse*.

The bus lurched forward again after letting some people off. Tried as she might, she couldn't escape the thoughts of the past. When she was younger, Sarah Thompson dreamed of being married with kids by the time she was thirty. Taking everyone on big family vacations to the beach or skiing in the mountains. Holidays would be spent together with extended family. Her parents would dote and compliment her on how beautifully well-behaved her children were. Her husband would have a good job and spend time coaching their son's little league baseball team. He would buy her flowers for no reason.

Sadly, that life was not meant to be. What should have been the perfect life for Sarah was just a shadow of a dream. All of those desires would have been great if it wasn't for the fact that life isn't fair. Things could, and did, get worse. Life had a way of ruining those dreams. That's when her sorrow arrived. That was when she first met her Darkness. Shortly after the death of her parents, the doctors diagnosed her with major depressive disorder. The term, *Darkness,* was her way of rationalizing and trying to deal with it—her pet name for it.

Sitting on the bus, just thinking about her dreaded curse, brought the familiar shadow of doubt over her thoughts. The shades of apathy pushed against her like a tangible fog. She knew better than to care about anything. It would only lead to pain.

The bus hit a pothole that made everyone jolt in their seat. The bone-jarring hit from the hard vinyl bus bench broke Sarah from her self-induced negative coma. The bus moved along the same route it did every night. It was mid-October in the Valley of the Sun, and this brought one beautiful thing about Phoenix. The summer heatwave was in its final stages, and the weather was finally starting to break. Fall in Phoenix seemingly only lasted about two weeks, but it came as such a welcome relief to the masses. It usually went by so fast that most people missed it entirely. The locals embraced this simple rite of passage as an end to the summer oppression and the beginning of the longed-for entry into the best part of Phoenix's weather. Wintertime is one of the reasons why people enjoyed living there.

Sarah adjusted herself in her seat as the bus rumbled and pitched forward again. Her feet groaned, and her back ached as she tried to get comfortable, but the chair would only give so much. Her body needed to relax, but her mind needed to rest even more. Thoughts of what she would do when she got home gave her a good feeling. At least there, she could finally unwind. A bath and a glass of wine would give her the proper self-indulgent mental vacation she needed. *Calgon, take me away!*, as her mom would say. She tried to stop it, but a smile crept onto her face.

As quickly as the smile appeared, it faded as tension returned to her lips, and her brow tightened. She was trying to hold on to the joys in her life as she felt her Darkness press against the tiny moments of happiness she tried to enjoy. Against her will, she felt the smile get pushed from her face.

The setting sun cast just enough light to see all around the inside of the bus even before the fluorescent lights came on. This bus ride was just like the hundreds of others she had taken before—the same routine with the same people. Knowing most everyone on the bus was both a feeling of comfort and disappointment. Seeing the same people meant that she had been riding on this blasted bus route too long.

There was Harold, the driver. He was a nice enough guy, but he *loved him some him*. Whenever he was not behind the wheel, he was working, and he never missed an opportunity to tell that fact to anyone who would listen. He was always asking Sarah to look at the size of his biceps. He came across a little arrogant, she mused, but if she were that fit when she was his age, she would be a bit full of herself too.

Behind him would have to be "*Maud*." Sarah wasn't exactly sure what her name was, but the woman reminded her of a Maud she used to know a long time ago, so that was the name she gave her. White hair, deep wrinkles, long cane, bitter and angry at whoever crossed her path. She was old in every conceivable way. She would complain if Harold drove too fast or too slowly. Sarah never knew where Maud went when she got off the bus, but the woman was never happy about getting there too late or too early.

Next among the motley crew of passengers would be Billy and Jill, who sat toward the middle of the bus. They were a cute young couple going to school and saving their money to get a house. Silly kids. Sarah desperately wanted to tell them that the future is not always as bright as it seemed. Cherish every moment you have right now because life is unfair, and it can beat you at any time.

Propelled by the sudden reminder of her own life, Sarah felt a weight press down on her like she was suddenly holding enormous sandbags on each shoulder. The floor pulled at her body as she leaned her head back, turning her attention back to the city rolling by outside the dirty bus window. The cooler temperatures always brought the people out of their weather-induced stupor. She could relate to that. During the summer, people would come into the café and complain about how hot everything was. Then they would sit in her section for hours, not wanting to venture back into the asphalt blast furnace. It seemed to happen every summer. People who could leave the valley were the lucky ones, but they would be coming back anytime now. Snowbirds, as they're called, came flocking in to nest for the winter, flying south to avoid the snow. Hopefully, the cooler weather would lift their spirits and bring the tips out of their pockets as well. The business had been slow, and tips weren't as good as they used to be, but then again, nothing was as good as it used to be. A heavy sigh filled her lungs as she dreamed about being one of those lucky ones someday.

The summers weren't always this draining, she thought, remembering the years when her parents would take her to the mountains. Even if it was only for a day, they would all get out of town to get out of the heat for a while. She knew it was also to make sure they spent some quality time together because it didn't always happen during the hectic work week.

The bus turned a corner as the shadows from the buildings along the road poured across the seats. Since the light of the setting sun was still pushing through the windows, this sudden darkness from the shadows made the bright fluorescent lights flare on and come to life with intensity. Out of the corner of her eye, Sarah noticed something on the bus had shifted. Something was different. She turned and forced her eyes to focus on each person, trying to see what had changed. As Sarah glanced from person to person, her eyes caught sight of what was different. A chill crept over her body as she saw someone new sitting in a seat she could've sworn was empty a minute ago. It was as if the person had just appeared on the bus. Although she tried, she couldn't seem to pull her eyes away from the stranger.

He sat directly across from the young couple, yet they acted as if he had been there the whole time. While the kids completely ignored him, Sarah felt something about this new passenger was anything but ordinary. Where did he come from, she wondered? She didn't remember anyone getting on at the last few stops. Someone could not have just appeared from out of nowhere. Maybe she missed him getting on, or he must have slipped on at the last stop. Perhaps Sarah was more tired than she thought. Shrugging her shoulders, she resigned herself to looking out the window again.

Though she tried to ignore the new passenger, the tiny hairs on her arm tingled as her mind urged her to look back at the strange, new rider again. Against her better judgment, something compelled her to look back in his direction. She didn't want to be rude and openly gawk at the man, but she kept staring right at him. He didn't move from where she first noticed him. For that matter, he didn't seem to move at all. His body was perfectly still even as the bus jolted and leapt along. His eyes were round and deep-set, and his nose possessed a distinct and memorable shape, gently curved with a subtle prominence at the bridge. His sharp features, along with his dark hair and olive skin, gave him a middle eastern look. The man's dark shoulder-length hair blended into the deep blackness of his clothes. It was not just any black attire, but it included an oversized black jacket —a full-length leather cowboy duster. The nights were getting cooler in Phoenix, but not *that* cool. The more she stared, the more she saw that everything the man wore was jet black. With black pants and a black button-down shirt, it looked like this guy was a cowboy hat away from a country music video. She laughed to herself when she thought of this K-Mart cowboy riding on his little pony. But it wasn't just his clothes that made him seem so creepy; it was the way he was staring toward the front of the bus. The darkly clad man focused his foreboding gaze on the driver's seat. He just sat and stared like a lion, stalking his prey, waiting patiently for the right time to strike. Sarah thought this guy would get up any second and pounce on Harold's back like a wild beast.

From where she sat, Sarah continued to study the strange man. She had met a lot of people as a waitress, but she couldn't remember someone making her feel the way this guy did. Just sitting on the same bus as him made her feel uneasy.

Sarah rolled her eyes and scolded herself for feeling so silly. *Oh well*, she thought, *here is another crazy person in a city full of crazy people.* The words were still bouncing around inside Sarah's head when the man suddenly whipped his head around and looked directly at her. His eyes met hers with such intensity that it sent chills down her spine. Her fingertips involuntarily came up to her mouth as she wondered if he knew what she was thinking. Her reaction was not so much from her thoughts as it was from this man's sudden, unwanted attention. His eyes were a mesmerizing shade of blue—the kind of blue that she remembered seeing in the calm waters of her parents' swimming pool. The more she helplessly stared at him, the more his eyes seemed to glimmer. They were radiating with a devilish illumination all their own. Every moment or so, a soft glint would appear like the way sunlight would reflect off the clear water. His eyes were such a stark contrast to his darker complexion that she swore they were not real. Contrasting or not, real or not, his eyes held her locked with indecision. Frozen and unable to look away, she felt a chill run through her blood as if his cerulean scowl searched her soul.

Panic gripped her as beads of sweat began to push their way onto her forehead. She felt like she was being exposed. As if every part of her innermost being was subjected to his view. Displayed for his pleasure. She felt violated even though this man never moved an inch toward her, which scared her deeply. She wanted nothing further to do with this mysterious person. Though she tried as she might, she could not tear herself away or break the power of his gaze. He had an inexplicable lock on her. Then, as intense as the man's expression was, his eyes suddenly changed to a gentler look. His expression transformed. He almost seemed like he had a look of concern for her. His eyebrows lifted, and compassion washed over his once rigid face. Without blinking, he slowly turned his head and returned his gaze to the front of the bus. As if Sarah might have been mistaken about the thoughtful look she saw seconds ago, the strange man's face went back to the cold and unreadable statue as he continued to stare at the back of Harold's head.

Sarah's face flushed, and she realized that she forgot to breathe while she was locked into the makeshift staring contest. The man had literally taken her breath away. With some minor concentration and a stupid smirk, her breathing came back, shallow at first. Each breath in and out felt forced, as if something pressed against her chest. She was compelled to look outside again.

The bus was approaching her stop. Stepping quickly to the bus's rear door, careful to avoid any further contact with the strange man, Sarah darted out the door and planted both feet safely on the warm concrete. Even though she didn't fully understand why, a sense of relief washed over her body as she turned to walk home.

It was then that she felt his eyes on her again. Her body became rigid as she turned to see the dark stranger beginning to move toward the back of the bus. Her legs felt as if the concrete had reached up and held her fast—stopping her from moving an inch. His penetrating stare held her eyes even as the bus lumbered down the darkening street. It was only after the bus finally turned the corner a block later that Sarah felt like she could move again. Her body relaxed as her heart began to beat again. Even though the air was still warm around her, she felt a cold breeze blow across her face. The chill was nothing compared to what she felt inside.

CHAPTER TWO

Sarah shook her head to clear her thoughts. Slowly at first and then faster, as if the momentary dizziness would somehow change the feeling the dark stranger gave her. Whoever that creep was, she was glad he was far away from her. Pushed by her nerves, she started to walk quickly across the street towards the grocery store. She debated with herself about even stopping, but she knew that she would not want to go back out in the morning. She was out of coffee, and that would be considered a crime in her house. She could survive without many things, but going through the morning without coffee wasn't one of them. Luckily, the small market was still open, so she raced over. Living alone made cooking more manageable, but it always meant that *she* would have to do it if she wanted to eat.

Looking up, Sarah watched the last few rays of the falling sun cast streaks across the darkening sky. The painted clouds held an array of variegated reds, pinks, and oranges. Sarah thought back to times when she used to enjoy such sights. There was a time when she was just happy to be alive. Or maybe that was just her wallowing in a feeling of barely being content. Those days were long gone, but even the pink hues that gave way to burnt orange waves above her warmed her spirit. Years ago, she would have stopped and enjoyed a sunset like this one. Years ago, she would have called her mom to tell her to go outside and look at the beautiful sky. Then again, it was years ago when she had a mom and a dad that loved her very much, but that's where all her joy was—in the past.

It has been said that time has a way of healing all wounds. From the time Sarah had lost her parents to a drunk driver, she had been trying to recover. To somehow heal her spirit and fractured soul. Time, though it seemed, had not softened all wounds. Especially hers. The only change that happened over time was when the pain gave way to numbness, which was the most challenging part to heal. It wasn't just the pain but the apathy. At least with the pain, you felt something. The doctors and psychologists said she would get better if she allowed herself to "let it out" or "feel something." But that was the problem. She forgot how to feel. She worked at making herself numb so much that she would stop not only the pain, but everyone else too. It was her way of dealing with everything. It was her safety net. It was her coping mechanism. It was her Darkness.

Sarah felt like she was born into the perfect family. Michelle and Peter Thompson were remarkable parents, and they loved her very much. The two met each other in high school and fell hopelessly in love right away. The joy and the desire for life were evident to everyone they knew. They loved God, and they loved people. As far back as Sarah could remember, the church was a big part of the Thompson household. Sarah's parents raised her to love life, to love people, and to love God. They would go to church every Sunday morning and Wednesday night like clockwork.

Sarah's faith in Jesus came from her parents and her upbringing. It gave her the strong, guiding force that she needed to make it through most of her teenage years. She would turn to God for answers about boys, school, friends, and the other torments of being a young woman growing up. During those years, she felt like God was listening, but now most of the time, she felt God was silently ignoring her cries. Things got quiet on the spiritual front. Contrary to the famous phrase, this type of silence was not golden. The more her prayers went unanswered, the more her faith waned.

In her mind, that's what made life so unfair. The good people suffered, and the bad people got to do whatever they wanted. She loved her parents. She thought about them all the time, but the memories of them were like a double-edged sword. The more she thought about them and their love, the more she was haunted by their sudden disappearance from her life. The day they were taken from her was the worst day she could remember. Even though it was so many years ago, it was still so lucid in her mind.

Even as she walked mindlessly up and down each aisle, she realized that she had been moving through the entire grocery store in a near robotic haze. Her thoughts of the past consumed her and sent her mind on autopilot. With a shrug of her shoulders, she put the few items on the counter to be bagged. She knew one thing for sure: her thirties had to be better than the last part of her twenties. She didn't even want to think about the possibility of facing her fortieth birthday in the same boat she was in now.

Picking up the small sack of groceries, Sarah walked out the sliding glass doors. The swoosh of the automatic doors brought warm air over her face as it pushed away from the refreshing coolness of the air-conditioned store. The sun was gone and the amber haze of the streetlights in the small parking lot showed only a few cars.

"I guess other people must have better things to do on a Satur ...," Sarah mumbled to herself, but her words got caught in her throat. Her body went rigid as she locked eyes with the dark stranger from the bus.

He was standing across the road, staring directly at her. The illumination from the single streetlight over him cast a deep shadow over the already dark figure. The black sockets around his eyes gave his face a skull-like emanation. Standing fully upright, he was taller than he looked on the bus. Her heart began to race, and fear began to fill her mind. Her eyes locked on him as he was staring back at her. Panic seized her for a moment as her mind tried to rationalize what she was seeing. It must be a coincidence. How else could this man be standing there, yet there was no doubt in her mind he was looking right at her. But how? There was no way he could have found her so quickly. Regardless of what she thought, there he was, standing less than fifty feet away, seemingly waiting for her. Was she even in the store long enough for him to get off the bus and double back? Whatever the reason, the strange man was there, Sarah knew that nothing good could come of it. She had to get out of there quickly.

Turning up the street, Sarah put her head down and quickly picked up her pace. Not wanting to overreact, she kept telling herself to just calm down. The sounds of her racing heartbeat mirrored the sound of her footsteps as they pounded down the sidewalk. She kept having to remind herself to breathe normally. Her mind urged her body to break into a complete sprint, but she didn't want to seem crazy. There had to be another explanation for why the man was standing there. It must have been a simple matter of coincidence, or maybe the man was waiting for another bus.

Suddenly, it dawned on her that buses didn't run down this street after five o'clock. Her bus was the last one. She glanced back to see if the man was still under the streetlight. She was hoping to see him fade in the distance as she walked, but that was not the case. Horror gripped her, and she nearly stumbled forward as she looked back to see the dark man walking up the sidewalk parallel hers. His pace didn't seem as hurried or frantic, but he kept up with her. If she didn't know any better, she could swear this guy was gaining on her.

Fear washed over her as Sarah turned back and kept walking. A little faster than usual, but slower than she wanted. She was only a few yards away from the end of the street. Maybe she could turn the corner and run the short distance to her apartment. She was so close to her apartment, yet the night felt like it was closing in all around her. Even the cars on the street seemed to slowly fade away into the growing shadows. She didn't have to look back again to know he was still there. She knew he was close—she could almost feel the weight of his stare on her again. That fear both propelled her feet forward while simultaneously trying to pull her back. With each step, she felt as if she was walking against crashing waves in the ocean. Each unseen, undulating wave was trying to slow her down. The muscles in her legs strained with each step forward. It took all that she had to fight against the growing panic in the back of her mind.

She was counting the steps as she rounded the corner. Knowing she could quickly run the short distance before the stranger even got to the corner, methodically, she thought of each action she'd need to take to get her front door open fast. She could push herself to make it home. Almost entirely around the corner, her body tensed as if it was ready to spring into action. She quickly took one more glance behind her to see if her stalker was close enough to catch her when she ran. Her body reacted before her mind could realize what she was seeing. Or rather, not seeing. Her eyes blinked a few times as she tried to focus, but there was no one there. The man was gone. Her mouth hung open as she stared down the vacant street where she first saw him. Nobody was there. Nothing moved. There was nothing out of the ordinary at all. The dark figure wasn't anywhere around. A feeling of both triumph and relief washed over her frazzled body. The air around her dropped by a dozen degrees as a cold breeze blew in from the empty road sending a shiver that felt like it went straight to her soul.

Regaining her composure, Sarah threw her shoulders back and stared down toward the grocery store one more time. The bright lights of the store blinked out as they closed for the evening. Slowly, she felt her strength returning.

"I must be nuts," she mumbled to herself. Letting out a heavy sigh, she gently shook her head and turned toward home. Maybe he wasn't following her after all, she thought happily to herself.

Turning to walk, she continued to look down the dimly lit street. Sarah brought her head around as her eyes tried to focus on something directly in front of her. Instantly her knees quivered as her eyes came to bear on the figure of the dark stranger. He was standing only a few short feet in front of her. His dark leather trench coat waved carelessly in the breeze as his sky-blue eyes glowed in the shadows cast on his face. He stared at her, just as he stared at her before. His eyes burned a hole straight through her very soul. There was a faint smell of dust and smoke in the air. The same way the desert smelled during a hot day in July. But this was October ... this was the city ... and this was impossible. There was no way this guy could have gotten past her, yet there he stood.

Her mind was racing with all the self-defense tricks she learned when she went to college, yet her muscles would not obey her commands. She thought of all the things she should do. The things she needed to do, but instead, she just stood there. She was frozen as if she was under a spell and trapped in her own mind. She couldn't control her own body. As much as her mind wanted her to fight, her body didn't comply.

Scream, damn it! Oh, God, will you please scream! Her mind was shouting at her to open her mouth and scream for help. Seconds felt like hours as time came to a complete halt. Opening her mouth, Sarah felt like she wanted to both vomit and shout at the same time. She pushed with all her might to release the air that was trapped in her lungs. All she needed was a simple shout to Heaven or to whoever would help her. But even as the breeze pushed past her, nothing came out of her mouth. The man was within a few feet and made no attempt to move away. There was no denying that he was there for her, and she could do nothing to stop him. The vacuum that sucked the voice from her throat also seemed to pull out her will to fight him. She felt her body fall limp as she dropped the bags of groceries. She collapsed to her knees as she hit the hard ground; the crunch of bone on concrete was audible. The fading afternoon heat pushed up from the pavement as her forehead pressed low. The resistance rushed out of her body like the air out of a balloon. She was powerless. The dark stranger had won. The fight was over, and not one punch was thrown. She was done. Whatever happened next, she just hoped it would be quick.

"Sarah Anne Thompson! Do not be afraid. I am not here to hurt you."

CHAPTER THREE

As the heat from the sidewalk pressed up against her skin, Sarah felt the voice pierce her consciousness. It hit her with as much physical force as an icy dagger being pushed into her skull. The chill itself invaded the very core of her being and slithered its way down her spine. Her body shook nervously from the power of his simple words. She couldn't bring herself to even look up at him. Her mind raced with the thought that this was the end. She felt her final breath catch in her throat as she waited for his strike. The feeling of anticipation made her body shake even worse. Sarah's mind plunged deep into thoughts of all the things she still wanted to do with her life. It was true what they said. Her life did flash before her eyes just before the end. Sadly, she regretted most of what she had done with her life up until that point.

For what felt like an eternity, she just waited there on the sidewalk. She thought about running or maybe the hope that someone might see her lying on the ground in front of this menacing lunatic. On any given night, this street would be busy with cars passing by or people out walking their dogs, yet there wasn't anyone coming to her aid. Someone else must have seen this man. They weren't even that far from the grocery store. This is ridiculous, she thought. Why wasn't there anyone else out tonight? Was she the only unlucky one that was going to be killed tonight?

The chill that gripped her body began to subside. The cold fear gave way to a new feeling. An odd, out of place, feeling of complete warmth and peace. Like the sensation that comes from drinking a warm cup of coffee on a cold morning. Contrary to everything she thought she should have been feeling at that moment, the warm feeling felt good. That was when the sharp voice came again and broke the silence.

"Stand up. You have been chosen for a very important task," the voice mused. His tone was penetrating. Resonating with a regal sound as if he were from another time and place altogether. The iciness she felt from his voice only a few minutes ago was starting to fade. She even felt some strength returning to her limp body, but now it was her catatonic fear that kept her from moving.

Sarah still could not bring herself to look up at her assailant. If he was not trying to hurt her, he sure had a funny way of showing it. She knelt in the middle of the warm sidewalk. Her face pressed down against the rough ground as if she was bowing before her attacker. The prey was cowering in front of a predator. She imagined how the jerk must have loved that. Her body did not respond to her efforts to stand, and the feeling of numbed fright still pulsed through her muscles. Her mind, however, would not stop racing through everything that was happening. His words kept repeating themselves over and over again. *You have been chosen.* There was nothing she could have given him unless he intended to rape her. This man was a crazy lunatic, but his choice of words was a bit ironic. Sarah chided herself, now was not the time for euphemisms.

After what seemed like hours, Sarah finally found the

courage deep within her to lift her head. Slowly, inch by inch, she raised her eyes. The first thing that she noticed was how dark it had become in the few minutes since she'd been lying there. Or maybe she had been there longer than she thought. How long was she lying in front of him?

Suddenly, the smell was back again. The strange odor of fire and ash. Like a bonfire in the desert. Her mind forgot about the smell as she focused on the man's shoes. They were boots, actually. Like the kind the cowboys might wear, except these were in perfect condition. They did not seem to be leather, but some kind of scaly skin. She had seen a pair like these before on an old customer of hers at the diner. Snakeskin! It was black snakeskin. The hem of his black slacks showed enough of the boot to see that everything was clean. Again, Sarah reminded herself to concentrate on all of these details to tell the police—if she survived.

Ever so slowly, she raised her head, studying every aspect of the man's clothes. Not wanting to get up to his burning eyes too quickly, she took her time. If he was not forcing her to get up too fast, then she might be able to delay him long enough for someone to stumble upon them.

His slacks were perfectly straight and pressed as if they had been ironed while he was wearing them. Shockingly, his hand was extended down to her as if he wanted to help her up. Was this guy for real? Confused by his gentlemanly action, she laughed inside at the thought of being raped or killed by the most helpful guy she had met in years.

As if driven by some kind of unconscious response, she reached her hand out to take his. When her hand touched him, Sarah felt the coldness of his skin. His palm and fingers were callused and rough. When her hand was entirely in his, he helped her up with ease. Her knees wobbled a bit; not sure if they could fully support her weight, but she found herself standing upright and looking directly at her would-be attacker.

"Again, I say. You have been chosen. Is there someplace that we can talk?" His eyes looked deeply into hers. His voice, which only a moment ago brought panic and fear now seemed to have a certain warmth to it. It soothed her and almost made her feel good to hear it. The shadows were still wrapped around his face like a black shroud. His mouth was lost in the depth of the darkness, and she could not even see his lips move. As dark as it was, his eyes were still drawing her in. They glowed, and she could not break away from the power of his stare until he spoke again.

"I am not here to harm you," he spoke smoothly. "I just want to talk."

"About what?" she responded with a quiver in her voice.

"Sarah, I have been watching you, and I believe you can assist me," he said flatly. He said it so calmly that she almost forgot that this man might try to hurt her or worse.

"Please understand that I just want to talk," he said, a little firmer this time. "Nothing more. Is there a place where we can talk?"

Without thinking, she blurted out, "We could go to my place. It is just over there." Instinctively, her free hand slapped over her mouth, not believing what she'd just said. There was a cacophony of voices screaming in her head. All were yelling the same thing. *Are you an idiot!?!?* She was offering the killer her own home to do the deed! All of the alarms were going off in her head, but she was in a trance. There was surprisingly something captivating about this man. He completely disarmed her. She knew this wasn't right, and yet, she was overcome with a peculiar sense of misplaced peace. There was no panic or fear at all.

The stranger still stood over her, not letting go of her hand. "That will be fine," he acknowledged. Politely stepping to the side, he helped her up and allowed her to pass. He waved his other hand down the quiet street in the direction of her apartment.

"Please," he bowed slightly. "Lead the way."

As much as she tried, she did not hear any other noises on the street. Finally, breaking his gaze, Sarah looked past him and down the road. There were headlights from cars, but it did not look like they were coming any closer. It looked as if she was staring at a picture. The vehicles were frozen in time, waiting for an invisible light to change.

Moving slowly, Sarah didn't attempt to run or fight off the polite stranger. He leaned forward and picked up her grocery bags. He did not attempt to give them back. It was as if her attacker was actually trying to help her. She simply moved past him and continued on the same path that she took night after night from the bus stop to her place. As she walked, she could feel his icy stare on her. She silently wondered if he was eyeing her up and deciding what to do with her once they got to her apartment. The fear that was so remarkably absent finally came roaring back. It raced through her body as she imagined all of the things this kidnapper would do to her. Just as she felt like she could not move forward any longer, fear gripping each step, she suddenly felt a warm sensation wash over her body, replacing the fear. Not the kind of warmth that came from panic or stress, but oddly it was the warm feeling that came from peace, like relaxing in a hot bath.

Once they got to her apartment, Sarah opened the door and went about her normal routine as if she had just come home from a typical day at work. Nothing out of the ordinary. Other than the tall, dark stranger that just followed her home and whom she voluntarily allowed to come inside her house.

Everything was as she left it, meaning the place was still a mess. She had clothes, both clean and dirty, lying on the couch. There were half-empty glasses filled with various liquids sitting on the tables at the end of her dust-covered couch. She felt oddly embarrassed that people would find her lifeless body in such a messy apartment. Maybe they would think that the killer made the mess before he left.

Sarah dropped her keys into a tray near the door just as she always did. As she took the small bag of groceries to the kitchen, she felt the knot in her throat lessen and her body relax. She felt stronger and more emboldened. She turned to face the stranger, but he interrupted her words with his own. This time his voice was more melodic and soothing.

"My name is Azrael, and as I mentioned earlier, I have need of your services," he declared in a calm and smooth tone. "You are to be given a mission." His features were more defined in the light of her apartment. His face was not as dark and cold as before, but his eyes were still vibrant and full of color. They radiated in sharp contrast to the deep olive complexion of his skin. His black hair came down to his shoulders and looked wavy and clean. This guy was certainly not a homeless person.

Then his words hit her as the reality of the situation came rushing back to her mind. Her services were *needed*? Was she to be given a mission? This man baffled her. If he was here to kill her, he was the nicest murderer she had ever heard about.

"Again, I am not here to harm you," he said in a booming voice that filled the room and her mind with the vision of a man shouting into a megaphone.

"Sarah Anne Thompson, you have been chosen." Waving his hand toward the couch, he continued in a much calmer tone, "Please sit."

Sarah was startled by the weight of his voice and by hearing her full name. How did he know it? She silently dropped the groceries and moved through the cluttered room. Her eyes caught sight of the man's hand. It looked as rough as she imagined it did. In addition to the visible calluses, she noticed many deep scars covering the olive skin on his hands and wrists. These were the hands of someone that has seen heavy physical labor or violence. Someone that is not afraid to get dirty and be rough. Someone that she knew she should avoid altogether. This made her even more uneasy as she sat lightly on the edge of the cushion. Begrudgingly, she turned her attention to the dark man.

"Let me tell you what you need to know," he stated flatly. "Simply said, I am not of this world. My role within your understanding of this universe is to take people from this plane of existence to the next." As he spoke, the one known only as Azrael paced from one end of the small room to the other. His steps were graceful and fluid as he moved among the piles of dirty and clean clothes. He turned back to her to make sure that he had her full attention.

"That is to say, I take their souls from this life to the next. When their time is done here on earth, I take them to their final resting place." Pausing for a moment to let his words sink into Sarah's currently frail psyche.

She began to shake her head back and forth. The anger, which so commonly partnered with her Darkness, came rushing forward.

"What? That's not possible! What in the hell kind of sick joke is this?" Her face reddened with heated anger as blood pulsed through her veins. She might not have been able to explain why she was so docile earlier when this man followed her back to her apartment, but she felt entirely in control of her emotions now.

"I can assure you that this is not a joke. My role is quite serious and not a jovial matter. But the comment about 'hell' *is* ironic." There was the slightest hint of a curl at the edges of his lips. A fact that did not go unnoticed by Sarah.

Feeling more emboldened by her anger, she pressed him further. "So, you kill people? Are you Death?" Panic mixed with a seemingly unhealthy dose of fury washed over Sarah. Her fear had subsided, and she felt more in control of her muscles. She started to stand up as she asked something that had just come to her mind. The thought of it calmed her anger long enough for the fear to return.

"Are you here to take me? Am I dead?"

The tall man moved towards her with the same graceful movements he showed before. Slowly, Azrael placed his hand on her shoulder.

"No, Sarah. I am not Death, nor am I here to take you away from this world."

Her legs felt weak as a wave of relief came over her. Even though she tried to start strong, her knees buckled slightly, and she fell back onto the couch. The plunge sent a fine layer of dust billowing in all directions. Her mind was still trying to wrap itself around what was now becoming stranger than the strange man himself.

Seeing that she was listening again, he continued, "My task is not to kill the people. The moment of their demise is something determined from the beginning. My duty is only to take the souls of the departed once they are released from their earthly vessels."

Shaking her head even harder this time, she forced herself to look away from his face. "I don't understand. This can't be happening!" Her voice had more force and authority in it than she felt she had, but she was glad that her attitude was finally talking back to this guy.

Azrael grabbed a small wooden chair from the dining room table set and placed it to face Sarah. Taking his time, he slowly and deliberately took a seat directly in front of her.

"The situation is what it is, regardless of what you believe or think about it. Just because you do not believe something does not make it false." Sitting fully upright, he continued.

"If you refuse to believe in gravity, it does not give you the ability to fly."

Azrael paused as he let her think about that thought for a moment. He leaned back into the chair as the wood creaked and complained under his muscular frame. "Tonight, when you first saw me, I was waiting to take my next charge to his final resting place."

His statement shook her back to reality. Sarah blurted, "You were there to take someone away? Who were you there to kill?"

Azrael paused for a moment and stared deeply into her eyes. Now it was his turn to shake his head in frustration. Even so slightly, he turned his head from side to side the way a father would do to a child that did not understand what he was saying.

"Dear Sarah. I just told you that I do not kill them. I just know when they are going to die, and it was my task tonight to collect the driver of the bus."

"Harold? You came for Harold?" she asked with a denying tone in her voice. "He is the strongest man I have ever known." She waved her hand toward him in disbelief. "I don't believe you … he is fit as a fiddle. I just saw him. He was fine."

"Again, what you believe does not change the reality of the situation, nor does it change the truth of what will happen." Standing up, Azrael towered over Sarah as she sat on the couch.

"Sarah, I will return to you soon. Then we will begin your commission." Without another word, he vanished from sight as if the shadows in the room rose up and swallowed the massive man whole.

Sarah just stared toward the spot where the stranger once stood. The room felt somehow smaller as she sat alone. There was still the faint acrid smell of dust in the air from where he was just standing. Whatever just happened, she knew that her life was about to change.

CHAPTER FOUR

Sarah tossed and turned the entire night through a fitful sleep. The once crisp sheets felt binding and heavy as she struggled within her restless dreams. Throughout the night, she found herself swinging her hands wildly in the dark, trying to defend herself from a stranger looming in the shadows of her waking dreams. When she finally stopped, it was the dull ticking of the wall clock that brought her back to reality.

She wearily laid her head back down on the pillow as she tried desperately to fall back to sleep. Her mind refused to let go of the thoughts of Harold Wilhenmeyer. The same reliable bus driver she had seen nearly every day over the past few years was possibly gone. She had talked with him, laughed with him, and even laughed at him more than a few times when he would get too full of himself. Overall, he was as close to a friend as she had. He had always treated her with kindness. He was a good man, or at least he seemed to be from what she knew of him. When people met him, they were always greeted with a warm smile. It was the first thing everyone noticed about him. The second thing was how he looked in his uniform.

Even sitting down at the wheel, Harold's muscular arms, tone chest, and a stomach as flat as a washboard could be seen under his off-white uniform. He was a man that took care of himself. Once someone found out how old he was, that was when they would really start to take notice of his physique. For a fifty-five-year-old man, Harold had the face and, moreover, the body of a thirty-year-old. He would brag all the time about his workout routine and his diet. Sarah thought about always bringing home some cannoli or a piece of pie and offering him some. Each time he would quickly tap his flat stomach and politely decline.

Now, as dawn rose, streams of sunlight cascaded into her apartment, chasing away the shadows from the night before. If it was only that easy to chase away the darkness that had been pulling at her mind. Her thoughts kept returning to the dark, dirty stranger who foretold her that Harold was going to die. In fact, if he was right, Harold was already gone. The mysterious phantom told her that he somehow took Harold's life and whisked him away to the hereafter.

Sarah took a moment and gazed at the clock. It was still ticking as her consciousness remembered the reality of time. The hands on the old wall clock reminded her of how quickly time can steal the moments of joy that all too often are taken for granted. The clock itself was a gift from her dad for her dorm room so many years ago. How many seconds have ticked away with little regard to the impact of what each one meant?

As if being snapped out of a daze, Sarah's eyes focused on what time that clock had on it, and she realized she was going to be late for work. She raced out of the door and practically sprinted to the bus stop. When she got there, she just paced back and forth periodically glancing down the street. Her agitated walk caught the attention of those sitting on the bench, much to the delight of the children waiting with them. Sarah was like a wind-up doll that walked to and fro.

Even though the morning sun was already warming the air around her, Sarah's skin chilled as if someone ran an ice cube down her spine.

The bus finally turned the corner, but it was still a block away. As if to mock her frayed patience, the bus drove so slowly that Sarah thought it would never get to her stop. As it approached, fate was taunting her once more. The sun was positioned perfectly to cause an intense glare off the windshield. No matter how much she squinted, Sarah couldn't see who was driving the bus. She hoped it was still the sharp outline of the muscle-bound driver.

When the bus came to a complete stop, the doors flew open with a swoosh. Sarah didn't mean to be rude, but she couldn't help herself as she pushed her way forward. The air was sucked from Sarah's lungs as she took a quick breath. In the seat where she greeted Harold every day was the body of an older, heavyset black woman. Sarah felt the blood flush from her face as her lips parted involuntarily.

The new bus driver sat in Harold's seat, patiently waiting for Sarah to get on the bus. After a slight delay, the older woman broke the silence. "Are you OK, miss?" the lady asked in a softer-than-expected voice. "You look like you've just seen a ghost."

"Yeah ... I just was not expecting ... um ..." is all she could get out as she continued to stare at the new driver. Stepping slowly onto the bus.

"Sorry, where is Harold?"

The older woman's face softened, and Sarah could see a glassy film fill the corners of the woman's eyes. A lump formed in Sarah's throat as she waited for the driver's response.

"Oh darlin'," she said as the plump, jeweled hand of the woman reached out and touched Sarah's still trembling wrist. "Harold passed away. Just last night."

Sarah felt the weight of a thousand days press down on her as her knees began to buckle. Each of those days in the past was one where she had said hello to Harold. Her hand gripped tight the entry railing, stopping her from crumpling limply to the bus's walkway. Sarah fought through the sadness and confusion, forcing herself to make sense of it all. She tried to clear her mind, but all she could do was stare blankly at the woman. Meekly, Sarah forced herself to speak. "How did it happen?" she said with an audible tremble in her voice.

"Well, we were told that he suffered a heart attack and died last night. Just as he was finishing up his last run, he died right there in his seat, just after he let off his last passenger." A small trail of a single tear rolled its way down the woman's plump cheek as she stared compassionately at Sarah.

"Thank Heaven that he was at a complete stop when it happened, or else it might have been worse. So sad. Did you know him very well, dear?"

Sarah's mind started to get foggy again. The driver's words seemed to fade away into a chasm of nothingness. Turning away from her, Sarah made her way down the aisle of the bus. She held tight to the back of each seat as she walked on. The confused driver just shook her head and let the other passengers on before she closed the door.

The sudden jolt of the bus and the weakness of her knees forced Sarah to fall into the nearest seat. The dark stranger was right. The man named Azrael was right. Harold was gone.

Sarah stared intently out the window and thought, "What in God's name is going on here? Why is this happening?"

Hours later, Sarah mindlessly moved from table to table at the cafe. She was still in the same dark cloud that surrounded her after she heard about Harold. The sudden reminder of death brought her own Darkness close again. As she took a tray of food to a table, she realized that she couldn't even remember getting off the bus and getting to work. Everything she was doing felt like she was on autopilot.

"Miss?" the man at the table called to Sarah after she put his meal down on the table. Turning around, Sarah noticed that she placed four plates of food in front of a man sitting by himself. He stared blankly at her and then at the table full of food.

"I didn't order this."

Sarah jumped in her skin and awoke from her hypnotic trance as if someone just snapped their invisible fingers. She stared down at the table full of plates and wondered why she just placed so much food in front of one man. Out of the corner of her eye, she noticed a pleasant-looking man waving timidly at her. He was sitting with a woman and two fidgety children. Their collective expression was a mixture of concern and frustration.

"I'm so sorry about that," Sarah said as she smiled awkwardly at the single man. "I just thought you looked hungry." Quickly moving the food to the other table, she made another set of apologies and raced back to the kitchen to collect her thoughts.

Just as she stopped to take a deep breath, Gerardo, the owner, walked in and moved tentatively over to where Sarah was leaning against a prep table.

"Are you OK? You have been making some strange mistakes this afternoon." His beautiful thick Italian accent was not enough to hide the disappointment in his voice. "This is not like you."

Looking up at him with her eyes wrapped in a veil of tears, she told him that someone she knew had just passed away today. Quickly putting his arms around her, he consoled her for her loss.

"I'm so sorry. Are you alright? Do you need to go home for

the day?"

Surprised by his words, she exclaimed, "No, it's fine. I'll do better with the orders. I'm sorry for screwing them up."

"Sarah, it's not because I care about the orders or mistakes. I want you to be OK. Come back tomorrow. We will be OK. Besides, it is not too busy anyhow. You should go home now and relax."

She knew he was right, and the café was pretty empty for a Sunday afternoon. Out of the fifteen booths, there were only five or six of them with customers seated. The high-top seats at the counter were nearly empty as well—save the regulars that would sit there all day. It was a good idea to take some time off.

The café itself was a cute place. With its Italian painted landscape murals, along with the backdrop of the brown vinyl-covered seats, the inside of the café looked like it was a 50's style diner stuck in the middle of Italy. Gerardo loved it, and his passion for making people happy through food showed every day. That was his gift. His taste in décor, however, was not so evident. The café was great, though, and she was thankful for the opportunity it gave her. She wasn't even sure where her life would be if Gerardo hadn't taken her in and offered her a chance to get back on her feet.

The more she thought about it, the more Sarah knew that she would rather be at home than at work, so she stopped arguing with Gerardo. She thanked him and said good night. Quickly she made her way out into the afternoon sun. Despite the date on the calendar, the Arizona heat was still intense as Sarah felt sweat form on her forehead. As she walked the short distance to the bus stop, she felt a sense of hesitation. Suddenly, a wash of dread came over her like the pouring of water, starting at the top of her head and falling to the bottom of her feet. She wondered if the feelings were from the heat or maybe from her fear of getting back on the bus. Each step closer to the stop brought her one step closer to the memory of the strange man that took Harold away. When the tan bus arrived, she secretly hoped that Harold would open the door and tell her it was a joke. A prank to make her laugh since it was so close to her birthday. The door opened, and a thin Mexican man sat in the seat. This was not a joke, and it certainly was not funny.

Sarah's eyes scanned the bus and looked at each face like one of those characters from a classic horror movie, looking around for any glimpse of the dark man, the angel of death named Azrael. After a few minutes of twisting her head around to see everyone, she gave up and started to relax. Maybe she would not see him again.

Sarah scurried into her apartment and closed her door quickly. Feeling exhausted, she pressed her thin frame against the back of the door and sighed. Her apartment was 'nice and simple' as she called it. Most of the furniture she got from the local consignment or discount store. From the old brown couch to the faded leather recliner, nothing actually matched, but it was all hers, and she always felt good to come home to it. The neighbors were a different story. Above her was a family of bull elk cleverly disguised as a single mom with three boys. Sarah didn't mind much. She knew that the mom, Emily, worked two jobs and made the best home she could for the young tornados. Sarah got so good at listening to them that she could tell which one of the three boys was above her, depending on how many steps it took them to get from room to room.

The neighbors on her left and right were OK as well. On her right was Mr. Murphy, a retired military man who spent most of his time at either the VA or the bar. He would always say that he was helping others in one place and helping himself in the other. Although he never mentioned which type of help was actually done at which spot.

On Sarah's left side was Mr. and Mrs. Shapiro. They were a nice couple that kept to themselves. David worked at a doctor's office, and his wife, who only went by the name, Mrs. Shapiro, came out to walk their small Pomeranian dog. The dog resembled a large piece of dryer lint with legs, but the bark was far worse than it should have been for a dog of that size. Each morning as it awaited its daily walk around the block, the sharp yap of the dog could be heard by everyone within a quarter-mile radius.

Closing her eyes, Sarah felt the heat of the outside world and the craziness of the day flow out of her. The peace immediately disappeared when she heard the coolness of a familiar voice coming from somewhere close. Close enough to be inside her apartment.

"Welcome home, Sarah. I have been waiting for you." The icy words floated to her like the distant sound from a fading dream. The voice resonated, ghost-like in her mind. For an instant, she wasn't even sure if the voice was just inside her head, or if it was actually coming from inside the apartment. Quickly opening her eyes and looking up frantically, Sarah realized that the sound was indeed coming from inside her place. She saw the tip of a black leather boot sticking out just around the corner in her living room. She knew where the voice came from and, moreover, whose voice it was. The *angel of death* was sitting in her apartment, and he was waiting for her.

A hand waved at her from just above the reclined black boot as the voice filled the small apartment again.

"Would you care to take a seat? I know you have had a troubling day."

A warm sensation pushed up from inside her chest as she listened to the man. Even though she knew he was sitting in the other room, the voice sounded like it was right next to her. Begrudgingly, she walked silently toward the living room like a child that was finally ready to take her punishment. She lowered her head as she dropped her stuff down on the small wooden table next to the door.

Though the light poured into the room through the flower-printed curtains, there seemed to be a shadowy darkness hidden within. As if the sunlight itself was creating gloom in the smallest places it could not reach. Seated in her favorite oversized, stuffed recliner, complete with imitation grandma-style doilies on each arm, sat the angel of death. He was simply relaxed as if he was an average person that had just dropped by for some coffee. His face was not as dark as she remembered, or maybe it was just the way the bright light was cascading across it. Either way, his eyes were still as intense as she remembered them from her nightmares. Almost too intense. She felt a pang of strange guilt come over her as soon as she met his stare. As if he knew everything there was to know about her. Like her soul was being ripped open for only him to see. Contradictory to how he made her feel, he sat comfortably with one leg crossed over the other, still wearing black slacks and the black leather trench coat. He might get around town quite easily, but his attire seemed to stay pretty stagnant. There was something about his look that surprised her. As his face brightened with a warm expression, he looked at her as if he were genuinely happy to see her. She moved reluctantly but quickly to the opposite end of the couch. It was the farthest possible seat she could take and still be in the same room.

"As you found out earlier today, Harold is gone. Do you believe me now?" The man's words broke the silence. The openness in his voice and the callousness of his words brought forth a feeling of frustration and anger that surprised Sarah. She paused for a moment—gathering herself before she spoke.

"I thought you told me that it didn't matter what I believed. You were gonna make it true anyway." She felt the blood rush to her face as her temper began to rise.

"My dear Sarah. You are correct; that is still true. It does not matter if you believe it or not; it is still true regardless. His words were as cold as before, but the lines in his face relaxed as he spoke.

"But if you are expected to act on a truth, you will need to believe in it."

Sarah was not expecting this logic. Her mind still wanted an argument, but she couldn't think quickly enough to respond. She needed something to satisfy the anger she had in her veins for the loss of her friend and the intrusion of her life. She wanted to take this guy apart, but her mind was overriding her body. As she processed his words, her body halfheartedly began to relax.

"Now that you are ready to listen, I need your help with my work," Azrael continued. "You will accompany me over the next few nights as I perform my duties."

Still trying to make sense of this man's very presence in her apartment, the gravity of his words made Sarah feel like the room was falling in on her. Her hands instinctively came to each side of her head as she struggled with his new command. Looking up intently, her eyes burned into him, trying to read his face. She was trying desperately to understand what he was implying. Was this angel of death going to take her around so she could help him kill people?

"I would ask that you please stop calling me the 'angel of death.'"

She had been looking directly at his face when she heard his voice, but his lips did not move. She listened to his voice as clearly as before, yet she knew it was only her mind that was hearing him. Panic came over her as she realized that this was no ordinary being. He listened to her thoughts and spoke to her within her mind. This wouldn't be good.

"Yes, Sarah, I can listen to your thoughts as well as speak to you without the use of an audible voice. There are many things that I can do, but you need not be afraid."

He must have known this would trigger something within her as a wave of panic washed over her. The abject fear swirled a sense of utter defeat within Sarah. Her shoulders sagged as if there were weights tied to each hand. This was a man; no …

strike that. This was not a man, but a creature. A creature that could travel through locked doors, move quicker than anything she had ever seen, and now had the power of telepathy. She concentrated as she looked the angel in the eyes and chose her next words carefully.

Taking a deep breath in, she resigned and uttered, "I understand, Azrael. What do you need me to do?"

"Good," he affirmed matter-of-factly. "I will continue to use my real voice, so it will not cause you to struggle. If this is easier, then we can communicate this way."

Feeling a sense of relief until she heard his voice in her head again. "But know this," Azrael's voice again whispered in her mind, "I can hear your thoughts, and I know what you are thinking just as you think it, so be wary of what your mind ponders."

After a slight pause, his voice continued again. But this time, it had a chipper tone to it. "On the other hand, you can also communicate with me if you need to tell me something without others hearing it."

Swallowing hard, Sarah felt her voice crack as she continued, "What do you need me to do?"

"Right. Here is what I need from you. You will accompany me when I go to collect the dying, although you will go to them before I truly take them." He paused to let that sink in. When she made no effort to interrupt him, he continued.

"I will send you ahead of me, and I will give you exactly one hour to spend with each of them. During this hour, you will be able to share with them nearly anything you wish."

When her mind understood what he really said, Sarah finally interrupted, "What?" Feeling the familiar sensation of frustration rising up from within her Darkness, she would not be so submissive. Her face flushed a deep shade of crimson, and her words were sharp as tacks.

"Are you kidding me? What would I say to a person that is about to die?" Sarah stood up quickly and began to pantomime. "Hi, my name is Sarah. You don't know me, but you are about to die. Lovely weather we're having, right?" She suddenly realized that her voice had taken on a darker tone as her words came out much harsher than she had intended.

"Please calm down. I understand your confusion. You must tell them about the most important thing in life."

Sarah thought for a minute as her blood began to boil. "What *important thing*? What *is* the most important thing in life?" Throwing her hands up in the air, "Haven't people been trying to figure that out for centuries?"

Cutting her off with a quick turn of his head, "Yes, they have been trying to figure it out for a very long time. Mind you … all people *were* given the truth as to the most important thing in life." Looking away, Azrael's face softened.

"Yet, sadly, most have forgotten what that is, and the world suffers even now because of it."

Looking back at her with his eyes blazing like blue flames, "You will know what to say because it will be on your heart. Share with the person what is the most important thing in your heart. But understand this … there are rules."

Sarah returned his gaze with a stare of her own.Quickly she blurted out, "Rules? What rules?"

"It is simple. The rules are this: you cannot tell them about me or their impending death. If you break either of those simple rules, I will take them immediately, and you will suffer the consequences." He let his last few words hang in the air before he continued.

"You can, however, share with them whatever else you wish, but it is imperative you tell them about the most important thing in this life. Just remember, you cannot break the rules of our arrangement."

Sarah sat slowly, not taking her eyes off of his lips as his words penetrated her anger. "What happens after the hour is up?" she snipped.

"After the hour is over, I will take them," he said flatly.

"What happens to them? Where do they go?"

"The choices they made here on the earth will dictate where they go."

Sarah thought about Heaven or Hell. She wondered quietly if everything her parents told her about life after death was real. Minutes passed as she stared at a small spot on the floor. "Where will I go when I die?"

Azrael paused for minutes before he answered.

"There are choices you have not made yet, Sarah. Your hour is not yet here." Standing up, Azrael towered over her petite frame. Even from a few feet away, Sarah felt like she was shrinking in comparison to this creature. Azrael continued to speak—slightly softer this time.

"After the hour is over with each person, I will return you to your home, and you will be free to go about your life until I need you again."

"What if I refuse to go with you?" Her back straightened in a veiled attempt at defiance. "What if I refuse to talk with them?" A mix of emotions washed over Sarah's thoughts as she tried to get her head around everything that was happening.

"You cannot refuse to go. We will go together. This is your charge, and it is not a choice." His voice had the authority of a teacher instructing a student on his expectations while taking the final test. Firm and to the point.

"As far as talking with the person, that, however, is your choice. At the end of the hour, I will take them whether you chose to speak with them or not."

His head turned slightly toward her, and his voice

lightened. "But I know you will do what is right and will talk with them when the time comes."

Suddenly, Azrael was moving. Quicker than Sarah's mind could comprehend. In a flash, he stood directly in front of her before she could even respond. "Also, understand this, Sarah Thompson; any refusal you might have to speak with them does not change the outcome of their situation. At the end of the hour, they will die. Regardless of what you think or believe. It is their hour."

Reaching out his hand to her, "Come. It is time to visit our first appointment."

CHAPTER FIVE

Before she had a chance to think about it, Sarah's left hand reached instinctively toward his. If she had allowed herself time to think about it, she would have told him off in spades. Yet as their fingertips touched, a surge pulsed through her like a current of electricity. For the briefest moment, she felt a single split-second of clarity that overwhelmed her with an unfettered, centering peace.

Sarah felt as if her body was sprung into the air. The pull of gravity tugged at her limbs like the upward sensation from a fast-moving elevator. As quickly as the pulling started, it stopped, and it was suddenly replaced by the feeling of weightlessness. Yet unlike the upward motion of being in an elevator, she was suddenly overcome with a floating sensation. No longer were her feet and body connected to the laws of gravity. She was suspended and floating in what she could only imagine how space might feel. Then, even though she knew there was no air moving around her skin or blowing through her hair, she felt the rush of being propelled forward.

Her mind was disoriented as the light around her faded.

The images of her apartment dissolved into muted colors as if someone turned a bright light bulb off in a dark room, and the afterglow could still be seen for a few seconds afterward.

There was no way of telling how long she was floating or flying, but she felt like it was only a few seconds before she felt a firmness pressing against her feet. She was standing on a solid surface again. Slowly, the light started to filter into her eyes. Much slower than when everything disappeared.

Sarah was no longer in her apartment. She had been transported somewhere else. Feelings of fear and panic grew inside her. Her heart was racing out of control, and her hands began to shake. Just as she thought she would have a full-blown panic attack; a sudden wave of peace welled up inside her. It washed over her like the coolness of a gentle breeze on a hot day. She started to relax. She was calm again. Her body reacted before her mind could control it. Whatever brought her this peace, was outside of her understanding.

She found herself standing in a doorway. The room directly in front of her had its door open, but it was dark inside. Not entirely black, but the light was much softer than the harsh fluorescent tubes that were humming somewhere above her head. Sarah's eyes started to adjust to the dim light just inside the small room. A bed with shiny steel rails was sitting in the middle of one wall. She thought it might be a hospital room for a minute, but the décor was too soft and tranquil. There were no harsh, sterile white walls or the typical things she remembered from all the time she spent in a hospital when her parents died.

Other than the fading light of the Sun coming from the open drapes, a soft dim glow came from a small lamp on a table next to the bed. This revealed a bare room with smooth tan walls that were wrapped around a light green carpet. An array of simple plants and pictures finished out the decorations in a place that could have been in a hotel—except for the hospital bed sitting in the middle.

It was then that she noticed a slight movement in the bed. A petite, frail woman was lying under the thick comforter. Her head was crowned with vibrant waves of tightly curled hair that seemed to blend in thoroughly with the bed's white sheets. She was awake yet paid no attention to the stranger standing in the doorway. Her soft gaze was fixed on a distant place somewhere outside the large window. Sarah tried to see what she was staring at, but she could only see the tops of trees swaying along the lower half of the window. On the horizon, the setting sun gave the clouds a fiery hue that painted the sky with beautiful pinks, reds, and oranges—another beautiful Arizona sunset.

The elderly woman must have sensed someone was watching her because she turned her head slowly towards the open door. It was then that Sarah heard the rhythmic beeping of a heart monitor. A spaghetti-like array of wires and tubes snaked from under the covers as they connected to small monitors. Everything was carefully and neatly concealed behind a partially opened curtain next to the bed. The lines on a small bank of monitors danced and kept time with her heart rate. The other screens displayed everything else you would want to know about a person.

For some reason, it was then that Sarah realized that she was actually in a new place. She was transported to a new location, just like Azrael said would happen. Taking that moment to better understand her surroundings, Sarah leaned back and looked down a lengthy, dull, white hallway. The stale, recycled air was ripe with the smell of rubbing alcohol and disinfectants. This had to be a hospital. As she spun her head in the other direction, she caught the sound of a woman's voice on the phone from just beyond the next corner. By the sound of the heated words, the woman had to be arguing with someone. When Sarah heard the woman use the term, *patient*, she knew right where the dark Angel of Death had brought her.

As if he were standing right next to her, Azrael's voice broke through her inquisitive search. "Time is short." The sudden voice startled Sarah and made her grab the sides of the doorway. The frantic commotion at the entryway to her room gave the older woman a terrible fright.

"Oh my," the elderly woman said with a frightened quiver in her voice. The frailty that echoed tenderly in the room gave Sarah a quick indication of the woman's advanced age.

"Who are you? I wasn't expecting anybody," the old woman asked as she strained her eyes to see the strange figure standing in the doorway. The bright light from the hallway gave Sarah a shadowy outline. The beeping from the heart monitor quickened as the woman tried in earnest to make out the face of her surprise visitor.

Azrael's voice came back into Sarah's mind. "Do not scare our guest and cause her to leave this earth before her due time. That would be in poor taste." Sarah cringed at the thought and the idea that she nearly killed this woman.

"Sorry, I was just passing through, and I was wondering if it might be OK to talk for a little bit." The words felt so odd in Sarah's throat, but they just rolled out of her mouth. It was the first thing that came to her mind. She had never been one for improvised speech, but she went with it, nonetheless. She took a deep breath and felt her nerves strengthen. At that moment, she committed to herself that she would make the best of this situation. It wasn't like Azrael gave her much of a choice. Did she even have an opportunity to say no? Could she just walk away from this woman?

"No!" The voice in her head came quickly. The gruff tone was complete with palpable frustration.

Sarah's heart was racing, pounding inside her chest in a mocked race to the sounds coming from the bedridden woman's heart monitor. Sarah's pulse quickly doubled the rhythmic chimes of the other woman's heart. Swallowing hard, Sarah asked with a dry throat.

"Would you mind if I came in?"

Still staring at her visitor, "Yes, yes. I supposed that would be fine." Trying to sit up a little, but the strength in her arms gave her little support. "It has been a while since I have had any visitors."

"Thank you," Sarah offered with a nervous smile as she walked into the room. Lucky for her, the shadows from the dark room could hide the frightened look on her face.

Moving to take a seat on the chair closest to the bed, she added, "My name is Sarah." Pausing for a second. "Sarah Thompson," extending her hand to greet the woman. Sarah could see the dark veins and bones wrapped tightly inside the pale flesh, taking the delicate woman's hand.

Just as Sarah settled into the chair, another dark outline suddenly appeared in the doorway. This time the person did not linger. A nurse, dressed in blue scrubs, walked with authority as she moved swiftly to the side of the bed. Her light red hair was pulled back in a tight bun.

"Margaret? Is everything OK? Your heart seems to be racing a little bit ... oh."

Suddenly, taking notice of Sarah, the nurse froze in mid-stride. Her hands floated in the air, just short of the equipment she was coming in to check.

"I didn't know you had a guest."

Sarah felt the eyes of the nurse study her intently.

"Yes. Yes. This is Samantha Timmons. She is here to chat with me for a while, dear." Looking back at Sarah and smiling. "It has been a while since I had a visitor. I believe she is with the church. Isn't that right, dear?"

Breaking away from the gaze of the nurse, Sarah stumbled over her words, "Uh, yeah. I am from the church. I was sent here to talk with Margaret." She nervously laughed inside at the fact that she didn't indeed lie about why she was actually there. She was sent to this woman, and she had to think the Angel of Death was associated with some kind of church.

"OK. I just wanted to make sure you were good. It has been a while since you've had someone in here, Margaret, so it's good to see you so cheery." Not taking her eyes off Sarah, the nurse directed her words away from the woman in the bed.

"Miss … visiting hours end in a little over an hour."

"Oh, OK," Sarah said sheepishly. "Thanks." She was beginning to feel a little uncomfortable. As if the entire day held any sense of comfort, this nurse made her feel downright itchy. Sarah suddenly realized that there must have been a check-in desk or something that a reasonable person would have passed when they came in. Since Sarah magically appeared here, she was sure she was going to have to provide some kind of explanation as to how she got past the nurse's station.

"OK. I'm sure I will be gone by then." Or at least she hoped she'd be gone by then.

The nurse's eyes scanned Sarah up and down one more time, then she turned on her heel and walked out. Before she left the room, she paused and looked one last time at Sarah sitting in the chair. The nurse was frustrated with the unannounced visitor, but there was obviously nothing she could do about it. Nurse Baxter ran a tight ship, and staunchly enforced her rules, but moreover, she was fiercely protective of her patients. When her job was to give the best comfort and care during the last few years of a person's life, she felt it was her duty to do her job with a caring attitude. And she did a great job at it. Margaret was no different. Margaret came to them a few years ago, and everyone felt an instant love for her.

As Sarah turned back to Margaret, she was struck by the bright smile emanating from a wrinkled face. Here was a woman that was genuinely happy to see her.

"Hi. So, you must be Margaret," Sarah said matter-of-factly. "How are you doing this evening?"

"Well, dear, I am dying. How do you think I'm *doing*?" she said with a wry smile. Margaret's candor stunned Sarah.

Sarah felt her mouth open as the words tumbled out before she could control herself, "You have no idea how right you are."

"What was that?" Margaret blinked her eyes rapidly and looked off to the side, and she brought her hand to cup her ear. "Sorry, Samantha, my hearing has been going bad for years."

Composing herself, Sarah blurted, "Sorry, I just wondered why you think you are dying. I mean, really … what makes you think that you are going to die?" Not wanting to correct her for calling her by the wrong name, Sarah just looked at her with wonderment.

"Well, look at me?" She gave a wave of her emaciated arms. "I'm not here to give birth." Margaret took a minute to laugh at her own joke. Her laugh was a gentle, comforting laugh.

Sighing slightly, Margaret lingered. "I have lived a full life, dear. I am ready to go."

Sarah's pulse raced at the honesty of the elderly woman. There was a silent pause in the room that brought a sense of tranquility. Even Margaret's heart monitor was beeping at a steady rate again.

"So, you are not afraid of death?"

"Oh, heck no," Margaret quipped with another radiant smile on her face. "Death and I are old friends. I have seen so many of my friends and family pass away over the years that I am comfortable with a visit from death."

Looking down and smoothing out her blanket, "Now that I am alone, you might even say that I am relieved." Lifting her green eyes up to look directly at Sarah. "I just wish he would hurry up and get it over with already."

Fighting back the sudden urge to cry, Sarah gripped the arms of the chair. Even more sudden was the impulsive urge Sarah had to tell the woman about Azrael and the real reason she was there. What would she say anyway? *Don't worry ... you'll be gone soon enough.*

Pulling herself back together and smiling at the woman, Sarah pushed her words through a cracking voice. "How long have you been here?"

"Well, if you are asking how old I am, I'm eighty-eight years old," she said with a sense of pride.

"Oh no ... I wasn't trying to be disrespectful," Sarah said quickly. "My mom always said to never ask a lady about her age."

"I know, dear," interrupted Margaret. "But I am proud of my age." Again, she occupied her hands by refolding the crease in her blanket. "Just as a young girl is excited to tell everyone around her that she is one year older, I am proud of my eighty-eight years on this earth."

Curling her feet up underneath her in the chair, Sarah asked inquisitively, "So tell me, other than your age, what are you most proud of?"

Margaret thought for a moment. Her eyes focused on a small piece of thread that had escaped the blanket. She softly replied as she reached to pull the fabric. "I have spent most of my life helping others."

After thinking for another moment, she added, "When I was young, I helped my mother take care of my smaller brothers and sisters." As the elderly woman continued to share, her gaze shifted to a far-off place, picturing her family from a long-since-forgotten memory.

"Sometimes, it was even some of the neighborhood kids too. As I grew older, I just always looked for ways to help others."

Margaret Masterson was the kind of woman other women aspired to be like when they grew old. She had lived a good life, and she was darn proud of it. She married her high school sweetheart, and they had been married for over sixty-four years before he lost his battle with cancer. They were married on the front porch of her grandmother's house on a warm spring day in Tulsa. Together, they raised three beautiful children, and they, in turn, gave them seven grandchildren, and four great-grandchildren. Sarah noted the way Margaret's eyes smiled as she talked about each member of her family. As this beautiful woman shared loving memories about her family, Sarah couldn't help but wonder where all of this woman's family were at this exact moment and why none of them were with her. Especially *right* now.

Feeling overwhelmed with guilt by proxy, Sarah blurted out, "So, where are all of your family living now? Are they spread across the country?" She hoped there were good reasons for their absence. Living on the other side of the country would be a good reason.

"Oh, no. My daughters live here in Phoenix, and my son lives in Tucson. They stop by when they can, but they all have such busy lives."

Sarah's heart tore in two as if someone was tearing a sheet of paper in half. Talking with this woman made Sarah realize just how much she missed her own mother.

As if on cue, Margaret piped up, "So tell me about your parents, dear."

Sarah felt her heart race as the sadness wrapped around her like a warm blanket. As if called into the room by its very name, the Darkness pulled at her mind. It was tugging at her emotions. It cried out to her, just as it did every time she thought about her parents. The Darkness wanted her to pull away from this evil world and run back to its comforting embrace. Sharing her thoughts about her parents was like opening the door to her demons and inviting them in. She often thought she was invincible and able to keep those demons at bay. She felt she was almost strong enough to rescue herself from her depression. Yet, it was the Darkness that always pushed its way forward, forcing her to feel weak and helpless again.

Sarah wanted just to smile and give the standard answer about her parents. The fake story where they were OK and living in Florida. That was easier to tell strangers. Although this time, she felt like it would be wrong not to tell Margaret the truth. There was nothing to fear in sharing with this sweet, old woman. As she started to speak, the words tasted foreign. After all this time, the truth still had a bitter aftertaste.

Sarah loved her parents. Peter and Michelle were both born and raised in Phoenix, which was a rarity in itself. They met at a church retreat at the age of seventeen. Michelle was the typical shy girl, and Peter was the hopeless buffoon that would do whatever it took to win her attention. In the end, he succeeded, and they went on their first date to a little restaurant where Peter knew the owner. Since money for eating out was a luxury, he agreed to clean out the entire storeroom to get a discount on the bill. The night was magical, and they laughed together the whole evening.

After high school, life tried to divide the young loves. Neither of their families came from money, so when the two kids got scholarships to different colleges, they were forced to be apart for nearly four years. Michelle went to study education in the cool mountains of Northern Arizona University, and Peter studied business at Arizona State University in Tempe. The young couple did everything they could to make sure they kept the long-distance romance going. On some weekends, Peter would gather some of his friends and take a road trip to Flagstaff. The friends would go off and party, while Peter and Michelle would spend the weekend just being together. Holidays and summers were spent back in Phoenix, and the couple was inseparable. At the end of each weekend, holiday break, or summer, they would pledge their love to each other and part one more time. Praying it would be the last time they would have to be apart. Michelle worked hard and got her degree in three and a half years, mostly because she was tired of being away from what she called "her true love." Peter graduated with honors and took a job at a local pet food warehouse as an office manager. Even though it seemed evident, and everyone knew it was coming, Peter had to build up enough nerve to ask Michelle's father for permission to marry her. He said yes, and then so did Michelle. Both sets of parents gave their blessing, and the wedding was beautiful.

The more Sarah talked about her parents, the more open she was with her new friend. She bonded almost immediately with this wonderful grandmotherly woman. As the conversation went on, Sarah found herself truly enjoying the exchange. This woman was engaging and lived an exciting life. The more they talked, the more beautiful this aged woman became. Her eyes were outlined by thick laugh lines. Each one told a story of their own. Inside the wrinkles, Margaret's eyes were tender and bright. They reflected the wisdom of living for many years.

Margaret had a lifetime of stories at her disposal, yet she repeatedly asked about Sarah's life. The warm smile of the frail woman was disarming to Sarah, and she found herself talking freely. It had been a long time since she had someone to talk with like this. Despite the feeling of picking at a mental wound, Sarah allowed herself to open up as she talked about the terrible loss of her parents, her former fiancé, and every other facet of her dysfunctional life. The woman's tender nodding and smile gave Sarah the encouragement she needed to continue on her rant.

"So, I really didn't mind the way they treated me since it was …" Sarah stopped herself in mid-sentence as she felt the cold touch of a hand on her shoulders. No one had come in, so this could only have been one person. She slowly turned her head to see the solemn face of Azrael, and Sarah knew something was wrong. It was at that moment, a distant sound caught her ear. It was like it was almost hidden from her before that very second.

Or maybe it was there, but her mind chose to ignore it. Yet there it was. Loud and quite distinctive now. The solemn sound of the heart machine as it screamed out its single, long tone. Quickly, Sarah turned her head from the monitor to Margaret and back again. Not knowing which one to believe. She was there a minute ago. *How did I miss her dying?*

"It is done. The hour is up, and she is gone." Removing his hand from her shoulder, Azrael quickly moved around to the front of Sarah's chair. Standing in between her and the now lifeless woman, he reached his hand out to the stunned Sarah. The sudden movement of the towering figure broke her stare. She mindlessly took his hand, but she couldn't take her eyes off the beautiful woman lying in the bed. Margaret's eyes were closed, and there was a wisp of a smile on her lips. If she didn't know any better, Sarah would have sworn that the old woman was just sleeping and dreaming a lovely dream. Sarah slowly stood up from the uncomfortable metal chair. She could hear voices and people running in the hallway just outside the doorway. Then dark clouds formed around her, quicker this time, as she felt her body grow light again.

An instant later, she was standing in the middle of her living room. The sound of the heart monitor still hummed in her ears. Sarah's stomach twisted, and her head spun. Feeling her knees growing weak, Sarah fell backward into her oversized green armchair. It was only then that she realized she was all alone.

Is this how it would be, she wondered. One minute he would be there, and the next, he would just disappear. Maybe he would be gone for good this time, she hoped. Perhaps she would never see him again. The thought quickly faded as a shadowy figure emerged from the kitchen doorway. An odd mix of rage, disgust, and remorse washed over her.

Azrael appeared in the doorway and walked quickly into the room. He was holding one of Sarah's large coffee cups.

The one she bought herself from the community yard sale last month. It was her new favorite, and he held it in his devilish fingers.

"Here, drink this," he stated calmly as he handed her the cup. "You will need it." Sitting quietly, he looked at her intently. She did not meet his gaze as her eyes locked onto something far off, not wanting to even look at his face for fear that she might do or say something she'd regret later. Stiffly, she took the cup and sipped the hot liquid.

It was admittedly quite good—chamomile tea, made with a bit of honey and lemon. Just how she liked it. The piping hot drink relaxed her as it went down her throat, each part of her body succumbing to the waves of warmth.

Contrary to the feeling of the soothing liquid, Azrael's voice was low and cold. Each word filled the room as if he was shouting through a megaphone, but his lips moved with only a whisper.

"Did you talk with her?"

Looking at him for the first time since the hospital, she took a few deep breaths, set the cup down on the end table, and tried to calm her nerves. As the anger and disgust subsided, confusion and frustration took their place. She tried so desperately to sort out what he was asking.

"Yes," she said weakly. "Yes, of course, we talked." The seconds seemed to linger. "She is … um … was a wonderful lady."

Azrael's voice was almost muffled by the clouds in her head. "Did you tell her what was on your heart? Did you tell her about the most important thing in life?"

"Yes. No. Maybe," she said undecidedly, shaking her head slowly from side to side. "I don't know. I think she was the one that told me about some of the more important things in life." Wringing her hands together, "She was a good person." Looking up at Azrael, Sarah's eyes were wrapped in a blanket of newly formed tears.

"What am I supposed to tell a woman who had experienced such a full and wonderful life?" Continuing without waiting for his answer, "She was actually waiting for you, you know. She wanted to die."

His voice returned to the cold, monotone sound. "Yes. I was aware of her desire to leave this world. Her time had not yet come until now." He gently placed a hand on her shoulder. "Search your heart, Sarah Thompson. In the future, you will know what to tell them. You must."

She could feel his cold grip through the lightweight material of her blouse. His voice was still ringing in her ears when she smelled the familiar scent of bone-dry dust. She looked up, and he was gone. Vanished again.

He may have been gone, but the reality of Margaret's death still stung in Sarah's mind. She could still hear the woman's frail voice. She could even feel the power and beauty of her words. And now that poor woman was dead.

"Gone," she whispered into the empty room. "Why does death hurt so much?" She pulled up her feet and hunched into as small of a space as she could muster. That was when the tears began to fall.

CHAPTER SIX

From somewhere far away, a cacophony of sirens howled in the background of his mind. The echoes of the gunshot rang over and over again with piercing clarity in his ears. He could see the small billow of smoke rise from the tip of his gun. He could smell the cordite. Sharp and pungent to his nostrils. All of his senses were heightened, yet he was frozen. Unable to move. He could not turn his head to look away, nor could he force his body to move. He just stood perfectly still as he watched the red stain grow wider and wider on the pure white blouse of the young woman. He was strong enough to look away finally, but it was short-lived as he caught her return stare. He met her eyes as she stared up at him. Then suddenly, her eyes began to blink rapidly as if to blink away the realness of the sudden attack.

David didn't intend for everything to go down like this. All he wanted was to get in the store, get the money, and get out. No one was supposed to get hurt. He just wanted the damn money! He just needed the damn money. It wasn't even for him. It was for his brother. The doctors told him that if his brother didn't have the surgery, he would die. David needed to save him. They were the only family either of them had left.

Then, as if from a distance, a new sound came pouring into his mind. It was the sounds of yelling and screaming that resonated back to him. Still, he stared at the woman as she began to cry silently. No screams or yells came from her. She wasn't the one yelling—it was a man's voice. The yelling broke him free from his catatonic state as David turned his head to see two men standing in the doorway of the payday loan store. In an instant, David noticed that the two men were completely different.

One man, the police officer, stood crouched down with his gun drawn. Pointing it at David and yelling at him to drop his weapon. He looked like any other beat cop that he saw around the neighborhood. David would have normally seen him as a simple man hiding behind a gold badge. Yet this one looked different as he stood yelling at him. This one looked scared. Was the cop afraid of him? Whatever it was, David didn't like it, but it was the second man that gave David the chills.

The other man stood just to the right of the officer. Dressed in an all-black suit with a black coat, the man stood completely upright as if nothing was bothering him. As if he was a spectator just watching a show. David knew right away that this man must have been a government type. FBI or CIA, maybe, but why would he be here?Perhaps the man was there the whole time, and David missed him when he cased the waiting area earlier. Either way, he knew he was outgunned.

For that split second, David thought about what he should do. Run? Fight? Give-up? As his thoughts raced in a million different directions, he noticed the way the fed-looking guy stared at him. The man's face wasn't angry or scared. It was as calm and peaceful as a sunrise on Sunday morning. Surreal against the context of the moment. The man just stared at David. The man's bright blue eyes implored David, but it wasn't to put the gun down or stop. His eyes conveyed peace—to be calm.

Everything happened so fast that David wasn't sure who moved first. David held the gun tight in his right hand, thinking about how many bullets he had left. He began to raise his left hand to tell the police officer to back up when he saw the flash of fiery light extend from the barrel of the officer's pistol. Then David felt like someone had punched him in the gut. It was a solid blow that landed square in his belly. It made him stagger back as he instinctively put his hand against it. David looked down to see his hand now covered in a bright red liquid. He collapsed backward and stared up at the ceiling. The realization kicked in. He knew he'd been shot, but there was no pain. Ever since he bought the gun, he imagined how bad it must feel to be shot. He felt the impact, but not the pain. As a matter of fact, he didn't actually feel anything as he lay there motionless. David saw the officer come over and kick the gun out of his limp hand. The cop was yelling at him, but David couldn't understand him.

That was when the government man came to stand over David. The expression on the man's face was wrought with sorrow. His eyes bore into David's, and he felt like the man was looking directly into his soul.

The hostages ran frantically as the man in black knelt down near David's head. He hoped the man would help him or save him—take him to the hospital or something. Instead, the man just rested his calloused palm on David's brow. All of the sounds washed away, and everything went eerily silent.

Softly, the man in black spoke. "Relax. Your time has come. It is over."

The warm morning sun rushed into her living room through an open window curtain. Sarah opened her eyes to see her apartment in all its typical dullness. The allure of the soft pillow was too strong. She decided to stay on the couch for a while longer, thinking about things. The tiny particles of dust in the air danced across the rays of sunlight like little snowflakes. Her gaze took in the tranquil scene as her mind drew back to a time when she would have spent hours just staring at the falling snow. Growing up in Phoenix, she knew sunshine and warm days. In those days, her family would take trips just to see the snow and enjoy the cooler weather in the mountains of northern Arizona. Sarah had some great memories of those days.

Reflexively, Sarah's muscles tightened, and her eyes closed tightly against the pain that came from remembering those forgotten days. A time when the darkness of her mind was more real than the light in the world around her. It was nearly five years ago when her parents were taken from her—ripped away by one man's ego. Too arrogant to not call a cab. Too overconfident to know what to do. Too drunk to control the truck. The accident ended the lives of the two most important people in Sarah's world. Subsequently, the tragedy nearly took Sarah's own life away from her. Even without the finality of death, the sheer heartbreak was responsible for consuming a large portion of her waking hours.

As the months progressed after her parent's death, Sarah found herself unable to function as a "normal" person. Or at least that's what the doctor said. Even her time at the accounting firm could not bring normalcy. The numbers that always brought her comfort started to become her nemesis. Sarah found working with reports to be confusing and frustrating. While she tried to hide the sudden lack of concentration, her bosses noticed it right away. Sarah had been talked to for making many grievous mistakes. Customers complained about the accounting firm's lack of accuracy, and the company knew they had to let her go. So, after being the shining new star in their firm, they cut their losses and fired her on one bright sunny day.

When the market crashed like a tidal wave of financial uncertainty on the entire country, Sarah's job prospects dried up like the morning dew on a hot Arizona day. Without a job, Sarah was forced to give her car back even though she only owed seven more payments on it. Her parents left her with more bills than the little insurance payout could handle. She tried going after the driver's insurance company, but he was uninsured. She was left with nothing.

A short time later, Sarah lost her apartment and relegated herself to some friends' mercy to stay with them. Her new living situation and the stress of her life caused one more thing to disappear from her life—Jimmy Goddard.

She had been dating Jimmy for nearly a year before the accident, and he was everything she thought she wanted in a man. He had the looks, the right attitude, and even the right job. He was a writer for a local news outlet, and he got the best seats for all the best concerts. In her heart, she knew she loved him and even had visions of them getting married one day. He was kind to her, and he lovingly helped her when her parents died. But when the Darkness of Sarah's life overshadowed and took hold of her frail mind, she withdrew from him too. Like the job prospects, Jimmy faded away from Sarah's world. He was selfishly filled with a fear that he would be pulled down into her Darkness. Little by little, her friends left her as well. She knew she was why they didn't want to be friends anymore, but her pride and attitude lashed out at them. Each one was given the riot act as they pulled away from Sarah's life. She didn't need them anyway. She was angry and hurt, telling them off and pushing herself deeper into her Darkness. It embraced her. It welcomed her like a real friend.

Alone and penniless, Sarah did what she felt she needed to do to survive. There was only one person that she could rely on to get her through this mess … and that was herself!

Days turned into years, and years felt like an eternity, but slowly the Darkness started to lessen. Gradually, Sarah began to learn how to live again. Soon light crept back into Sarah's world, just as the sun rises with the dawn to signify a new day has come. Sarah woke up one morning and felt like she had been in a coma for years. She felt like the Darkness was there, but it was just a muted memory, faded and dull. It was as if a heavy blanket had been draped over her head for longer than she could remember. Now, it had finally been pulled away to reveal a world she had almost forgotten. Lying in bed on that morning of her rebirth, she stared at the rays of the morning sun pushing through the drawn shades. Something so simple looked so beautiful. Tiny pieces of dust moved silently in and out of the shaft of light. She could see the sunlight for its sheer beauty again. Looking around at her life, she saw the devastation that her depression had caused. She was standing in the middle of a crater caused by the mental explosion that literally destroyed her life and pushed everyone away with its blast. She was all alone, but at least she felt like she was herself again.

Not wanting to go back to the same routines or even the same people, Sarah scraped together some money and moved to the west side of Phoenix. Only a short way away, but it gave her a completely different life altogether. She had wished that enough time had passed since the collapse of her last job. She hoped to get a job in an accounting firm somewhere or maybe even do the books for a small business. She had been wallpapering the downtown business sector with her resumé for hours when she stopped at a small café for a bite to eat. It was there that she met Gerardo. He had been looking for a part-time waitress, and she took the job right away. That was only a year ago.

With an income and a sense of direction, Sarah took baby steps and tried to rebuild her life. She got an apartment and even began reaching out to the people in her past, apologizing for the way she acted. Her days were much brighter, mainly in part to the intense Phoenician sun but also to her resolve to keep her Darkness at bay. 'Each day is one step farther away from your past' was her motto. Most days, it was easy to stay positive, but there were some days that the Darkness nearly won out.

Sometimes it would only take a small trigger to let the Darkness overtake her. Like popping the plug out of the proverbial dam, an angry customer, a sad movie, or a story about a drunk driver would bring the heavy black blanket back to her mind, and she would instantly shut down. She started to recognize the Darkness for the enemy it was. It would stalk her and wait until she was weak before trying to devour her like a ravenous lion.

Now Sarah sat perfectly still on her couch. Letting her mind reflect on the past. She wasn't even sure if the warm tears that washed over her face were for the past or the present. Indeed, they couldn't have been triggered by the old woman she had just met the night before. She barely cried after her parents died, yet here she was, blubbering like a silly schoolgirl over this random lady. She tried to fight it back, but the feeling was too strong to stop. Or maybe it was because she was too weak to resist. Either way, the wave of emotions came upon her like a surge. The sobbing grew with intensity as she began to feel the heavy blanket seamlessly wrap around her mind again. Slowly, her eyes closed as she let herself fall deeper into the Darkness.

"It is OK to cry," came a resonating voice from somewhere close.

Like a muted call in a dream, the voice carried its way through the fog that was beginning to cloud Sarah's mind. Her eyes popped open, and she whipped her head from side to side —looking for the intruder that broke into her rare moment of peace. As she wiped the tears away with the back of her hand, she found herself looking at the black jacket of what must be something left over from her nightmares. It was him.

"It is OK to cry, Sarah," the voice came again. "Death is a hard thing for the living to understand. You are allowed to mourn. You are supposed to mourn, but you are supposed to grow out of that mourning and back into life. It is time for you to live again."

Sarah sat up on the couch and took in the full image of what was sorely becoming more and more of her reality rather than a nightmare. Unable to open her mouth and satisfy him with an answer, she continued to stare back at him.

"It is those poor souls that forget they are still living, and the others are the ones that have died." Staring intently at Sarah, Azrael crossed his hands in his lap and interlaced his fingers.

"The ones that keep themselves in the mourning place will find themselves dying a slower and often, much more painful death. You know what I am talking about, do you not?"

Nodding her head slowly. Sarah reminded herself that this being was not of this world. She felt her pulse quicken as she took in the memories of her Darkness and the pain of loneliness. Her arms instinctively wrapped around her body as if a cold wind had just blown through.

"But I came out of it."

"True," he mused with the briefest of smiles. "You are stronger than most of the rest. You have a certain spark inside you that was not ready to give up this life." Leaning forward to put his face even with hers.

"What lies at the core of this spark is what I need you to share with others."

Standing up, Azrael reached his hand out to her. "Come. We have further business to tend to."

Snapping to attention, Sarah stood up. "I can't go anywhere looking like this," making a point to wave her hands up and down her body in an animated display of futility.

With a crescendo, she raised them over her head and cried out, "I'm a wreck."

"I see nothing wrong with you." Waving a hand of his own up and down in front of her.

"Come, our hour awaits."

Sarah followed his hand and saw that her clothes were

changed in an instant. No longer was she wearing the clothes she fell asleep in on the couch. She was now in a casual navy-blue pants suit, and it looked fully pressed. Reaching her hands up to her hair, Sarah felt the wavy curls bounce as if she had worked on it all morning. She quickly moved over to the mirror and was stunned by what she saw. Not just the hair and makeup, but the woman that she used to be. The woman she remembered from her past. *Wow, this guy is good*, she thought. Placing her hand in his, she felt the weightlessness come over her again.

CHAPTER SEVEN

Sarah came out of the emptiness and fell into a world so bright that it burned her eyes at first. By the weight of the glare, she fully expected to be standing in a hospital again. In fact, the light seemed so bright that she could have been at the gates of Heaven itself. As her eyes got used to the light, Sarah realized she wasn't anyplace too special at all. In fact, she was in someplace that looked like an office with the sun shining brightly through large glass windows overlooking the city skyline. From the angle, she was facing east and very high up. Camelback Mountain was off in the distance, surrounded by the ever-present layer of brown dust. *Gotta love Phoenix*, she thought, *blazing sun and dust clouds.*

The office itself was a modest, almost sterile-looking room with minimal décor. Everything else looked in order except for the large wooden desk. It was dark wood with evidence of many years of use. A small black chair sat behind it, but the style was nothing compared to the desk's one-time elegance. The morning sunshine incessantly poured through the floor-to-ceiling windows, reflecting brightly across the top of the desk that was blanketed entirely in white papers and tan manila folders. Stacks of paper and notebooks filled the "in-box" to the point of overflowing. The temperature in the quiet room was stiflingly warm as the morning sun slowly heated the room. There was a smell of cheap aftershave in the stagnant air. Her nose wrinkled with disgust as the invasive scent overtook her nostrils.

"I thought I was here to talk to people … what am I supposed to do with *this* mess?" she asked as she turned around to find herself alone in the small office.

"You have to get the job first, toots," shouted a deep voice from the other side of the sturdy wooden door. Sarah gawked at the plain brown door. It was set against a blank white wall with just a miniature nameplate to the door jam's right. It read, 'Jason Wingfield – Councilman – 7th District'.

"Well, what are ya waiting for? Christmas? I don't have all day. Get in here!" The voice was louder and gruffer this time— tinged with a noticeable hint of agitation.

Sarah looked around the room once more to make sure this voice was talking to her. Seeing she was utterly alone, it must have been directed at her. Slowly she moved toward the closed door. Reaching for the handle, she was startled when the door suddenly opened away from her. Framing the door stood a stocky man in a white dress shirt, bright yellow tie, and grey slacks. Even though it was early in the day, slight sweat rings marked each armpit of his Stefano Ricci shirt. The buttons on his shirt seemed to strain against the mass of his stomach. What was left of his receding hair was pulled straight back and held tight by layers of gel. A wall of pungent odor hit her as the air rushed past her from the open door. He was definitely the source of the cheap aftershave smell. At first glance, his round face showed the anger that was present in his voice. As quickly as she could blink, the gruffness washed away from his face when his eyes focused on her. The deep lines on his plump cheeks creased as a smile lit up his face.

"Why … hello there. Won't you come in?" the man said as he backed up and waved his hand into his office. The voice was much more subdued and subtle now. The tone reminded Sarah of a salesman trying to change tactics to please a customer.

"You don't seem like you are too eager or excited about the job. Are you sure you want to be a secretary?"

Standing frozen in the doorway, Sarah looked at the man with instant contempt. "I am actually not here for an interview." Taking a deep breath, she pushed her shoulders back, and she marched into the man's office. She thought she felt strong enough, but it was more like a fly going into the spider's web.

"I'm here to talk with you," she said with as much false confidence as she could muster.

He openly leered at her as she walked past him. "OK, your choice, but it looks like you would make a great secretary," he said with a grin. His eyes studied every curve of her body.

Sarah could feel the eyes of this man undressing her as she walked through the office. Once inside, she turned to him and opened her mouth to speak.

"I am …"

"You can have a seat over there," he interrupted as he walked around her and over to his desk. "I really do need a secretary." Taking a seat and leaning back in the chair, he smiled.

"The last one didn't like my 'hands-on' approach to management," he gestured with mock air quotes around the hands-on idea.

Chills ran up Sarah's spine as mental images came to her about what he meant. She knew what this man was implying, and she didn't like it at all. She gripped the tall back of the soft leather chair. Standing behind the barrier gave her a weak sense of security, similar to the wooden chair a lion tamer would hold against a roaring lion. Whatever the obstacle, she wanted to keep something between herself and this man. Gathering her strength, she tried to speak up again.

Seeing Sarah's apparent objections to his comment made him laugh with a hearty bellow. Even from across the desk, Sarah smelled the whiskey on his breath.

"Well see," interrupting her again. "I need someone who can help me out around here."

The last few rips of laughter made his stomach ungulate beneath the lemon-yellow tie. Tapping his plumb fingers on the arms of the oversized chair as he stared at Sarah's neckline.

"We have tons of work to do." Pausing again. "Are you sure you aren't from the agency?"

"No, I am not from the agency," Sarah blurted out a bit quicker than she intended. Forcing herself to stand tall in the face of this brut, she dug her nails into the soft leather of the padded chair back, "I'm here to talk with you about something significant, or at least that is what I am supposed to do." An awkward pause followed as Sarah realized that he was not listening to her. Even though he was staring at her intently, it was apparent that his mind was elsewhere.

Feeling her skin crawl, Sarah forced her words out, "What do you think the most important thing in life is?"

Hearing the tail end of her question, the Councilman lifted his head up and looked Sarah directly in the face. "The most important thing in life is power. Plain and simple. Power." Leaning back again, "The one with the most power is the one that controls everyone else. That, my dear, is the most important thing."

Changing his expression, he furrowed his brow and asked, "Why do you want to know?"

"I've been sent here to talk with you about a crucial matter." Sarah could feel the dryness in her throat begin to tighten. "You could say that it is a matter of life or death."

"Well, then I guess I better pay attention," he replied sarcastically with a chuckle.

Feeling empowered with unknown strength, Sarah stood a little straighter. "I'm here to talk with you about the most important thing in life, but I'm not so sure what it is myself."

"Like I said, power is the most important thing," he said with a bored expression.

"What about other things like love and God?"

The words unconsciously poured out of her mouth before she knew what she said. It was the only thing she could think of in that split second. Those were the two things that her mom always told her were most important. She began thinking about how her mom talked about God, and how much she

loved being together as a family. It was strange that she thought about her here. Maybe this was what she was supposed to talk about with this man.

Eying her warily, "Do you know who in the hell I am, lady?" He paused for a minute even though he knew it was a rhetorical question. Jason Eugene Wingfield was a career politician and a perpetual degenerate. He learned early on in life that people are useless unless they are being ordered around and manipulated. His father, a life-long politician, taught Jason that people were like cattle. Feed them scraps of the truth and then milk them for all they are worth. Once they have been used up, take them out to be slaughtered and clear the path for new constituents.

Once Jason discovered the intoxicating rush of being in power, he sought it wherever he could find it. Whether it was a high school student body president or a college dorm chairman, he sought the control that came from power. He even tried to weasel his way into a local lodge just so he could run for the council board. The rush from being in charge wasn't the whole reason. It was the feeling that he was superior to others. He tricked or suckered them into believing his lies, and it became like a drug to him. He was above them, and they put him there. To him, it was the same as them hoisting him up on their shoulders and parading him through the village. He was their king, their master.

When Jason took office or any authority position, it took an act of Biblical proportion to remove him. He would bribe, lie, cheat, and slander his competitors to make sure he kept his position. His motto was *'whatever it takes.'* Sometimes, he ran with the darker circles of society. It was the back-alley deals and clandestine meetings that made him feel a little like a mobster. It was through those dealings that the young Jason Wingfield was guided toward the city government. The Pentero Mafia from Los Angeles wanted someone on the inside of the Phoenix government to give them the edge they needed to take over the criminal underworld. Wingfield was their man, and they pulled the strings to get him on the path to mayorship.

"Well, I can buy love," he said apathetically as he slammed his hands down on the desk. "And if I wanted God, well sugar, I could buy him too!"

Sarah was stunned at this man's disregard for God. She might not have been a perfect believer in the God of Heaven, but even she would not go so far as to say such things. She shifted uncomfortably from one foot to the other. The heretic stared at her legs as she moved.

Feeling the anger well up inside her, she blurted out, "Well, what about death? What if I told you that you were going to die?"

This comment caught his attention, and the Councilman snapped his head up to stare directly at Sarah's face again. Eying her up to see if she was bluffing or trying to threaten him.

"Look, lady … I don't know who in the hell sent you, but I can tell you this much. I don't take lightly to people threatening me."

Pushed forward by the effects of the adrenaline, Sarah just stared back at the obese man. "I have it on good authority that you are going to die soon."

The color drained from his face as tiny beads of sweat began to form on his furrowed brow. "You tell your boss to go to hell! No one threatens me and gets away with it."

Standing and leaning forward over the desk, "I pay too many people in too high of places to take this kind of crap from you!"

The fear of the man's anger mixed dangerously with Sarah's desire to see his reaction as she pushed him further, "If you knew you only had one hour to live, what would you do?"

The Councilman could see the fear in Sarah's eyes. All of his years in politics told him that this lady was bluffing. She was trying to get him to react. She almost had him going. He was almost running around scared in his own office.

"Well, toots," he exclaimed with a nervous laugh. "I would do so much coke and get so many broads that I wouldn't care what happened to me." He knew that this would offend her, and he liked it. The tables were turned, and he was making her feel uneasy.

The last of the adrenaline that gave Sarah her fierceness was gone. It left her with a heavy feeling in the pit of her stomach and a sour taste in her mouth. This man disgusted her, and she needed to get away from him as soon as possible. She wasn't going to wait for the full hour. There were too many things this creep could do to her in an hour.

"I think we're done here," Sarah said boldly as she turned on her heel and cleared the short distance to his door.

Still chuckling to himself, Wingfield shouted, "Are you sure you can't stay for some dic-tation?" This brought an even bigger roar of laughter from the fat man.

With the sounds of the evil laughter behind her, Sarah

quickened her pace. In her anger, she slammed the door behind her with an audible thud. Feeling somewhat victorious with her last little jab at the obscene man, Sarah's lips curled up in a slight smile. Her stride was long and confident as she walked quickly toward the door on the other side of the small office. As she walked out of the little receptionist's office, Sarah found herself looking out into a sea of cubicles. The room was electric with activity. Phones were ringing, and people were shouting at each other over the short gray dividing walls that made up their 9-to-5 workplace 'cell'. Some of them looked up at her, but most just ignored the random woman that came from the Councilman's office. Sarah took the opportunity and made a hasty retreat to the bank of elevators just beyond the main entrance.

Sarah fought the compulsion to look back as she waited for the elevator. Pushing the button a second time, she glanced at her watch. Doing a quick calculation, Sarah had been at the office for about fifteen minutes, tops. *Would he be dead in forty-five minutes*, she wondered? It would serve the man right. He was not a good man at all, and she hoped that this might have even been a blessing in disguise. Maybe someone with ethics and morals might take over the vacant position after Azrael took Councilman Wingfield away.

Slapping the button a third time, Sarah felt a slight wave of panic rush over her. Did she tell this creep too much about Azrael coming to get him? A sense of dread crept in as she scolded herself. In her head-strong arrogance to try and put this guy in his place, she might have broken the one rule with the Angel of Death. Would he be coming for her later because of it? She replayed the conversation in her head, careful to remember what she told the man. After another second, the doors opened up, and she stepped into the empty elevator.

She turned quickly and hit the button for the ground floor. Just as the mirrored doors closed, Sarah suddenly realized she was not alone. In the reflection of the polished metal, a tall, dark figure stood just behind her. His cold, blue eyes were staring at her in the polished image.

"Oh God," Sarah exclaimed, clutching her chest over her heart. "You scared me!"

"You have no idea," came the deep, monotone voice from behind her. Sarah turned to look at him. Intensity tightened his features as he stared at her.

"You did not finish your task."

"Actually, I thought I might have said too much," she said softly, as she thought about what she had told the crude man. Sarah looked at Azrael's dark complexion to see if she could read his response, but it was like a rock with no emotion. Only his ice-blue eyes flared with a strange mixture of anger and sadness. If he was upset with her or overjoyed with her, the rest of his face didn't show it.

"It seems that you told him what was on your mind and not what was on your heart," he said dryly. "When I mentioned that you had a spark about you, I did not mean the kind of spark that would start an explosion."

Sarah felt the wave of red wash over her face as the heat from her glowing skin pulsed in her cheeks. Turning her face back to the elevator doors, Sarah did everything she could to avoid his gaze in the reflection of the mirrored doors. She thought again about what she told the Councilman. In retracing her conversation, she remembered the vulgar things the lewd man said to her and how she felt in his presence. The feelings of helplessness brought a new kind of heat to Sarah. The feeling of guilt melted into anger as she reminded herself that the Councilman was going to die. Instead of feeling remorse for the disgusting man, she had a feeling of utter apathy. He was going to die, and she had an unsettling comfort that came from knowing that fact. The man deserved to die.

"Who deserves to die, Sarah?" The words came quickly to

her mind. Reflexively, her eyes looked at the dark man standing behind her. She watched, but his lips did not move. "Who is the judge that decides which people are to be punished? If wrongs have occurred, who is the judge that decides what punishment should be associated with what transgression?" The questions kept floating through her mind.

"Are *you* that judge, Sarah?"

The question stung her like a slap across the face. His voice was still as chilling as it had always been, and his words carried the weight of a sledgehammer. A fresh pang of guilt welled back up inside her.

"If they committed a crime or hurt people, then maybe they deserve to be punished." Her voice was a little louder than she intended as she felt the burn of conviction rise up to meet the feelings of guilt.

"Can there be forgiveness," he questioned.

Sarah paused as her eyes searched for some deeper meaning in Azrael's face. "Forgiveness of what?" she quipped. "Forgiveness of the wrongs they did? Well, sure, maybe." She shook her head. "I don't know. I am not the one that can offer those kinds of people forgiveness."

"That may be true in a deeper sense, Sarah," he said as he leaned in closer. "But what about the good people that do bad things? Should they be forgiven in the same way that bad people are when they do evil things?

Sarah had always believed that most people were good by nature. Sure, there were some whackos, but being a waitress, she'd seen plenty of decent people too. Sarah knew most of them had good hearts. Even if they didn't tip well, she mused, she knew most people were inherently good. She didn't even know if some of her customers were church leaders or ax-murderers.Some of them just needed to have someone listen— someone to be kind to them.

"I guess so," she said solemnly. "But what about those people that are sorry for their mistakes? Can there be room for forgiveness no matter what they have done?"

After a slight pause, Azrael gave a heavy sigh. "Yes, Sarah. There is forgiveness for all." He reached his hand up to place it on her shoulder. His voice was no longer cold but yielded a fatherly tone.

"Most people want forgiveness, but their desire for it is to merely appease their sense of guilt. Their hearts are not truly repentant, and they do not seek after forgiveness in the right way."

He lowered his eyes to the floor. Maybe it was the shadows cast from the elevator's ceiling lights, but he actually looked solemn. His deep voice filled the small room, "Simply saying you are sorry is not enough."

CHAPTER EIGHT

In the middle of the police station, the commotion had died down after the recent payday loan store shooting. The clock ticked as minutes marched toward the end of a shift that was not coming to an end nearly quick enough for Michael Wolfe. The desk he was sitting at was like so many of the other desks, but his had piles of papers and folders that threatened to topple at the slightest nudge. The overall detective's office space was tranquil for this time of day. That was the way Michael liked it. A chance to get some things done that he normally wouldn't have gotten a chance to do.

He was an average-sized man, but his tight muscles showed his natural strength. His brown hair was kept military short. He learned to love the haircut from his days in the Army. He liked it simple. He liked it clean. That was one of the reasons why he chose to become a police officer in the first place. He saw that there was a sense of black and white about things. The law was either broken or upheld. Too many people tried to dance in the gray areas of life without making a decision or taking accountability. That is why so many cases were given to him. He had a sense of finding out who the person behind the crime was. He was rarely wrong about a suspect, and once he started an investigation, it took an act of Congress to get him to stop.

He sat in the shadow of a manilla tower that held many of those exact cases. Hundreds of files containing dozens of unsolved murders and ongoing investigations. Most of them were cases other detectives had given up on a long time ago. This was how he became a detective so early in his career. He was only thirty-two, and much younger than most of his peers at the station. As an officer on the street, Michael had a knack for noticing things the other investigators missed. Mostly, he would pick up something that was out of place.

His big break came in a case where the suspect had taken a bus ticket from the victim and used it to make his escape. Michael was one of the first on the scene and noticed the victim wore an ID bracelet with a Los Angeles address. Looking for some other kind of identification, he found a receipt in the man's pockets for a café that was just across from the bus station, only a few blocks away. The victim did not have luggage with him, but there was suggestive evidence of a struggle, and something dragged through the dirt away from the scene. When the detectives arrived to comb the scene, they ruled it a random mugging. Michael didn't feel this was a good enough assumption. He felt there was more to this crime than met the eye, so he walked down to the bus station to see if the victim's name was on any bus manifests that had recently left the area. His name came up on a bus that was destined for Los Angeles. The bus was stopped before it got to Blythe, California and the suspect was caught with the victim's wallet still on him.

Today, however, he was not working on one of his many case files. His shoulders were tight, and his forehead wrinkled as his fingers flew quickly across an oversized calculator. An open checkbook flapped wildly in the other hand. He studied it as he would typically scour a crime scene. He just knew that something had to be wrong with it, but after an hour of looking over it, the only thing wrong with the checkbook was it belonged to him. It told the sad true story of his finances or lack thereof. He was an honest cop and never took anything that wasn't his. He was happy with what he earned, but then his bosses came to him earlier in the year and asked him to take a pay cut because of city budget problems.

Now his wife, Tori, was seven months pregnant with their first child, and his savings were slim. He desperately wanted to give his family the lifestyle that his wife was accustomed to, but it wasn't easy on a detective's pay. His wife had a small job at a local boutique, but the doctor warned her that she needed to stay off her feet, so she was forced to quit about a month ago. Now, Michael took overtime and off-duty work whenever he could get it.

Closing his eyes and leaning back, he pressed his hands against the desk. Quickly opening his eyes, he thought he heard the files on his desk start to shift. Spending the morning picking up and re-filing a ton of paperwork was the last thing he wanted to do today. As he thought about it, a folder on top of a six-inch tower started to slide. Grabbing it quickly, Michael sighed as he placed it gently back on the crest of the mountain. Rubbing his eyes with one hand, Michael took a cup of cold coffee in the other. Just as he brought the stale cup near his nose, he suddenly wondered just how old the coffee might be.

The rush of movement at the far side of the office interrupted his thoughts. The main office door swung open, and an older, overweight man shouted for Michael. He was wearing a dark blue suit that did little to hide his weight. The tie, which Michael could have sworn was a clip-on, draped wearily across the expanse between the jacket buttons.

"Hey Michael, there was an overdose down at the capitol building. It's got your name written all over it ... ya want it?"

Looking at the mountain of other cases and then at his checkbook, he replied, "Yeah, sure. I'll go have a look."

He took a large swallow from the cup before he realized too late that the coffee was older than he thought it was. Much older. Grabbing his coat and taking a swig out of his water bottle, Michael jogged out to his car.

When he got to the capitol building, the place was filled with people. It was something you would expect when a dead body was found at a government office. There were always more on-lookers and rubber-neckers than actual police officers working the crime scene.

Moving his way to the front of the crowded office, Michael learned of the late Councilman Wingfield. He knew the deceased. Rather, he knew *of* the deceased. Wingfield was well known for his shady dealings and his outright attack on the police department's fiscal budget. Michael knew he had to play this one cool, or else he might just smile at the justice of it all. The victim had overdosed on one too many cocaine lines, and it should be a simple case to close.

The councilman's office was a mess. Papers were everywhere as if a whirlwind had blown through the high-rise office. The desk had everything thrown to the floor. Based on the damaged lamps and furniture, something quite violent happened. *Maybe this would not be an open-and-shut case after all*, he thought to himself. When he examined the body, Michael concluded that the victim was the one that destroyed his own office, or at least he was trying to stop the person that did. When he looked at the amount of cocaine on a mirror in his private bathroom, he knew the toxicology report would show the cocaine levels in this guy's bloodstream were more powder than platelets. Quick enough to bring on a drug-induced rage, but what triggered the outburst?

Michael called one of the officers taking notes. "Hey, do me a favor. Get me this guy's phone records from his office line and his cell phone." He waved his hand at the body, "Something happened just before this guy went nuts and trashed his office. I want to know who he talked to."

"Yes, sir," the middle-aged officer said. There was more than a hint of disdain in the man's voice. Michael had heard that tone many times. Many people didn't take too kindly to a guy younger than them making detective.

"Thanks," Michael said with as much enthusiasm as he could muster.

"Witnesses claimed to have seen a woman leave the Councilman's office shortly before the body was found," the officer finished.

After talking with a few witnesses, Michael's intuition found it curious that none of the witnesses saw the woman enter the office. They just saw her leave. He asked for the forensics team to get fingerprints. It turns out, it was perfect timing. The cleaning crew had been there just this morning, and everything had been wiped clean from the previous night. The prints they pulled were easy to find and clean to read. Their search turned up only three sets. One was the victim's, a second belonged to the person that discovered the body, and the third must have belonged to the mystery woman.

"I can have those prints for you in a few hours," said the lead investigator. He was a tall man in his mid-thirties with a large puff of blond hair that practically blocked his left eye. "Where do you want me to send them?"

"Email 'em to me," Michael said as he pulled his hand through across his head and let out a heavy sigh. *How in the hell does he even see the fingerprints*, Michael thought with a hint of jealousy.

"I'm heading home to spend some time with the wife."

With that, Michael left the crime scene with as much fanfare as when he arrived. Walking out, he noticed most people were already back to work as if nothing had happened. Maybe it was the way they coped with death. Perhaps it was because they just didn't care about what happened to the Councilman. Either way, their behavior made it easier for the investigators to do their jobs, which was good.

The drive home was uneventful. These days, Michael tried to spend as much time as he could with his wife. If there were reports to be completed or research to be done, he would rather do it at home if he could.

When he arrived back at his house, it was empty. Even though the sunlight was still at its mid-day peak, there were thick shadows across his front yard. The fact that he lived in a desert never stopped him from maintaining the only house on his block with a green front yard. The large mesquite tree gave great shade across the front of the house and made the summer temperatures a little more bearable on the front windows. He also made sure to have a thick layer of green grass to lower the temps around the house. Michael had always dreamt of playing ball with his son in the grass, and now that he lived in Arizona, his dream was just a little harder to keep up. The house was a modest one in a good neighborhood. Not bad for the money, considering he bought it only after the real estate market crash.

Michael went in and set his laptop up on the kitchen table. Starting the coffee maker, he noticed a note from his wife telling him that she was out with her sister and would be back soon. Relegated to being alone for a while, he turned on his laptop and scanned the want ads for some extra work. Hours had passed, and Michael was frustrated. He pushed away from the table with a disgusted look on his face. There was plenty of work out there for a simple security guard, but the pay was so low that he might as well stay home. It wasn't worth being away from Tori. He knew something would come up.

Just then, a ding came from his laptop, telling him that he had a new email. Opening it up, he found himself looking at a file on Sarah Anne Thompson with a note attached from the forensics investigator.

> Detective Wolfe: Here is the file for the person you requested. Her prints were on the doorknob and a chair in the office. Oddly enough, nothing on the desk or any other part of the office. Good luck.

Her file showed a typical, boring life. No prior convictions. Not even any tickets. Basically, she was a decent person when it came to keeping the law. They had a copy of her fingerprints from a background check her church did on her many years ago. He opened a link that contained a picture of her from her driver's license. A pretty looking woman. Brown hair. Brown eyes.

"Then why in the hell were you at that creep's office just before he died?" he questioned aloud.

Getting up to get another cup of coffee, Michael heard the front door open and the gentle sound of laughter coming up the hallway. It was Tori, and her sister, Lisa. Michael loved his wife, and he was glad that her sister was around to help keep Tori from being lonely. Moreover, he was thankful that Lisa kept Tori off her feet for most of the time. He generally liked his sister-in-law. She was a good person with a caring heart.

Lisa was a nurse at a fancy retirement home over in Sun City. It seemed to be the place where all local Phoenicians went to retire. Tori told him that Lisa had always wanted to help the elderly. Even when she was young, Lisa would help out around their grandparents' house. Lisa was good at it too. She had the patience and the love it took to be that kind of nurse. The incredible strength it took to stand by a person who was facing the end of their life was something not many people could handle. For all the good qualities that Michael appreciated about her, he also knew she was a bit of a busybody and tended to stick her nose into other people's business.

Despite the one glaring flaw, Tori loved her sister, and he loved that about his wife. There were even times when he felt like Lisa was more excited about the baby coming than he was. This was something he would never openly admit to his wife.

Tori was ecstatic about being pregnant. She didn't have the morning sickness or weight gain that had terrified her. Tori had everything going for her. According to the ladies at the doctor's office, Tori was one of the lucky ones. All that Michael knew was that his wife looked beautiful when she was pregnant.

"Hi, Hun," came the voice from the hallway.

"Hey, babe. I'm in the kitchen," Michael called back. He poured the rest of the coffee down the drain. He loved coffee, but his wife loved it more. Well, she loved it *before* she got pregnant. Now she was trying to eat and drink healthier for the baby, so she quit caffeine cold turkey. Out of respect for her healthier choices, Michael stopped drinking coffee around her. Still, he didn't have the same willpower to stop altogether.

"Smells like you were having coffee," she said as she walked through the door, holding some shopping bags from the local department store. Setting the bags on the table near Michael's open laptop, she continued, "Lucky dog. God, I miss that stuff."

Walking up, he kissed her softly and smiled, "You'll have it again one day."

"Yes, and then we can all drink it around you again," said Lisa with a smile as she walked into the room, holding the remaining few bags. "Hi, Michael."

"Hey Lisa," Michael replied with a worried look on his face as he looked at the bags. "Did you girls, umm, have fun?"

"Yes! Lisa bought us some things for the baby," she said in a high-pitched squeal of excitement. She grabbed his hand with both of hers. "Come see what we got." They made it halfway out the kitchen door when they heard Lisa's voice.

"Hey, wait … who is this woman," Lisa said with a curious, alarmed tone to her voice. Michael looked over and saw her reading the file that he still had open on his laptop screen.

"Eh, she's a nobody really," he said as he briskly walked over and began to close his laptop. "Someone I might need to talk to."

Tori laughed and punched Michael on his shoulder. "Yeah, Michael is out looking for skinnier women!"

"No! Seriously." Pushing the lid back open, "Who is she? I have seen this woman before."

"Really?" Michael asked quickly. Now Lisa had his undivided attention. He stared at his sister-in-law as she stared at his prime suspect.

"Where, Lisa? Where did you see this woman?"

Still looking at the picture, Lisa told them about the strange woman that appeared from out of nowhere and stayed with one of her patients for a little bit. She lifted her eyes to meet Michael's expectant gaze.

"Crazy thing is that the patient she was with died, and by the time we got to her room, this lady was gone." Pointing at the screen and then waving her hand up in the air, "She was gone. Just like that." Lisa punctuated her statement with a snap of her fingers.

A chill ran up his back as he saw a pattern forming. This couldn't be a coincidence. Michael placed a hand on her shoulder and used his police investigator's voice, "Are you sure this is the woman?"

"Absolutely! That is definitely her," Lisa said as she turned to look at Michael. "Who is she?"

"When was this? When did you last see her?" he asked as he ignored her question.

"Just last night."

Michael swallowed hard. He stared at the picture of Sarah Thompson for a long time. His instincts knew that something was going on, and he had just stumbled on to a bizarre turn of events. There must be something more to this woman. Could this be the early stages of catching a potential criminal? He had to talk with Sarah Thompson.

◆ ◆ ◆

Joey Hampton sat in the break room for a while, spinning a bottlecap from his soda. Everything around him was quiet. Almost too quiet for this place. It was always peaceful this early in the morning. Once the bell rang later, everything would be a loud mixture of machines and men. He got to work early today with a purpose in mind. Today, he was finally going to talk to the boss.

As Joey's shift ended yesterday, he asked his boss if he could meet with him in the morning. He had had enough of how things were running on the production floor, and he had to tell someone. As he sat there, his hands balled into fists—thinking about how the other guys acted when he told them what they were doing was illegal.

The McMillan Bottling Company had been in business for fifty-six years. Bottling some of the finest locally crafted beers in the tri-city area. Initially started by Roy McMillan and handed down through two generations. Roy's grandson, Gerald, now ran the plant since he turned 30 about ten years back. They made it a point to take care of its employees and the community. Even during hard times of the last recession, the McMillan's were known to give random bonuses and even directly pay some of the employees' mounting debt.

Joey jumped when he heard the doors open down the hall. The morning shift would be coming in from the parking lot. Even though he knew the morning crew would be coming in soon, he still felt a sense of foreboding. He stood up and quickly made his way to the boss's office. He could stay in the waiting room without drawing any unwanted attention. As he approached the office, he noticed the light coming from under the door jam. His luck was turning. The boss was in early, and he could talk with him before anyone else got there.

He heard voices as his hand reached for the door handle—deep, rough voices. The boss was not alone. Leaning his head in closer, he started to make out what they were saying.

"What do you mean the last batch was light," questioned the voice Joey knew to be Gerald McMillan.

"Yeah, boss. We stayed last night to run the last few batches ourselves. We only used the material you told us wasn't in the inventory, so it wouldn't show up missing." It was a voice Joey wasn't sure he recognized. It might have been the 2nd shift manager, Travis.

Another voice pushed in, "So, when we ran the second batch, the total came out about 250 gallons short. We put everything into the drums just like you asked."

Joey stood frozen by the door. There weren't supposed to be any drums in the product line. Everything went into either bottles or kegs.

"Well, we have to go with what we have. The buyers will need to wait until next month to get the rest. I'm risking a lot just to make these extra batches: the missing inventory, extra usage on the production line ..." McMillan declared. "We need to get the stuff drummed and shipped out before my father or any of the old-timers find it."

Joey stood up straight. There was something illegal going on. He wasn't mistaken when he counted the inventory. He was right, but wait, was the boss really in on it? It almost sounded like he was the one setting it all up. That couldn't be right.

As he stood in front of the closed door, confusion gripped his mind. He thought about all the times when the boss stayed late. Everyone assumed he was working hard. Ensuring the company would survive the tough times. Joey was so stunned by this conflict that it tore at his mind. In his mental stupor, he never heard the person coming up behind him. The last thing he heard was the sound of rushing air and the faint whistle of something moving quickly toward him. Then everything went black.

He wasn't sure what hit him or how long he was out, but he felt throbbing from the back of his head. Each pulse was like white lightning behind his closed eyes. He could barely concentrate long enough to listen to the voices that were standing over him.

"There goes our safety bonus," he heard a man say as he chuckled. Joey felt strong hands pick him up, and the sudden upward motion made him want to vomit. As he opened his eyes, he saw two men standing about two feet in front of him. Another man was standing a little bit away. His vision became a little clearer, and he noticed he recognized two of the men. He was right about the voice. One was the night manager, Peter. The second one he knew was Hector from the Receiving Department. The hands that lifted him roughly and put him in the chair, belonged to Jones, the security guard. The third man standing behind the first two men was not like the others. He was someone Joey had never met. This man was not dressed in factory clothes, but instead looked like a gangster or a mafioso type. Wearing all black with an oversized coat to conceal the large caliber weapon he most certainly had hidden. Probably the enforcer.

"So, what are we gonna do with him Boss?" Hector asked in a nervous voice. The room was silent for what felt like an eternity. Finally, McMillan stood up and walked toward Joey. The other two men stayed back, but the enforcer followed at the boss's heel. When the gunman got into the light, Joey could see the long leather trench coat that the man wore. No matter what was under that coat, it was the man's eyes that shook

Joey. The intensity with which the man stared at him with was staggering. The cold blue eyes gripped him with such power that Joey could physically feel it.

Even as McMillian's hand came up and Joey saw the gleaming of a knife from out of the corner of his eye, he still could not take his eyes off the other man. Joey knew he should have been afraid, but strangely, he wasn't. He felt the pressure against his chest as the knife came plunging down but there was no pain. Surprisingly, he felt an odd sense of peace as McMillan brought the knife back up again—this time covered in his blood. The edges of his vision started to fade away as the vibrant blue of the man's eyes glowed like beacons in the darkness. Then, in a sudden flash, even those were gone, and there was nothingness.

CHAPTER NINE

Sarah's head was spinning by the time she made it back to her apartment. Her heart jackhammered in her chest. She wasn't quite sure if it was from the craziness of the morning or the fact that she kept glancing behind her every few feet. The way her new overlord kept appearing and disappearing provided her with a healthy sense of paranoia. It was only after Azrael vanished from inside the elevator that Sarah realized she would have to find her way back to her apartment. Lucky for her, she had the day off, or she would have had to squeeze a cab fare out of the new dark-cloaked taskmaster.

Walking home, Sarah replayed the scene over and over again. Remembering the words he said. She knew he was right, but she wasn't about to let him know it. Besides, it was pretty rude of him to leave her in the lobby of an unfamiliar office building miles away from her apartment. Despite her anger, her own guilt figured the abandonment was what she deserved for not doing exactly what he asked her to do.

The entire bus ride home, Sarah's mind was filled with thoughts of Margaret and Jason. Two people, seemingly on opposite ends of the personality spectrum, have been taken from this earth in the past twenty-four hours. One, a beautiful, angelic woman, and the other, an obnoxious, evil man. One she wished could have stayed longer, and the other one she couldn't wait to get away from. Yet, there were two commonalities between them. First, both were taken away by Death himself. And the second common denominator was a bit trickier to nail down. Somehow, she was supposed to tell them the very same thing. Something that was so important that a dying person needed to know. She was a person that could barely plan her life one day in advance, and here she was expected to help people figure out the most crucial thing in their life with only one hour to go.

Ignoring the obviously misplaced trust in her by Azrael, the more she thought about the differences between the two people, the only thing she could use to connect them was death itself. The mysterious leather-clad man foretold their death down to the minute. She wrestled with her own mixed emotions as she thought about what Azrael had done to them. She was angry about Azrael taking away Margaret, but she was happy that he had taken Jason. Like two sides of the same coin: one good, one bad. Yet either way she replayed it in her mind, Azrael was the devil. He consumed people and took them from this earth.

Once she got home, she tried to occupy herself by cleaning her apartment. Part of it was to give her something to do while she tried to process everything that was going on in her head. She also figured that if Death were to be coming over as a frequent houseguest, she should have a presentable place.

"Oh, God, what am I thinking? The only person I've ever had back to my apartment more than once is a demon from hell," she yelled out loud.

That's when she stopped in her tracks. Still holding on to the throw pillows, she wondered what God would think about Azrael. Did God allow this demon to have that much control of

His people? These *were* His people, after all, right? They were His creation. Where was He in all of this? As she cleaned, she grappled with the idea of a loving God that would allow the devil to have his way on earth. She remembered that the Bible mentioned something about God being the ruler over everything. She thought that meant the devil as well.

Frustrated and tired, Sarah plopped down into her favorite chair. An old Lazy Boy recliner that she bought second-hand a few years ago. It had the perfect arrangement of springs and pads to envelop her after a long day's shift. It would help her soothe her tired muscles after being on her feet all day, but this time, the chair felt different somehow. Adjusting her position a few times, she thought it might just be in her head. Why not—everything else was going wrong in there.

Once she finally found a comfortable position, Sarah decided to stay there. She snickered to herself as she defied the call to complete the rest of the cleaning that still had yet to be done. It was her way of selfishly rebelling against what *had to be done*. The thoughts of Azrael and all the people that have died tugged at the fringes of her mind. She felt sadness like she hadn't felt in a long time.

It wasn't long before her eyes grew heavy, and the comfort of her favorite chair pulled her down. Just as sleep took hold, her lips parted, and she whispered, "Death sucks."

Everything had come together perfectly. Months of planning and years of dreaming had all led up to this day. This was her special day, her wedding day. Sarah had dreamt of the fairytale wedding ever since she was old enough to play dress-up in her mother's closet. Today, everything had to be perfect. She would be the beautiful bride in white. Her handsome husband would be waiting at the end of a long aisle, flanked by all of their closest friends and family. The entire crowd would be welcomed by the gentle sounds of classic loves

songs being played by a harpist on the balcony. An array of soft oohs and aahs would mingle with the murmurs of onlookers as she entered the back of the church. Now that dream was finally here. It had finally come true.

The women to each side of Sarah moved in relative unison, like little bees hovering over the same beautiful flower. Each one encircling the bride, primping, and adjusting with final touches and details. A flurry of hands worked bright, baby white carnations into her magnificently braided hair. The other woman stood silently next to the pair, arranging another set of flowers into the bouquet. A beautiful mixture of red and white roses, along with garden lilies, then wrapped in an elegant lace tassel that hung down a few inches past the stems.

Sarah stood in front of a full-length mirror and tried to absorb every second. Every moment was filled with future memories. Even though sunlight poured into the room from the nearby windows, Sarah still glowed brighter than the rays of light in her dress. The imagined light emanating from her dress radiated its beauty to fill even the darkest shadows in the room. She wore a white dress, trimmed in lace. It clung to her body with a perfect fit, contouring her like a finely wrapped present. Gently she pulled the edges of the frock out to each side to let the fullness of the dress flow out.

"You look wonderful, my dear," her mother said as she finished pinning Sarah's hair up after she put the last flower in with a sense of accomplishment. The pride that Michelle Thompson felt for her daughter on this special day was palpable. A single tear formed and fell away from her moist eyes as she tried desperately to hold back the flood of emotions. She was trying to be strong for Sarah. They had both agreed that if one started crying, they would both be bawling within seconds. Michelle didn't want to be the first one to cry, so she fought hard.

"Thanks, mom," Sarah said as she looked at her mother in the reflection in the mirror. "You look amazing too!"

"You both look fabulous," came a deep voice from the doorway.

Her dad's voice filled the room. "My two angels decked out in their Sunday finest."

"Well, I hope she won't wear this to church," Michelle joked. "I mean, she does look lovely, but I think she might stand out among the other parishioners." She turned to face the man still standing in the doorway. "Besides, would you want to go to church in that monkey suit?"

"Heck no," he shot back quickly as he ran his fingers inside his tight collar for the hundredth time. Peter Thompson wasn't a big man, but he filled out the rental tuxedo with the best of them.

"I think this thing might have shrunk since I tried it on."

"Or maybe you have been having too many of mom's cookies, huh, Dad?" Sarah smiled as she watched him enter the room. "How do I look, Daddy?"

The tall man slowed his walk as he approached his daughter. Running his eyes up and down the bride as an artist might look at a perfect painting. His smile filled his face as he reached out to embrace his daughter's shoulders. She felt his firm grip wrap around her. He was comforting her with his strong touch, the way only a father's embrace can do.

"My sweet baby girl," he said as he looked down at her. He was nearly a foot taller than she was. "You look simply amazing." Tears escaped from his bright blue eyes. "I am so proud of you. You make an amazing bride. Jimmy is a lucky man." Peter wiped the wet trails from his cheeks with the back of his hands.

"Dang it, Daddy!" Sarah exclaimed. "You were not supposed to cry! We had a deal!" Try as she might, her eyes wrapped themselves in the wash of her joy-filled tears.

"Oh, no!" Peter said defensively, putting his palms up in protest. "That little agreement was between you and your mother. I never would have agreed to it. I knew there would be no way I could hold it together on my only daughter's wedding day." With that, the three of them began crying, filling the makeshift dressing room with a symphony of muffled joy. They held each other tightly for a while longer, not wanting to let go, but each of them knew they didn't have much time.

"It's time, everyone," came another voice from the doorway as if on cue from the clock ticking in their heads. The wedding coordinator smiled as she entered and instantly began to check Sarah's makeup. The woman was nice enough, but a real taskmaster. She was petite in stature but a giant in attitude. No one, not even the pastor, would dare challenge her once she had an idea about a wedding. These were her projects. Her babies, if she was forced to admit it, and she wouldn't let anyone else change them. This worked well for Sarah and her mother because neither of them was any good at organizing such a special event. Sarah knew that if her mother had more input, the wedding would have taken a completely different look. It was also wonderful to have the coordinator stressed out, so Sarah could enjoy the time leading up to her special day.

The tiny shrew-looking woman gave Sarah the once-over with the scrutiny of a jeweler inspecting a rare stone. Finally, the coordinator smiled and tucked a stray hair up behind the bride's ear.

"You look perfect, Sarah. How are you feeling?"

"A little nervous, but I think I've got it under control," Sarah said with as much hope-filled confidence as she could muster.

"You'll be fine, I'm sure. Just like we practiced." The coordinator smiled once more and turned to leave the room. "Michelle and Peter? I believe you both know what to do."

"Yep!" Peter quipped. "I just have to get her down the aisle without tripping over the dress." Perfectly timed, a piano's muted sounds poured in from the main sanctuary, filling the room with a beautiful signal. This meant the bridesmaids would begin their procession down to the front of the church, accompanied by her soon-to-be brothers-in-law.

Sarah took a deep breath as her dad came to stand next to her. She could see he was nervous. Maybe even more nervous than she was. Taking in a deep breath, she could smell his cologne, which made her smile one more time. She loved everything about her dad. He was the perfect man. Smart. Funny. Caring.

Together they walked out of the door and into the short hallway that led to the main lobby. It was lined with white roses and carnations that gave the room a spring feel even though it was the middle of January. Sarah felt a little more light-headed with each step, barely able to control the nervousness roiling just under her skin. It was probably just nerves, but she thought they were mixed with a tinge of excitement and even a tiny hint of panic.

A small lamp in the far corner of the receiving area cast a slight amber haze around the room. Sarah wasn't sure if it was the light, but everything around her had a tiny shimmer to it. She again blamed it on her nerves and gripped her father's arm just a bit tighter.

When they finally came to the doorway that led into the back of the sanctuary, it swung open with unseen hands. Sarah's mom was standing across the lobby in front of the double doors that would take them into the main event. She smiled as she watched the two of them approach, tears still waiting to escape her brown eyes. Sarah and her father glided across the room and stood facing the main doors. Michelle took her place by Peter's other side.

They stood, arm in arm, in front of the large wooden doors that separated them from the mass of people. Just on the other side, her future husband would be standing and waiting for her at the end of the aisle. Sarah could not help but be taken aback by the realness of it all—all her dreams were about to come true.

Time seemed to slow down as the doors began to open. A dazzling white light poured in through the growing crack between the entryways. Getting stronger and filling the lobby as the doors opened fully. Sarah lifted her bouquet to shield her eyes from the brightness. As her eyes adjusted, she suddenly became aware that there was not just one light source but two lights. Two balls radiated in the space directly in front of her. The spheres were somehow suspended in mid-air. Right where the altar should have been. Instead of watching the bride enter the sanctuary, every head was turned toward the glowing orbs.

Sarah turned to her dad, who only looked back at her and smiled. She quickly looked over at her mother with a confused look on her face. Michelle had a sad smile on her face as she stared at Peter, not even paying attention to what was happening in the church. That was when she heard the sound. A harsh and brutal sound of a gnarling engine filled the air as the glowing orbs began to move toward them. All eyes seemed to watch the machine as it thunderously accelerated down the aisle.

A rusty grill of an old pick-up truck formed between the floating lights giving shape to the mechanical monster bearing down on them. It coalesced from nothing and came at them with an ungodly speed. Sarah broke loose of her father's arm as she tried to pull them out of the way of the oncoming vehicle. As if her hands were grabbing at smoke, Sarah's fingers went through her dad's tuxedo. They passed through the material and his body as if he were a ghost.

Frantically, Sarah looked back at the oncoming lights—they were almost on top of them now. There was no time left for them to get out of the way. She shut her eyes tight and desperately reached for her dad's arm again. Where was he?Sarah stiffened as she felt the rush of wind hit her, blowing her veil back. Waiting for the impact she knew was coming. The end would come soon.

CHAPTER TEN

It had been hours since the sun set, leaving the room washed in shadows save for the faint glow from the streetlights below. Sarah woke with a shutter, still curled up in the old recliner. The throw pillow she was clutching was soaked with sweat. The strange feeling of the moist fabric against her face brought her out of the dream-induced coma.

Laying still and keeping her eyes closed, she tried to piece together the fragmented parts of the dream. Still, as she was awakening, the images faded away. All except for the truck and its headlights. Those were perfectly clear in her mind's eye. A chill raced over her skin as the panic gripped her again. It felt so real. Too real. She thought she could still smell the faint odor of truck exhaust floating in the air. Even the roar of the truck's engine still echoed in her ears. Slowly, both faded away as well, yet she could still vaguely remember the sound of a woman screaming far away. She remembered how the woman's scream even overpowered the harshness of the truck engine. The more she thought about it, the more the haunting wail echoed through her mind. Sarah wasn't sure if the scream had been something real or the remnants of her fading dream. Either way, she knew the scream was her own.

As she sat there for a moment, her mind tried to make sense of the nightmare. She didn't want to believe it, but she knew all too well what the dream meant. At one time in her not-too-distant past, she had it all, but everything was ripped away from her. The only thing she felt now was the familiar feeling of sadness mingled with anger. This toxic mixture was the perfect breeding ground for her depression.

Even as she thought this, she felt her Darkness creep up on her, sensing her weakness—her brokenness. She wanted to get up and shake off the Darkness like an old blanket, but she couldn't move a muscle. Or maybe she didn't want to. She did not even have the energy or the ambition to tilt the chair back, so she just sat in numbed silence. It had her right here where it wanted her. Truth be told, it was right where she wanted to be. Like a gentle lover, her Darkness held her close as her eyes closed again.

In the morning, Sarah found herself lying in her own bed. She wasn't even sure how she got there, but she felt the coolness of the sheets against her damp skin. Thankfully, she didn't have the truck dream again, but the woman's scream still echoed through her mind. The sound hung whimsically between awake and dreaming. The resonating cry was filled with so much pain, pain she forced back down to the recesses of her mind as she released herself from the dreamlike state.

She missed her parents and seeing them again was the one thing she longed for. They felt so close in her dream, and she even smelled her mom's perfume lingering in the air. To have them so close yet mercilessly yanked away again. This was nearly too much to handle. New wound over old scars. That was when she started to cry. Warm tears slowly dropped onto her pillow as she wondered if she was cursed. Was she forced to relive her worst fears and most painful memories over and over again? Was this what her life had come to? Faded nightmares of hope-filled dreams.

She curled her knees to her chest and laid perfectly still. It was easy to fall back into her Darkness. Even then, she could feel the long, cold tendrils snaking around the fringes of her mind. Sarah knew that feeling all too well, and she knew better than to give in again. She had to fight it, but the draw was too strong—like the beckoning of a lover that was trying to seduce its mate. The intense luring drug them ever closer to an edge from which they couldn't pull away.

She fought to open her eyes, to physically try and push back against the blackness from which her mind was trying to pull her deeper. Reluctantly, Sarah uncurled herself and stretched a quivering hand toward the side of the bed. With all the effort she had, she pulled herself up and sat silently on the edge of the bed. One minute went into two, then to five. Slowly the Darkness faded, coldly reeling back to the depths of her mind. She was lucky this time. She was able to break away from its hold. Closing her eyes again, she knew she had to keep her Darkness hidden. She could not dance so close to the edge again. She needed to keep it locked away so it couldn't hurt her again. Not again.

Sarah took a deep breath and stood up quickly. Her head pounded from the night of crying. Pulling herself into the shower, Sarah decided to go to work early. She was scheduled for the day shift today, and she privately hoped that it would serve as a distraction from what had been going on.

Thankfully, the day did progress much the same as any other. Customers came and went as the hours flew by. The tips were great, and she enjoyed seeing some of her regulars. Throughout the morning, she tried to hide some of the worries on her face with a forced smile. She knew how to play the part of a normal person. The smile would block the pain, and the sarcastic humor would deflect the sadness. She got away with it for the most part, but the ones that knew her best were the first to ask her what was wrong. With a shrug and a wave of a hand, Sarah would reply to each of them with her standard, non-committal, "I'm fine," or a "Just tired."

The only time she struggled with lying was when a cute little boy named Kenny kept asking her the same question over and over. *'How are you doing*?' the adorable three-year-old repeated. Over the past few months, Kenny and his mom had been coming to the café for lunch. Every Tuesday at 12:30, like clockwork. He was a good kid and minded his manners. Much better than most kids his age. Heck, better than most adults for that matter. Sarah loved his cute curly hair and adorable dimples. After Kenny asked for the umpteenth time, she finally told him that she was trying to work through some complicated 'big girl' things. He seemed to be satisfied with that answer because he stopped asking her.

Thinking about everything going on, it was actually a fantastic day. Her mind only went to Azrael a few times, but she would allow herself to push those thoughts away each time. She was even able to keep her mind from wandering to the pain of her dream. She was lucky enough to be able to rebound from her Darkness this time, but she didn't know if she could have the strength or even the desire to resist again.

As busy as she was, Sarah's *normal* day came to a complete halt when she noticed a newspaper sitting on a table as she was clearing it. It was a copy of today's Arizona Republic. The front was folded so only the top story was visible. The title was all Sarah needed to see to make her heart fall into her stomach. She slipped quietly into the booth and read the article. *Councilman Wingfield found dead in office—Mystery woman in connection sought for questioning.* The article didn't give many details, but it did say that a mysterious woman was seen leaving the Councilman's office just before the body was discovered. Police had not identified the woman, but they had a few leads and wanted to talk with her only as a *'person of interest.'* Sarah's pulse raced, and her palms began to sweat. *This couldn't be happening,* she thought. She was so wrapped up in her thoughts that she did not see the man standing next to her until he sat down on the bench seat across the table from her. She looked up at him as he took a wallet out of his coat pocket. Flipping it open, she saw the detective's badge. Her heart went from racing to a dead stop.

"Is that an interesting article you're reading, Miss Thompson," the man's voice questioned. "You are Sarah Thompson, aren't you?"

Sarah looked toward the voice and saw the silhouette of a man, but it was the glimmer of a gold badge that her eyes could not break away from.

Sarah responded weakly, "Yes."

"Good," the man said succinctly. "My name is Detective Wolfe, and I would like to ask you a few questions." The man flipped the wallet closed and slid it back into his brown jacket pocket.

Sarah suddenly found it tough to swallow. Her tongue felt like it had doubled in size. Still staring at the now empty table, she mumbled, "'bout what?"

"I would like to talk with you about where you were yesterday morning." He added after a slight pause, "And where were you on Sunday night for that matter?"

Startled, she looked at him with a frightened expression. "Wh … what do you mean?" Fidgeting with her fingers, "I was here on Sunday night, and then I went straight home." Realizing that her voice was a bit higher pitched than usual, she continued, "And yesterday was my day off, so I ran some errands and then went back to my apartment for most of the day."

The Detective stared at her with a blazing glare. "Really? What time did you leave work on Sunday night?"

"Around five o'clock. Why?"

"Well, Miss Thompson," taking out a pad of paper and flipping through it. Coming to a page with a bunch of scribbled notes on it, "I have a witness that said you were seen at the Valley of the Sun Retirement Home in Sun City around six o'clock." Looking up at her again, "That is a pretty far drive to get there from here. Can you tell me why you went there so fast?"

Even Sarah was unsure if she fully understood the real reason why she went to see Margaret. Thinking that the truth might be the best option, Sarah said calmly, "I went to see a friend."

"OK, this friend wouldn't happen to be Margaret Masterson, would it?"

"Yes, Margaret was a wonderful woman, and I was thankful to spend some time with her before she passed away."

"Uh-huh," he said mindlessly as his eyes looked intently at her facial expressions, trying to see if she was lying. "So, you knew she died?" he asked but added more before Sarah could speak. "Cause my witness said she saw you there before Margaret died, but not after."

"I heard about it yesterday. Terrible news." Sarah was trying her best not to freak out.

His eyes stared into hers. Searching for the truth. After a moment, he continued, "And speaking of yesterday, where you were yesterday morning around nine-thirty?"

"I, um, I'm not sure of my exact schedule. Why?"

"Just curious. What were you doing at Councilman Wingfield's office? Was he a wonderful man too?"

Sarah inadvertently gagged at the thought. Knowing she had no real reason to be around that grotesque man, Sarah felt herself get uneasy again. "I have no idea who you are talking about." The lie tasted bitter in her mouth.

Letting out a frustrated sigh, he tilted his head down as he looked at her. "I'm talking about the death of Phoenix City Councilman Jason Wingfield." He tapped his pen on the newspaper, sitting off to the side. "The man's office where we found your fingerprints. Then we talked to a bunch of witnesses that saw you leave his office in a hurry."

Slamming his hand down a little too hard, "Care to tell me how your fingerprints got in the Councilman's office, Miss Thompson?"

Sarah jumped at the sudden sound. She knew that she had better come up with something quick. "Um, I had gone to see him about a complaint I had about the city buses." She knew this had some truth to it. She had gone to the city council to talk about the bus routes not too long ago. She just hoped that this particular Councilman was somehow associated with the bus routes.

There was a long pause as the Detective just glared at her. Sarah knew she had to get out of this conversation. Luckily for her, Javier, the daytime cook, shouted her name from the kitchen and told her that her plates were in the window. It took Javier yelling her name twice before she came out of her panic-induced state. Suddenly remembering she was supposed to be working, Sarah jumped out of her seat.

As she was standing up, the Detective spoke again, "Did you and the Councilman talk about anything else other than *buses*?" He said the word with a bit of a sarcastic tone. "You do realize that you were the last person to see the Councilman alive, correct?"

Looking towards the kitchen for a moment, she turned her attention back to the table. Locking eyes with the man, Sarah felt frozen.

She spoke with a slight quiver in her voice, "I didn't know he died until I saw the paper this morning. He was not a very nice man for a woman to be around, so our conversation was brief." Speaking the truth finally broke the fear this man had over her. "I told him about my concerns, and I left. That was it."

Sarah turned away and started walking toward the kitchen. The short distance felt like it took an eternity to span. All the while, she could feel his eyes boring into the back of her head as she walked away.

She stood for a moment in front of the pick-up window, trying to gather her composure. She took a deep breath and reached for the plates of food. As she started moving toward her waiting customers, she fought the urge to look over to where the detective would still be sitting in the booth. She hoped he would just go away, but as she came to the end of the counter, her worst fears were realized. The police detective had moved to intercept her.

"Miss Thompson," he said in a low, firm voice. "You were seen in the room of an elderly lady just before she died and at the office of a prominent city official shortly before he died." As Sarah tried to walk past him, he continued his questioning. "How is it that you met with these two people just before they died?"

Pausing for a moment, Sarah took a deep breath and looked him straight in the eye. "Look, sir, I have a job to do, and I have no idea how or why those people died."Moving around the detective, she added, "Maybe it was just a coincidence."

The detective moved quickly to her side so he could still see her face as he spoke. "Ms. Thompson, I have a job to do too," he said in a voice that was a little louder than she would have liked. "And I don't believe in coincidences. There is something you are not telling me, and I will find out." With that, the detective turned and walked out of the restaurant.

The plates of hot food seemed to grow heavier in her hands as she watched the detective go out to his car and leave. After dropping the food at the tables, she walked back towards the kitchen area. As she passed the counter, she saw a business card where the detective had been standing. His name was Detective Michael Wolfe, and he added a small hand-written note on the back. *Call me when you are ready to talk. I'll be in touch.*

Sarah finished her shift in a tormented flurry. The visit from the police detective gave her a scare even though she knew she hadn't done anything wrong. She decided to walk home instead of taking the bus when her day was done. The new bus driver seemed nice, but the whole ordeal just reminded her of the mess her life was in. She figured the walk would also help her think and hopefully get to the bottom of her dilemma.

Turning to walk up Central Avenue, she realized that her feet didn't hurt nearly as badly as they usually would after a busy day at the café. The air was still warm, with the fading traces of summer refusing to give way to fall. No matter what she was feeling on the outside, her mind traveled back to the problems of the day. Azrael kept coming to her mind, and she thought desperately about what to do with him. It was like a love-hate relationship. While she didn't want to see him again, she knew she had to. He had the answers she needed.

As she walked deep in thought, the daylight faded, and dusk had taken hold of the passing time. Shadows fell across her path, dark and deep, yet the darkness in her heart was far more foreboding. Even the fading light had given an ironic parallel to her fading spirit. The restless emotions in her heart were warring with the logic of her head. A person cannot appear and disappear out of thin air, she repeated over and over to herself. Nor can a person predict when another person would die unless they were the one causing the death. Azrael was all these things and more. She knew he was a thing to be feared and not taken lightly. Then again, neither was a Phoenix police detective with an itch to arrest her.

Each footstep brought her closer to home but seemingly farther away from any answers. Now that the police were involved, she couldn't act like this was just some kind of a dream. This was real, and she had to deal with it. Not even a dream, really, more like a nightmare. A nightmare that she was praying she would wake up from at any moment.

CHAPTER ELEVEN

As Sarah walked, the tall downtown buildings began to play a game of peek-a-boo with the sun. The evening shadows from the structures bathed the landscape in its darkness as the sun pushed through the gaps between the tall towers. She made her way to Jefferson Street before noticing how the sun was setting faster than she thought. Was she walking slower, or was it later than she realized? Either way, she didn't want to be downtown alone at night. Raising her arm to hail a cab, Sarah's heart jumped when she heard the voice coming from behind her.

"Leaving so soon?" The familiar voice came from out of the ever-increasing shadows.

Weakly, Sarah lowered her outstretched arm as she began to turn around, her face frozen in disbelief. Azrael emerged from the darkness as if his body were part of the shadows themselves.

Staring at him, she spoke in a light, frail voice, "I was wondering when you were going to show up."

Tilting his head to the side, his ice-blue eyes crashed against her defenses like a tidal wave against the rocky shore. "Actually, I was about to say the same thing about you. Our next guest is just around the block, and I have been waiting for you to get here."

She winced at the word, *guest*. Disgusted by his use of the phrase, Sarah just glared back at him. He used the word as if the place he was taking them was a day spa or something. Trying to compose herself about the *'guest'* word, his other choice of words struck her like a slap across the face. He was here waiting —for her. *How did he know that she would come in this direction*, she wondered? Sarah thought about it for a moment and knew that she did not tell anyone at the restaurant that she was walking home.

"OK, wait a second," she quipped with a resonantly frustrated tone. "How did you know I would be coming this way?" Sarah moved closer to him. Closer than she would typically have, but she was getting angry. "Are you stalking me again?"

His 6'2' frame towered over her as he looked down with a mixed expression of anger and sympathy. "Sarah." He paused. "I am with you always, and I know what you are going to do before it happens." The muscles in his jaw relaxed, softening his expression.

"If that means I am stalking you, then yes. But I believe it means that I have a vested interest in the tasks that you need to complete."

Sarah's face started to redden, and her hands clenched into fists. Sensing that his answer was not received well, he changed tactics. "You see, Sarah. Your task is to reach these people before their time is up. This is about them." Standing next to her, he seemed to grow three inches in height. Raising his voice with a deepening boom, "In sixty-one minutes after you meet them, they will be dead. *You*, however, are free to go on living your life. This is about *them*, not you." Repeating his last statement, Azrael let his words hang in the air.

Sarah paused as she realized he was right. She felt the anger flow from her body like the air let out of a balloon. The redness in her cheeks turned from a burning frustration to an embarrassing glow. She knew she shouldn't be the one doing this, but these poor people were going to die, and for some reason, she was the last person they would talk to beforehand.

Putting her head down to hide her face, "Ok," she said sheepishly, "Let's go." He put his hand on her shoulder again as Sarah closed her eyes. She waited for the feeling of weightlessness, but it didn't come. Instead, she felt the tall man pull her along by her coat as they walked down the street.

The night had fully covered the city with its darkness as the weak, amber streetlights came on. While they walked, the lights from the passing cars illuminated the bundled bodies of a few homeless people milling around the streets. Most looked like they were settling in for the night, while some looked like they were getting ready to start their day. Most looked docile, but some would flail their arms through the air as if they were swatting away an invisible swarm of bees. Or maybe they were just throwing punches in the air to ward off the reality of life.

Stepping over a bedroll that a man set up against a newspaper stand, Sarah felt Azrael pull her to the right. The streetlights quickly faded as they went deeper into an alley. The air turned cooler as they walked away from the heat of the asphalt. The dust from the dry ground gave an eerie look of a fog holding just above the ground. As Sarah's eyes adjusted, she looked at the reason for the dust cloud. A man was shuffling from side to side as he looked out the end of the alleyway and into the street.

Turning to scan the darkness, Sarah noticed that she was now alone. Azrael was gone, and there was just the seemingly dancing man at the end of the corridor.

Is this the man, she thought as she watched the ragged figure turn his head away, peering out into the opposite street.

"Yes." The voice came as a mellow-toned voice from deep inside Sarah's head. "Talk with him."

Sarah swallowed hard against her dryness, and fear caught in her throat. The man was a simple silhouette cast against the bright lights of the streetlamps just beyond the passage. As she approached, she could see the realness of the man take shape. He stood only a few inches taller than she was, but that was because he had a noticeable slouch to his body. His shoulders looked as if they were being pulled down by a burden of some unseen weight. If he had stood tall, he would have towered over Sarah. She made a mental note. The coat he wore hung on his body like a child wearing his father's clothing. The ragged material shifted half a second after he moved as if he was wrestling against it every time he turned. His head twisted wildly from side to side as his wide brown eyes scanned in all directions. He didn't focus on any one point but kept searching, trying to locate something just past what she could see. When his face turned toward the dull light, she could see his withered skin stretched across his cheekbones. His dark, leathery skin had deep creases that spoke of long days of hardship and suffering. His beard pulled in against his gaunt features like a sheet thrown over a skeleton. Of all the things that surprised her the most, it was the smell of the stranger that jumped out at her and attacked her nose like a mule kick. The pungent smell of urine mixed with sweat and vomit nearly overwhelmed her as she fought to keep moving forward.

"Excuse me," Sarah said tentatively, unknowingly putting her hand to her nose.

Like a flash of lightning, his head whipped around and stopped when he saw the woman standing so close to him. His eyes blazed white-hot with anger, and his body seemed to grow in size. She could see the whites around his sunken eyes as he glared at her. Then, like a cat, he leaped at her. Moving quicker than any man she had seen as he spanned the five or six feet that once separated them in the blink of an eye. His grip felt like iron as he grabbed her shoulder. He pulled her to the right with a quick jerk that nearly took Sarah off her feet. He pressed her up against brick wall as he brought his free hand up to her face.

"Are you here to kill me?" he asked in a gruff voice, pointing his filthy finger at her. His eyes never looked away, boring a hole through the back of her head.

Sarah's heart raced out of control as she imagined this man tearing her to shreds with his bare hands. She tried to move, but his grip pressed her harder. Each movement from her brought a tightening of his hold on her. He had her pinned, helpless to stop him.

Frantic, she exclaimed, "No, I am here to help you!"Taking a quick breath in, she tried to calm herself. "Not to hurt you," she somehow forced out through her dry throat.

She felt the vice grip on her shoulder release, but he still held her against the alleyway. His head began to look around, up and down the alley again.

"Well, maybe not you, but they are out there. Watching me," he said with a soft tone in his voice. The smell of his breath was nearly as overpowering as the stench that came up from his body.

Sarah felt the blood come back to her face as she breathed out the single word, "Who?"

Snapping back to look directly at her again, he leaned closer to her. "The bastards that took my angels," he told her in a hushed tone. "They killed my Angela and Kimmie, and now they are trying to kill me!" As he said the words, he reached into his pocket and took out a picture of a clean-cut, handsome man standing next to a beautiful blond woman and a smiling little girl. Sarah could only assume that this lunatic was the man in the picture. The crazed man just stared thoughtfully at the photograph. When he spoke, the anger was gone—replaced by the voice of a broken man.

"We were so happy. It all happened so fast," he said as wetness formed in his eyes. "We were all at home when I heard a noise outside. At first, I didn't think anything of it. Then came the pounding on the door." Sarah saw the look on the man's expression change. A mixture of fear, sadness, and anger twisted his face. "As soon as I unlocked the door, it came pushing back at me. It all happened so fast. They were so strong."

The man slowly paced back and forth as he told his story. "I failed. I tried to stop the door from opening. I tried to stop the evil from invading our house." Then the tears broke through and washed the dirt from his cheeks in tiny lines. "I tried," he whispered.

Sarah could see that pain in this man's eyes. She listened intently as he kept talking. "What happened?"

"I failed them," he replied softly. "I tried to keep the devil out, but when his demons pushed through, I lost my balance and fell. The last thing I remember was falling and seeing dark figures coming to get me."

The police report told the rest of the story. Randy Garwood had been knocked unconscious from the impact of his head on a table as he fell. The home invaders ransacked the house, tearing everything apart and stealing anything of value. The assailants found Randy's wife and young daughter hiding in a locked bathroom. The flimsy door was forcibly broken open, and both of them were murdered. When Randy woke, his hands were tied loosely enough to remove the straps. He found the bodies of his wife and daughter in the bathtub. It was later assumed that the assailants left Randy for dead because of the head wound. He was cleared of any wrongful doing with the case, and the assailants were never found.

Sarah looked down at the picture in the man's hand as a single tear drop fell on the image. He released her shoulder and held the picture tight in both hands. Stepping backward as if in a trance, Randy's body swayed like a ghost. He was no longer moving wildly or searching for something unseen in the night. He just moved slowly backward until his back was against the wall on the opposite side of the alley. Staring at him, Sarah suddenly felt an overwhelming sense of pity for this broken man. He lost everything. She heard him mumble to himself over and over again, *'they're gone.'*

Stepping closer to him, she asked him who had taken them away. "They did! Aren't you listening?" His voice cracked as the words punctuated between his sobs. "They came in and took my loves from me. I wanted to stop them, but they took them anyway." His knees finally gave out as he allowed his body to press against the wall, sliding down. Tears flowed openly from his cheeks, following now familiar trails through his dirt-covered face.

Sarah found herself suddenly saying a silent prayer. Instinctively reaching out to touch his shoulder, she remembered what it felt like to have someone ripped from her life. The pain of her memories washed over her mind like a stinging cold shower. The hot tears flowed from her own watery eyes as she thought about her parents. The still tender emotions came with a mix of anger and sadness. *Life's not fair*, she thought. No one should have to endure this kind of pain.

"I'm so sorry," she said softly. She knew the words were of little comfort. She knew they were more comforting to her than to him. In this world, there was nothing that could comfort his loss. Nothing that could take away his pain.

She mustered up the strength and cleared her throat. "I'm not here to take you away, but someone will be coming very soon." She touched his shoulder a little tighter. "He is going to make all of this pain go away."

"Good," he shouted! The sudden outburst startled Sarah. "I have been waiting for a long time for them to come back." Still holding the picture, he began to look from side to side again. Pushing his way up, he yelled, "Come and get me, you bastards! Finish what you started, you cowards! I am ready this time!" His hand went inside his clumsy jacket and pulled out a large knife. The light from the streetlights caught the glint of the large blade. Sarah knew right away what it was and jumped back.

"Oh God," she screamed. Her words were drowned out by the crazed man's rants and loud mumblings. She tried to back up even farther, but the unyielding concrete wall seemingly pushed her forward. Randy looked off into the distance and shouted into the void of darkness. He staggered forward, tumbling out of the alley. Screaming and cursing at some unseen evil that was only in his mind. Sarah stood frozen with fear as she tried to make out his words. She could understand a few bits and pieces as the man staggered farther and farther away from her. 'It is time,' she heard him yell. Panic and self-preservation made her legs refuse to follow after him.

As his words faded, she heard him cry out one last time, "They are coming!"

Lowering her head, Sarah just turned and made her way back down the alley. Away from the cries. Pushing herself to get distance from the man in pain. Inside, she hoped she would be able to walk away from her own pain as well. Maybe it would be better for this man to die, she thought. It would be better for his pain to stop. This man's life was taken from him when his family died, yet he was left alive to suffer in torment. His mind gave way long before his body did.

The chill of the breeze came through the dark alley and brought Sarah back to her senses. She picked up her pace a little and rushed back to the bus stop. She knew the man would be dead soon, and the angel of death would come to take her back to her apartment. She didn't want to wait for that; she just wanted to be alone. She just wanted to forget about all of this mess.

The trip home brought her no solace. The stillness of the apartment brought her little comfort, and the smell of the crazed man still clung to her like a thick mist. Grabbing a glass of red wine in her hands, she looked intently at the clock. It had been more than an hour since she met the man in the alley, and she wondered if he was dead.

"Yes," came a booming voice from what felt like everywhere at the same time. "That man is dead, and his pain is gone." The words seemed to echo in her tiny apartment. "And gone, too, is his chance to hear what you needed to tell him! Gone forever while you sit here and medicate yourself in a pool of your own self-pity!"

"That is not fair!" Sarah sat upright in the chair, knocking the glass of wine to the floor. The red liquid instantly stained the beige rug.

"You said it yourself, Sarah! *Life is not fair!*"

It was her voice resounding in her head. The dark angel was using her own voice to mock her. The blood pulsed through her veins as anger welled up inside and she shouted into the night.

"Fine! Fair or not, I shouldn't have to be the one that has to go to these people. I am not their savior!"

A softer voice blanketed her mind. "I am not asking you to be their savior. I am asking you to talk with them and share your heart with them. You cannot save them from dying, but you can help them."

"I cannot help them or save them, but you ask me just to sit there and watch them die!" Sarah knew she wouldn't find him in the apartment, but she kept looking around the room as she yelled. "I don't want to be that person." The frustration flowed out of Sarah with each sentence like a deep exhale. "I don't want that responsibility." Finally, she fell to her knees in exhaustion and surrendered.

Softer, almost like a whisper, she continued, "What kind of monster asks a person to do that? Why am I being punished?"

"Dear Sarah, you are not being punished. You were chosen because you are so very special. This is a gift. Not a punishment. Rest now, and we will talk again later."

Sarah felt her body give way to sleep, and her muscles submitted to the strain. Her mind, which moments ago had raced with panic and frustration, was now calm and relaxed. Night came over her, and she slept.

CHAPTER TWELVE

The opposing smells of burnt toast and fresh coffee filled the room just before Michael opened his eyes. He had a restless night's sleep while his mind kept trying to force him awake with its own set of worries. He knew his lack of sleep was nothing compared to his wife's inability to get comfortable. Ever since she hit her third trimester, Tori couldn't get a good night's rest. Between the baby kicking and the constant heartburn, she was lucky to get three or four hours of sleep at a time. It was good that the doctor put her on bed rest, but it didn't stop Michael from worrying about her. Grabbing the covers and pulling them over his head, he remembered the not-so-distant past when his wife would be able to sleep in, and he would be the one burning breakfast. Knowing he would have to face the day at some point, he reluctantly shed the covers and got up.

When he walked into the kitchen, he was taken aback by his wife's beauty. Even with her shoulder-length auburn hair in complete disarray and her mismatched PJs, she still took his breath away every time he saw her. It was the same reaction he got from the first moment they met.

They were both much younger then. Michael had seen her at a friend's house a few times and thought that a good-looking woman like that must have a boyfriend. She was finishing up her education degree at Arizona State University. He was attending the police academy at the time, and he had never been shy around anyone except her. She would later tease him that he acted like a little schoolboy whenever they ran into each other. After some coaxing from his friends, Michael built up the nerve to ask Tori out. Their first date was amazing. He instantly fell in love with her laugh and zeal for life. Thirteen months later, they were married. Since then, she has put a smile on his face every day since. That was a little over seven years ago. Time had flown by, he thought, but he could not stop thinking about how she still looked exactly the same as the twenty-one-year-old schoolgirl.

"Good morning, Hun," she said with a smile. Pivoting on her heel so she could grab another mug, she stopped to kiss him. "I made your coffee. Extra strong, just like you like it." Tori loved coffee, but when she had read all about what she could and couldn't eat or drink while pregnant, she stopped drinking caffeine altogether. This made her act of love even more special to him. Even though she couldn't have any coffee, she endured the fresh ground beans' intoxicating aroma and the percolating goodness as she made him a cup. Recently, she started drinking herbal tea instead. She would claim it was just as good, but he knew it wasn't the same.

He sipped the hot coffee and took a seat with her at the small kitchen table. The plate in front of him was covered with delicious-looking cheesy scrambled eggs—his favorite. The source of the burnt toast smell was also sitting there, giving a Ying and Yang effect to the meal. He ate it and smiled as if it was the last meal he was ever going to eat. He even grinned at her as he chewed the blackened bread.

"Sorry for bringing work home the other day," he said in between bites. Swallowing hard, "I have this strange case, and it keeps bugging me."

"That's OK, Hun," she said as she winced in pain just as she brought the tea to her lips. Tori reflexively grabbed her side. Letting out a little moan and placed her hand on the spot where their future daughter was kicking her in the ribs. She put the cup down just before she closed her eyes.

"Is she still kicking pretty hard?"

Taking a sharp breath in, she replied in short little words. "Yeah. She is getting pretty strong."

After a few minutes, Michael noticed the peace that returned to his wife's face. His future soccer player must have moved her kicks or stopped them altogether.

"I'm sure you can hardly wait to get her out here, so you can kick her back, right?"

"That would not be a very nice thing to do to our baby girl," she said in a playfully accusing tone. A slight smile parted her lips, "But she sure does deserve it sometimes. I am going to remind her of all the times she kicked me while I carried her." A pause caught her as she looked down at the bulge under her cotton pajama top. A small tear formed in her eye as a broad smile appeared on her face. She was happy and already thankful to be a mommy.

Taking his eyes away from his darling wife for just a moment, Michael noticed the clock on the kitchen wall just over her shoulder. With a flurry of movements, he shoveled the last few bites of eggs into his mouth and mumbled to his wife about being late. She barely saw him get up, but she jumped up with him at the same time.

"Can we talk about the baby's room when you get home," she asked as she chased him around the house while he got ready. "I have some ideas about how I want to finish the decorations." The only response she got was a nod as he finished his coffee and raced out the door. Lately, that was the only response she ever got from him when she talked about spending money.

The day started as ordinary as any other. Sarah woke and got dressed for work without even thinking about the homeless man or the argument she had the night before. Even the wine stain was gone, and the glass was in the sink. Sarah just wished she could have a whole day without the police or the harbinger of death visiting her.

Work at the café was a welcome break from the craziness surrounding her life over the past few days. Even Javier was in a good mood, which usually meant the food came out better. And better food meant better tips. She liked that. The truth was that her tips were incredible all morning, and her outlook wasn't so grim after all.

She even had a chance to sit down and enjoy her favorite breakfast while on her break. Just the sight of a simple fried egg snuggled inside a piece of toast brought back warm feelings. As her family called it, Eggy-in-the-Basket was a simple and fun way to eat her breakfast. Every time she ate it, it would remind her of lazy Saturday mornings with her mom and dad.

These days, she would use the breakfast tidbit as a running joke with the chef of the café. Despite his culinary degree, Javier had never heard of this creative delicacy. Once she taught him how, he was willing to make it for her; and each time, she would remind him that he didn't know everything about cooking.

She loved working at the café. Gerardo's Little Italy was founded in the early '90's when Gerardo bought a rundown old post office building. The red brick front with the white trimmed windows and doors reminded him of growing up in a small town outside of Florence, Italy. He purchased the property with an inheritance he received when his elderly parents passed away. They both worked hard their whole lives so Gerardo and his sisters could have a better life. To honor them, he took the money and built something that his parents would have liked. A place that warmed the heart as well as the belly. When customers walked into the café, their senses were delighted with the smell of fresh-baked bread and the sounds of classical Italian opera. Both were the loves of Gerardo's mother. He was practically raised eating freshly baked bread alone and listening to his mother sing while working in the kitchen. He took all of her recipes and brought wholesome, Italian family-style cooking to Phoenix.

The morning passed by quickly at the café. Sarah was thankful that she hadn't thought about any of the outside negativity. It got even better around noon when she received a pleasant surprise. A friendly face from the past walked through the door and surprised Sarah.

She had known Nadine Gomez since their freshman year at ASU. They took English 101 together and both cried at night because of the reading list. Together they pushed each other to finish the class. Nadine got a B, and Sarah ended up with a C +. It was OK by her because she just wanted the crazy reading list to end. A mutual hatred of all things classical literature brought them close, and they stuck together through all four years of college. They were the best of friends and a much-needed source of soundness. Sadly, everything in life has a season, and so did their friendship. Sarah lost contact with her just after graduation when Nadine married the student advisor for their dorm. Micky Burton was a nice enough guy. Pretty cute and he treated her well—that was good enough for Sarah. After the wedding, Sarah went from the bride's maid to a social outcast. Their circles didn't cross much after that, and they quickly lost contact. Over the years, they exchanged Christmas and the occasional birthday cards, but that was about it. The last thing Sarah knew about her was that she had a few kids and was living in Tucson. And now she was standing on the Saltillo flooring in the middle of the café.

When they made eye contact, both women took only a moment to remember each other. After that, it was like they were both in college all over again. They ran to the center of the dining room and warmly embraced. Sarah noted that the hug was a little tighter and lasted a little longer than she would have expected. As she pulled away, Sarah noticed more than a few tears in the woman's eyes.

"Oh my gosh!" Nadine said in between the squeals of delight. "How are you doing? Sarah, you look amazing!"This last outburst brought another tight embrace.

"I'm doing OK, thanks," Sarah replied with an enthusiasm that seemed a little more fake than she meant it to be. It wasn't that she was *not* excited to see her old friend. It was just that she was not proud of her current circumstances, nor did she fully understand the most recent events even to know if they were good or not.

Right away, Nadine knew something was wrong. "You always were a terrible liar." She held Sarah at arm's length as she pushed a lock of flaxen hair out of her eyes. "Seriously, how are you doing?"

A smile broke out across Sarah's face, and a slight veil of tears covered her eyes as she tried to change the subject. "Whatever! I'm doing fine. Besides, you were always the one that I needed to lie for. How are you doing? What brings you to this neck of the woods?"

Still holding on to Sarah's arms, Nadine looked her in the eye. "To be honest, I am not sure at all. I just got done with a meeting here in town, and I started to head home when I had the strangest, overwhelming urge to try this place. I had heard a lot of great reviews about this cute place, and I felt like I needed to come in right now." After a short pause, she added, "And now I know why."

Sarah was so excited to see Nadine again and didn't want their impromptu meeting to end. She desperately wanted to catch up with her old friend, so she asked Gerardo if she could take her break a little early. They went over to a booth behind the register that didn't typically get used.

"I thought you were still living in Tucson. Are you back in town?"

"Yeah. For about six months now." Nadine let out a heavy sigh. "Micky and I got a divorce about a year or so ago. I tried to stick it out for the kids. But after a while, he stopped caring about his children, and I stopped caring if they saw their dad or not." She popped her head up. "And now we're here."

"Wow! I'm so sorry. The last thing I heard was that everything was good. What happened?" Sarah reached out her hand and gently placed it on Nadine's fidgeting fingers.

"Well, the jerk cheated on me with his secretary." Tears began to well-up in the corners of her eyes again. "He said he had fallen out of love with me. As if that was a thing. I was devastated. The kids were crushed." Nadine looked out the window as she continued. "It wasn't long before he just signed over everything and left—short and sweet divorce. He would come around every once and a while to see Noah and Megan, but even that stopped." Nadine chuckled a little as she wiped the tears off her cheek with the back of her hand. "And now I live with my mom in Chandler." Looking back at Sarah, she added, "Actually, I am much happier now."

Just as Sarah was about to respond, Nadine started up again. Cutting her off so she could change the direction of the depressing conversation.

"So, tell me, what is going on with you?" Wiping the tears out of the way without smearing her mascara, she added, "Tell me why God brought me to this place?"

Surprised by the odd-sounding statement, Sarah's

defensive sense of humor kicked in. "Well, that's a name I didn't see on the list of reservations."

"Now, don't you poke fun. I'm serious. I believe things happen for a reason. It was no accident that I came in here today. God had me bump into you, and I am thankful for it."

A lump formed in Sarah's throat. She had remembered wishing she had someone to talk with about all of the craziness going on in her life. Now, out of the blue, here was an old friend telling her that God brought Nadine into her work. There were so many things that she wanted to say; so many things that she needed to get off of her chest.

Just before she opened her mouth, a strange tingle went up the back of Sarah's neck. It was like someone was rubbing an ice cube down her spine. Off in the distance, she could see the busboy putting dirty dishes into a tub, yet the sound of the dishes clanging together faded out. It was like the volume was being turned down in her head. Then a dark, cold voice came rushing through her mind.

"Remember your obligations," Azrael said coldly. "You are not to mention me or your visits."

Seeing the change in Sarah's expression, Nadine was now the one reaching out to touch her friend's hand. "Are you OK, Sarah? You're as white as a sheet."

Sarah felt the blood come back to her face as the volume returned to normal in her head. Blinking a few times, she looked embarrassingly over at Nadine and confessed, "I'm OK. I have been having some nightmares lately, and I just thought of one when you mentioned God calling you in here."

"Well, let me assure you that God is not the subject of nightmares. He saves people *from* nightmares." Straightening up a little in the seat, Nadine told her about how she came to know God shortly after her divorce.

"I was a mess, and God saved me from that. He saved

me from myself." Nadine squeezed Sarah's hands tighter. "He showed me true love and taught me about serving others." After a short pause, she added, "He saved me from the hopelessness in this life and gave me the promise of eternal life with Him in Heaven."

Sarah listened and tried to follow along. She remembered how her parents would talk with others about God and their deep love of Jesus. She also remembered that this was the same God that took her parents away from her and ruined her life.

Sarah felt her jaw tighten as the bitter taste of God's *love* came back to her mind. "Well, I'm sure glad that you are better. And if God is the reason, then I am happy for you." Looking down at the table, "I've learned that God has a different plan for me. I have not found the same joy from it as I once did, and certainly not the same peace."

Thinking for a second, Nadine knew something was wrong. This wasn't the church-loving person she remembered. Nadine racked her brain thinking of what would cause someone to walk away from God's love. She remembered the times when Sarah would talk with her about accepting God's love and forgiveness. Now here she was, the one talking with her friend about the unmatched love that comes from the Heavenly Savior. Nadine said a silent prayer to herself and asked God for the strength and wisdom to talk with her friend.

As if being shocked, Nadine lifted her head and cautiously offered, "If this is about your parent's death, you have to know that God was not responsible for that drunk driver. God didn't cause that terrible accident."

Now it was Sarah's turn to feel shocked. She was amazed at how close Nadine's words were to the truth. She felt her heart pound inside her chest. Sarah's mind raced for a way to change the subject.

"I hear ya." She nervously shredded the white paper napkin in front of her. "It's just that I've had some strange dreams lately.

They've really got me thinking about some things." She paused for a few seconds, then took a deep breath and steeled herself. "Let me ask you something. If you had a chance to talk with someone just before they died, what would you say?"

"Well, heck. That's easy," Nadine exclaimed as she smacked her palm down on the table. "I would tell them about Jesus and make sure they were ready to meet their Maker."

A long silence filled the space between them as Sarah just stared at her old friend. Nadine knew enough to let someone process what she was saying when she talked about Jesus. Too often, she found herself stepping over her own words, and the power that came from hearing the truth got lost in the mix.

Sarah's mind kept playing the words over and over as she began to see what her old friend was talking about. "Do you think that is the most important thing in life?"

Nadine leaned forward slightly and looked Sarah straight in the eyes. "Yes, I do," she said matter-of-factly. "A person needs to be told about the afterlife before they get done with this one. The most important thing about life isn't death, but what comes after." Nadine noticed that Sarah was struggling to process what she was saying.

"You should talk with my pastor about it. He is a great guy, and he really knows what he's talking about—the Bible and everything it has to say about death. He can help you."

Still thinking about what Nadine said, Sarah noticed that Gerardo was looking at his watch and made a quick glance in her direction. Suddenly realizing the time, Sarah grabbed Nadine's hand.

"Sorry, I gotta run. My break is over. If you could write down your pastor's name and a way to get a hold of him, I'll see if I can talk with him."

Standing up quickly, Nadine hugged Sarah. "Sure. Sure. I will write it down and give it to you before I leave." Sarah took her friend to a table in her section and suggested some of the better parts of the menu. It was a lovely lunch, and the ladies continued small talk between customers. When Nadine left, they hugged again, and she made Sarah promise to keep in touch.

After that, the rest of the day went along without a hitch. Sarah genuinely had a smile on her face. To make the day even better, Gerardo also told her that she could head out fifteen minutes early so she would be sure to catch the bus. Just as she was handing out the check to her last table, she noticed a new person at a table in her section. Renee, the young teenage hostess, didn't tell her that she had a new table. She should know better than to seat a person in her section just before her shift ended.

As she walked up to the table, she started to untie her apron. "Sorry, but I am done for the day. Robyn would be right over to take your order."

The air in the room seemed to get cold with each step. She felt her stomach tighten as she came close enough to the table to see the dark-cloaked stranger sitting at the table. She caught the familiar acrid dust and leather smell just as she made eye contact with the angel.

"Good afternoon, Sarah." His voice was as calm and cool as ever. "Would you please join me for a moment?"

Drawing her strength from somewhere deep inside. The sight of this being fought against the joy she had just felt throughout the day. "As a matter of fact, I do not want to sit down." Coming around the table to look straight into his blue eyes, "I am not supposed to sit down with the customers during my shift, and besides, I have a bus to catch after my shift."

"Believe me, Sarah." He was staring at her as he waved his hand. "I do not think that anyone here will have a problem with you sitting down."

Sarah looked around the crowded restaurant and felt a chill creep up her spine. She watched the wave of his hand and noticed that everything froze in mid-motion. One customer had a fork full of meatloaf that stopped just shy of his open mouth. Robyn looked like a statue as she poured a cup of coffee. Even the steam that came up from the cup was frozen in mid-air as if someone had hit pause on a video. Someone did, in fact, hit pause. And that someone was staring right at her. Waiting for her to sit down.

Turning back to look at him, she quipped, "Neat trick." Taking a seat opposite the steely-eyed man, Sarah felt her anger flood her veins as the peace she felt floated away like a wisp of smoke from a distant fire. Her joy faded away until there was nothing left but raw irritation.

Continuing to stare at him, she waited for a response to her sarcasm. The Formica tabletop felt cold to the touch as she brought her hands up. The pause seemed endless and pointless; Sarah ended it by taking the chance to get a few things off her mind.

"Do you know that the police are harassing me? They said they saw me at Margaret's hospital room, and they have my fingerprints from the councilmen jerk!" Her hands balled into fists. "What have you gotten me into?"

"You are only doing what you have been asked to do." His lips moved tightly. "Nothing that you are doing goes against any law—man-made or otherwise."

Sarah took a few moments to look at him squarely. She hadn't taken the time to genuinely look at him since the bus. She was either too afraid or too angry. Even though she was angry now, it still didn't stop her from studying his face. She noticed the subtle features of his clean-shaven face. There was a softness in his skin. His olive complexion was mild and perfect, creating a sharp contrast against his dark hair and ice-blue eyes. For a moment, she felt her anger dissipate. A sense of peace came over her, and she relaxed. Even her hands unclenched involuntarily. She began fidgeting with the placemat on the table.

His voice had a relaxing tone to it. She found that she honestly enjoyed the sound of it. It reminded her of someone reading a familiar story. Strangely, she even found herself liking to hear him speak, although she would never admit it to him. He would probably get egotistical about it. In fact, when he wasn't yelling at her, his voice had a firmness to it that seemed to encourage and inspire her. Strengthen her spirit. She was not sure why he would want to encourage her, but it reminded her of how her father spoke, and she liked it.

With the same resonant tone, he broke the silence. "You are to serve the tasks of the higher purpose and not the affairs of man."

Feeling much calmer than she should have been, considering she was stuck in a frozen world, she simply shrugged her shoulders in acknowledgment. "If I am supposed to be serving a higher purpose, then why won't this higher purpose tell me what I am supposed to be telling these people?"

"Sarah, that is for you to know and to share with others." His lips formed a tight smile. "Not everything needs to be done for you. Some things you must figure out first, although I believe you already know the answer. You may just need someone to help you rediscover it."

Sarah thought about what Nadine said. "My friend thinks I should talk with her pastor about learning what's the most important thing in life."

To that, he simply responded, "Let the wise listen and add to their learning, and let the discerning get guidance."

Sarah stood perfectly still as she tried to figure out what he meant. He continued, "Come. We must depart, so we will not be late for our next charge."

Though she was getting a little used to this routine, she

would still hear the word *'victim'* whenever he spoke about the people she was going to meet.

CHAPTER THIRTEEN

When Sarah felt her feet touch solid ground again, she heard the sounds of traffic. Not wanting to get caught off-guard, Sarah thought it wise to start paying better attention to her surroundings. As the darkness faded, the intense light was so bright that it forced her to shield her eyes. The light, she realized, was coming from the sunlight all around her. She found herself standing on a street corner somewhere in the city. Cars hurried past her, and nothing seemed out of the ordinary. The street sign showed her that she was at the intersection of 16th street and Bell Road. This was in the northern part of the city. Not too far away, but far enough that she wouldn't have normally traveled this far unless it was an emergency.

"I guess this is an emergency, right?" she asked no one in particular. When she finished looking around, she finally looked down at her clothes. Her uniform was gone, and she was wearing a beautiful blouse and her favorite pair of jeans. Her hands hesitantly touched her body. Trying to get her mind to accept what her eyes were seeing. She patted her back pockets and found a small notebook and pen. This was a little odd. Now

Azrael was giving her props to work with. She felt more like a puppet rather than a helper.

Movement caught Sarah's eye as she suddenly realized that she was no longer alone on the sidewalk. A young blond girl was briskly walking straight toward her. From her youthful look, the girl couldn't have been more than sixteen or seventeen years old. She had a backpack slung over one shoulder and was busy typing away on her cell phone. The girl's wavy blond hair and athletic physique made her look like a young Barbie doll. As she approached, the girl's face lit up with a bright and sincere smile when she noticed Sarah. Instinctively, Sarah returned the smile and extended her hand toward the young girl.

"Hi. My name is Sarah Thompson. Would you mind if I walked with you for a bit?"

The girl took Sarah's hand and shook it tentatively. "Hi. My name is Charlotte."

Seeing the apprehension in the girl's eyes, Sarah put her palms up and smiled. "Sorry to bother you. I am not a stalker or anything like that." A nervous laugh escaped her lips. "I was just wondering if I could ask you for your thoughts on a subject."

Charlotte's eyes brightened, and her voice increased in both octave and speed. "Oh, you mean like a podcast or something?"

Sarah saw her chance to get this girl to talk, so she ran with it. "Yeah, sort of." Shifting from one foot to another. "I am doing some research for a task I have been given. It is all about how short life is."

"Great!" The blond curls bounced when she spoke. "Can you share the link for it when you're done?" Rolling her eyes, her tone became noticeably sarcastic.

"My academic advisor told me this morning that I needed to do some community service activities and become more involved with my extra-curricular activities. She would love to see that I am helping you."

Sarah was stunned at how easy this was to get the girl to talk. She thought about how she would have run in the other direction if a stranger came up to her and wanted to talk about how short life was. Now came the time for the real question. Turning, Sarah started to walk alongside the girl. The traffic passing them along Bell Road made a rushing sound, and she had to raise her voice so the girl could hear her.

Taking a deep breath, she asked, "So, what would you do if you knew you only had a short time to live?"

Snapping her head towards Sarah, she exclaimed, "Oh! We had a question like this in our ethics class! Most of the guys just said that they would party and go crazy." Laughing out loud, she added, "I have always felt that I should help people. I mean, even if I was the one dying, I would still want to help people, right? To do something good before we go."

"Sure," Sarah nodded in agreement.

"I have been given so much that I would like to help those that don't have as much. My mom and dad taught me to try and help those that are less fortunate." Cocking her head to the side, "Well, I guess if I was the one dying, then I might be the one less fortunate. Huh, kinda ironic. Don't ya think?"

Sarah felt the intensity of this girl's enthusiasm. It was a bleak contrast to the realization that she would be dying in less than an hour.

"Yes. A person that only has a short time to live would be the least fortunate one." The rush hour traffic started to pick up, and the two women subconsciously quickened their pace as well.

"What would you miss in life?"

Charlotte thought for a moment. "Well, I think I would miss the good times. I have plans for college. I just got a scholarship to cheer at the U of A. Don't get me wrong, it is not just about me. I would hate that my mom and dad would be sad if I wasn't around. They don't really have much fun by themselves. I am the only fun one in the family!"

The more they talked, the more Sarah found herself genuinely liking this young girl. She was like the little sister she'd always wanted. Most of the younger people that came to work at the café did not have this girl's positive attitude or zest for life. It didn't seem possible that she was going to die soon. *Not possible, and not fair*. Sarah had to stop herself from getting too angry. Her mind raced back to how Margaret Masterson was ready to die after leading a full and abundant life. Then she thought about the vile councilman and the crazy homeless guy.Both of them were better off dying. One because he was evil and the other because he was in so much pain. In her opinion, death was the best thing for both of them. Now there was a young life—so full of enthusiasm. It was not fair that this girl had to die too. Sarah's mind raced with ideas; there must be some way to help her. Maybe Sarah could find a way to hide her. To keep her safe. Perhaps if she made the girl change her direction in life, she would see tomorrow's sunrise. There had to be something Sarah could do.

The girl's blonde curls kept bouncing as she continued to walk away from Sarah. Her young voice was filled with a high-pitched, excited tone. Turning her head and looking toward Sarah, then she stared off into the distance as she thought about the different things she would miss and the dreams she had for the future. Each word broke another small piece away from Sarah's resolve. Panicking, she glanced at her watch, realizing the top of the hour must be getting close. She had to think of something and fast.

Sarah looked up as they approached 7th Street.Frantically thinking of how to save this precious young woman. Suddenly, her eyes caught a glimpse of a shadowy figure standing directly across the six-lane street. There stood the angel of death. He was waiting for them. Her muscles froze in place as her eyes focused on the man standing on the opposite corner from where she and Charlotte walked. Her momentum nearly pulled her over as her feet became like magnets, stuck to some unseen metal surface under the sidewalk. The same could not have been said about her new friend as the young girl continued to walk forward. Charlotte casually looked right where Azrael was, but she made no comment or gesture about the strange-looking man. The killer stood next to the crosswalk sign as it flashed—beckoning with a mocking gesture for them to come to him.

Try as she might, Sarah's throat tightened around the words as she tried to yell. Her mind raced for a way to warn the young cheerleader before she reached the other side of the street. Charlotte stepped just out of arm's reach as Sarah's hands waved hopelessly in the air. The bubbly girl just kept talking and walking, happy that she had a person that would actually listen to her dreams.

Sarah looked past Charlotte as she turned her attention back to the dark figure. He was watching the girl intently. It reminded her of the first time she saw him. The way he stared at Harold, the bus driver, with the same ground-leveling gaze. In a vain attempt to scream, Sarah opened her mouth and tried to yell at Azrael.

"You can't have her!" Sarah's voice boomed and echoed in her head, but no sound came out of her mouth.

As she observed the scene unfold, Sarah saw the car coming out of the fringe of her vision. Like a freight train, the car moved incredibly fast as it barreled toward both of them. Just as Charlotte stepped into the street, the dark blue sedan raced through the red light, missing two cars by inches. Cross-traffic cars slammed their brakes to avoid the would-be collision. Oblivious to his surroundings, the driver of the four-wheeled missile was looking down as the car headed right at Charlotte. Sarah's eyes widened as the vehicle crossed the intersection without slowing down. The driver wasn't even paying attention. He didn't even see Charlotte!

The sudden loss of not having her new friend right next to her must have caused Charlotte to stop for an instant. The young girl turned to look over her shoulder, turning her body away from the oncoming car.

Everything happened so fast, but Sarah's mind processed the scene as if moving in slow motion. Her attention was glued to the oncoming car, but it was too late to do anything. She could not even close her eyes in time to avoid watching. The hollow sound was deafening to Sarah's ears as the girl's petite body was struck by the speeding metal ram. Charlotte's body floated through the air like a ragdoll thrown by an angry child. White smoke erupted from the screeching tires as the driver suddenly realized what was happening.

The car slid hundreds of feet before it finally came to a complete stop. But it was far too late. The young girl's lifeless body landed a few dozen feet from where she was hit. Her body lay motionless with her feet on the sidewalk and her head twisted backward. The once blond curls, now turning red, set a gruesome contrast against the dark black asphalt.

It was the anger that tore Sarah's eyes away from the horrific sight. The muscles in her legs tightened as she tried to lift her feet to run. She wasn't sure if she would run to help Charlotte or run to attack the dark angel. It didn't matter because her feet were stuck as if they had become part of the sidewalk. With laser precision, Sarah's head snapped straight as she looked directly at the angel of death. He stood motionless, still waiting on the opposite corner—a statue in black staring at the ground where the dead girl's body came to rest. The dark figure seemed to deflate like the air that slowly escaped from a balloon. Azrael's once tall and lean stature seemed to diminish. His shoulders slumped as his head tilted down, and he stared at the ground a few feet in front of him. The commotion from the accident was just to his left, but he did not look at it.

Studying him intensely, Sarah noticed a look she wasn't

expecting on his face. His lips pouted, and his ordinarily tight jaw was slack and limp. He truly seemed to be sad.

Her voice finally came back to her, and she shouted with all her might. "How could you have killed her, you devil," she screamed. "She was so young." Her voice trailed off as her vision got blurry from her tears. Sarah's body grew instantly weak. The last thing she saw was the ice-blue eyes of Azrael as he raised his head to look at her. Like the lights getting suddenly turned off in a dark room, Sarah's world went black.

It was around five o'clock at the police station when Detective Wolfe made it back. He had been all over town finishing up various interviews on the supposed suicide case of Councilman Wingfield. If the case had been assigned to nearly any other detective, the case would be closed, and the file would probably have had dust on it already. Instead, Michael found himself interviewing people about the councilman's past habits as well as his current associates. Officially, none of them were considered suspects or accomplices. Still, the police department's higher-ups wanted to make sure they had all the answers to the questions that had not even been asked yet. If the issue of drug use in a public office were to come up, and it often did in a case like this, then the department wanted to have every angle covered.

Michael was tired just sitting at his desk; he needed the *real* police work to be finished. He always thought it would be his physical abilities and shrewd guile that would make him a great police officer. Ironically, he never knew it would be his excellent typing skills that would get worked out the most. Filling out reports consumed the majority of his time. He had only chased down one criminal in his entire career, and only had two high-speed pursuits in his car. Both ended with Michael catching the bad guy, but the action was short-lived compared to the hours of paperwork that followed. It was much easier to drive the car while chasing down the perpetrators than it was to document every second of the chase.

An hour of writing and typing had gone by and Michael was finally done. Aside from the slight cramp in his hand, he was pretty satisfied with the write-up, although he was not 100% confident in the contents. He did what he was told and wrote what he was supposed to write. Sarah Thompson was mentioned as a person that visited Councilman Wingfield before his death. Still, nothing was mentioned about the likelihood that she had anything to do with it. Michael knew something was wrong with the whole thing. He told his superiors about how he had identified the key witness at the scene of both deaths. They didn't seem too impressed after he was pressed for details and was forced to admit that the elderly woman died from natural causes. Couple that with the fact that he had no objective evidence that Ms. Thompson was even there at all. Detective Wolfe was forced to exclude the information altogether about Sarah being at another death. He was told it would just look silly when the case was reviewed by the city officials. His boss made it sound like it was in *his best interest* and so he avoided any undue negative backlash. In his gut, Michael felt that there was more to the story. He took his notes and created a file of his own about the strange woman.

Afterward, he looked at the completed case file and smirked with a sense of accomplishment. Glancing at his watch, he realized that he could still catch his Lieutenant before he left for the day. This way, he could at least get the case file turned into the prosecutor's office and finally out of his hair. Michael jumped up and grabbed his coat, careful not to disturb the ever-present pile of dossiers that he still had not finished yet. These cases would have to wait until he could get back to them—now that his highly visible case was '*done.*'

When he found his lieutenant, he was in the computer lab reviewing some videos that had just come into the station. Lieutenant Lloyd Bradder was standing over the two technicians running the controls as if he were a director giving orders for a live telecast of the Super Bowl. Michael generally liked his boss and felt that he was doing an excellent job keeping the precinct chaos to a minimum. Even if he was a bit gruff, Michael knew his boss was a good cop. Lloyd Bradder graduated from the police academy over thirty years ago and finished at the top of his class. He would be the first to remind anyone of that fact whether or not they ever asked. Overall, he was a pretty smart cop and had great instincts about people. Bradder was on the quick path to the upper echelon of police management. Yet, it was his attitude and appearance that were shunned by some of the political elitists. Stocky and bald with a protruding belly, everyone knew their superior officer would not be able to pass the police academy physical entrance exam if he had to retake it. The man liked his beer as much as he enjoyed loose women. Those things all combined to create a toxic slurry that severely limited his career and took him far off the fast track to upper management. It only took a few drinks at a local pub to get him complaining about how his career had topped out. Instead of being the golden child, he was a bitter has-been, but he was good at hiding it from the captain. To make sure no one went over his head, he was sure to not come down too hard on his team. He was still OK in their eyes, and that was about the best he could ask for.

Michael didn't see what the others saw. He genuinely respected his boss and looked for ways to learn from him. Sometimes he knew what not to do as a detective as much as things to do right.

Michael walked up to his boss and tapped the completed case report against the inside of his palm as he waited. The Lieutenant's head slowly turned. The look of annoyance was evident on his face. Meeting the detective's eyes, the frustrated man grabbed the folder from Michael with a particular swiftness mixed with anger. He flipped it open and started to mumble to himself as he read through it.

Michael felt good about the report, so he knew he had nothing to worry about. Just over the shoulder of his slightly shorter superior, he could see what his lieutenant was yelling about a few minutes ago. It looked like a scene from one of the intersection traffic cameras somewhere in the city. The shot's angle was set to see cars that might have run a red light or something. He watched in mild curiosity as the technicians were replaying a scene over and over again, trying to get a clear view of what looked like a car accident.

It only took a few scenes to see that it was an accident involving a car and a pedestrian. It looked like the car completely ran through the red light. From the footage, it looked like the car actually swerved directly toward the young woman as she stepped into the crosswalk. Michael could easily see that the light was red, and the car never hit its brake lights. A sour feeling came over him as he watched the young blond woman, actually, more of a teenager, get thrown through the air by the impact. The scene replayed over and over, each time from a different camera angle. Michael noticed that the teenager could be seen turning her head away from the car and staring back at another woman standing on the corner. The other woman did not move. She just turned her head and watched the car as it approached. There was something about this scene that made Michael feel uneasy. Not only the horror of the accident, but something else was wrong with this picture.

That sour stomach instantly tightened as his mind finally focused on what the problem was with the scene. The woman standing on the corner was the same woman that he had just interviewed. The same woman who was present at two other seemingly innocent deaths. Michael watched as Sarah Thompson's face appeared over and over again. She was on the screen from each angle as the different videos came up. He was absorbed by the sheer impossibility that this was the same person. The room's volume seemed to lessen to a point where he could only hear his own heart beating. His short, shallow breaths were pulsating along with the pounding of his chest.

Michael placed a hand on each one of the technician's shoulders as he leaned forward. Almost touching his nose to the screen. The montage of video feeds stopped as he realized how hard he was pushing on the techs. They both stared up at him with a look of weariness and frustration.

"Sorry, guys," he said as he leaned back away from the screens. "I have met this woman before." Pointing his finger up at the screen, "Is there a feed that shows more of her? I need to know if this is who I think it is."

"Sure, Detective." Clicking away at his keyboard, the younger tech brought up a new video feed. This one was from directly across the street. "This is the best one we have of her."

"Thanks," he said as he studied the screen. "That has got to be her." But just as Michael finished his sentence, the woman disappeared from the center of the screen. It was as if someone put a new feed up on the screen—one without the woman being there.

"Wo, wo, wo! Hold the phone!" Not taking his gaze off the screen as the video looped, his eyes scanned the fullness of the screen. Searching for the missing suspect.

"Where did she go?" He watched as Sarah was there just before the accident. Then she yelled something, but she was not looking at the girl any longer. From this angle, Michael could clearly see that she was looking almost directly at the camera. A few seconds after the accident, the woman disappeared. The screen remained the same, but the woman was gone.

"Yeah, that is strange." The older technician typed a few commands into the computer just as the screen went into a tighter loop and zoomed in on where the mystery woman was standing. Over and over again, the woman was in the frame and then she disappeared without any movement.

"There is probably a glitch in the feed. We might be missing a few seconds." Shrugging his shoulders, he added, "It happens sometimes."

Michael looked at the time stamp on the feed. He watched intently as the timer ticked away the seconds. Each frame of the video was synced to a tenth of a second. There was no missing time as the number clicked in its proper sequence. The feed went through its progression, and there didn't seem to be any evidence of a missing piece of coverage. The woman indeed just vanished.

"Just before she disappeared, she was yelling something," Michael said with a panic in his voice that he was trying hard to hide. Finally, breaking away from the screens, he whipped around and stared keenly from tech to tech, moving slowly face to face.

"Do either of you guys know how to read lips?"

Bewildered, they turned to look at each other for a second or two in disbelief before answering. There was a faint smell of cheap aftershave and cigarettes that filled the tight area where the three men were wedged, and Michael's patience was wearing thin. The techs knew the detective was about to blow his lid.

"Um, there's a guy that works the second shift. I think his name is Andy Miller," said one tech. "He's pretty good at it," offered the second. That is all Michael needed to hear.

After giving the techs strict orders to have the tape viewed by their colleague and report back to him immediately, Michael left the room and hurried back to his office. He did not even notice the Lieutenant had left the room. Michael thought he might have to add to the report he just turned over if his hunch was right about Sarah Thompson being at the scene of another death.

When he got to his office, he called his supervisor and asked what it would take to get a surveillance person to put a tail on Sarah Thompson while he worked out some details. He needed to know where this woman was going and who she was coming in contact with. They might just be her next victim.

CHAPTER FOURTEEN

The morning broke to reveal a gloomy day. Thick grey clouds rolled over the horizon and gave the morning a miserable feeling. Sarah saw the dark clouds in the distance. They were a beautiful sight against the mountains in the background. Maybe Phoenix would finally get some of that much-needed rain. Despite the outcome, overcast days were a rarity in Phoenix.

As Sarah got off the bus, she looked up and thought the weather set the perfect stage for her first visit to a church in over five years. Over the years, she held a particular disdain for organized religion. If God didn't care to come to her house, why should she bother to go to his? Although she had to admit, his house was better than hers. The walkway up to the actual church was simply beautiful. The sidewalk was lined with plush, green grass. A perfectly manicured hedge formed a small wall, and she could even see some good-sized trees off in the distance. She would have expected this much greenery at a business or maybe a church in the nicer parts of town like Scottsdale or Paradise Valley, but not out here in the southeastern part of Phoenix.

New Life Christian Church had been in Phoenix for over a hundred years. About fifteen years ago, the congregation moved their church from a small location downtown to a much bigger one in the suburbs. The main sanctuary could seat over two thousand people. The church would regularly be rented out for major concerts. The outside terrace led to a lobby that was lined with tall columns. Each entryway made the church look more like a city government building rather than a house of worship.

Just past the main building was a series of prefab buildings. Some of them had miniature paintings on the outside that gave instant understanding they were children's classrooms. Handprints of different colors and sizes created a rainbow effect that surrounded a picture of Jesus with his arms outstretched.

The second prefab building was a simple white structure with a few modest trees and bushes outside. As Sarah walked up, the breeze blew a bit stronger and a lot colder. She knew this was just another ominous sign that she shouldn't be there.

When she entered the main door to the office building, Sarah was expecting to see a regal set of desks or maybe some statues surrounded by stained glass windows. Instead, the reception area was relatively ordinary and straightforward. Two soft-looking chairs had evidence of more than a few years' worth of wear. They were set on each side of a small wooden table. If it wasn't for the array of Christian magazines sitting around, the office would have passed as any other office. Soft music was playing, and Sarah realized that she was a bit disappointed about the music as well. She expected to hear some kind of Benedictine Monks' prayers playing to the sounds of the choir's rendition of Amazing Grace. Strike two, she thought. Yet, more than the mounting sense of disappointment was a deep feeling of peace —that this place was a bit more normal than she expected. She knew she was just projecting her own bias and an anxiety. The whole place looked like it was more relaxing and less rigid than she anticipated it was going to be, and for that, she was grateful.

Just as the door shut behind Sarah, a young woman came into the office area from down the hall. Her walk almost looked like she was skipping. Her eyes met Sarah's, and a broad smile came across her face.

"Hi! You must be Sarah Thompson, right?" the woman said in a perky voice. As big and bright as her smile was, it was overshadowed by the near-glowing neon orange shirt she was wearing. It had an outline of a cross with the name of the church scripted underneath. In bold letters, it read, *In all things, work heartily as if working for the Lord* – Galatians 3:23.

"Yes. Yes, I am," Sarah said hesitantly.

"Great! I'm Ginny!" The woman took Sarah's hand and shook it so hard that she practically ripped it off at her shoulders. "Pastor Allen is expecting you." The young woman turned with a bounce. "I can show you to his office." Sarah was led down a small hallway lined with random pictures. Some of the people were standing in front of a newly built water well in some foreign country. Some were simply snapshots of older people, probably senior members of their congregation. They passed a few closed doors and small alcoves before stopping in front of a plain white office door. Ginny knocked softly and opened the door. Leaning in, she announced Sarah's arrival.

"Pastor? Sarah Thompson is here for her appointment."

Sarah thanked the woman, who simply smiled and responded that it was her pleasure to help. Stepping into the office, Sarah felt the all too familiar feeling of disappointment rise inside her once again. The office was ordinary and lacked any sort of overt regality. She expected the pastor's office to have more of an overtly religious feel to it. The plain walls were lined with light brown bookshelves. Each one was overflowing with books of all shapes and sizes. Opposite his simple wooden desk was a small sitting area with a few chairs around a tiny brown coffee table. As she glanced around the room, she expected to see a large, felt picture of Jesus or an enigmatic crucifix with him staring down. Instead, this place looked just as normal as everything else.

A short man with a big smile rose from behind the desk. He was about as tall as she was, maybe even shorter. It was his eyes that caught her, though. His soft green eyes were smiling brighter than his round face was. A look that exuded a feeling of joy that was nearly infectious right from the start. This was finally something that met her expectations. His face was what you would expect from a person that loved God. As Sarah looked at the man, she felt like he was the exact image of what a man that loved helping people would have. This is just what she needed to see at that precise moment.

"Good morning, Sarah." He extended his hand as he came around the furniture. "My name is Ryan."

Sarah greeted him with a firm handshake and looked him straight in the eye. She was trying not to show how crazy she felt inside. Police were chasing her. She was now in the habit of watching people die. And oh yeah, there was a silly angel of death guy that kept appearing in her life and transporting her around as if he was the ghost of Christmas past. Nothing too crazy about any of that. As she stared at him intently, his voice broke her concentration. It was a relaxing, almost disarming voice. If he wasn't a pastor, he would probably make a great salesman.

"Nadine has told me a little about you. She said that you had some questions about death. What would you like to talk about this morning?"

Sarah didn't know where to begin. Her head swirled with all the angles from which she could approach her situation. How could she tell him what was going on without giving away the truth and breaking her obligation to Azrael? She decided to just come right to the point. She took a deep breath.

"Well, Pastor. I wanted to ask you what the most important thing that should be on a person's heart before they die is?"

There, she said it.

Ryan's eyes widened as he leaned back in his chair.

"Wow," he said with a deep exhale. "That is a great question!"

He looked down at the table for a moment as he thought. "Well, I would have to say that the answer can be as deep or as simple as you need it to be."

Smiling sheepishly with a sense of relief, Sarah said, "I guess simple is good."

"OK. The answer is Jesus."

Disappointment washed over Sarah's face. This wasn't exactly the answer she was looking for. This was the kind of response that left more questions than answers.

"Okay," she said as she elongated the word into three syllables. "What is the deeper answer?"

With a broad smile on his face, "Well, I guess that is the beauty of your question. That answer is also Jesus."

Sarah's disappointment went to frustration as her face reddened, and her hands gripped the arms of the chair. Her eyes stared mercilessly at the man. This guy was either crazy or screwing with her head.

Seeing his guest's reaction to his answers, he sputtered, "Sorry, please let me explain." Ryan knew he misjudged the seriousness of her question. He gave her the standard response that every four-year-old is taught to give in Sunday school. "You see, Jesus is the simple answer to the question." He leaned back again and brought his fingertips together. "God sent his son to the earth so he could have a relationship with us that he didn't have before. In the Bible, John 3:16 tells us that God sent his only begotten son, that whosoever believes in him will have everlasting life. That is why I can say that Jesus was the simple answer for someone that was about to die."

After a slight pause, "The thought of forgiveness, going to Heaven, and never perishing might be important to them."

Sarah knew the words from the Gospel of John. She mentally recited them to herself as the pastor spoke. She knew the verse from a time when she would go to church with her parents. It was *THE* verse that all good little Christians knew by heart. And now, she found herself looking at it in a whole new light.

"I guess I understand," she offered quietly.

Pastor Allen knew he was at least getting through to the young woman. Now to go father.

"The deeper question is answered by the reasons why Jesus is the simple answer to what is the most important thing to a dying person."

The pastor's voice got more serious. "Can I share some more from the Bible?"

She just nodded silently as he reached for an ordinary-looking book from his desk. As he was leafing through it, it struck her that this was his Bible. It looked like any other weathered, old book. It was not at all what she thought he would have. It was not colossal book at all, nor did it thump when he set it on the coffee table in between them. She was just about to make a comment about it when he found what he was looking for.

"Here it is. 1John 4:8-10—*Whoever does not love does not know God because God is love. This is how God showed His love among us: He sent His one and only Son into the world so that we might live through Him. This is love.*"

Pastor Allen raised his finger into the air as he read. "*Not that we loved God, but that He loved us and sent His Son as an atoning sacrifice for our sins.*" He brought his hand down and quietly shut the book.

"Sarah, God sent Jesus to us as a guide—so we could find

Him again. It was a true relationship that was lost due to sin in the Garden of Eden. God showed us how to love him and to love each other through this relationship." He paused for a moment to collect his thoughts.

"See, when Jesus took the cross and died for our sins, it was an example of how far God would go to get us back into that right relationship with Him. He sent His innocent Son to suffer and die at the hands of guilty men so we could be cleansed of our sins."

Pastor Allen could see his words sinking in, but he couldn't tell if they were making sense to her. Without encouragement, he continued.

"Jesus told us in the Bible before He died that He was the Way, the Truth, and the Life. No one could get to the Father without going through Him. A dying person would want everlasting life, but they don't know how to get there. When I go to the terminally ill ward at the hospital, I go there to talk to them about Jesus and the need for them to embrace Him as their personal Savior."

There was a long pause in the room. The sound of the clock ticking on the wall was the only reminder that time was moving.

"Sarah. If I may, can I ask who your savior is?"

The question was so simple, yet Sarah never really thought about it much. She grew up in a Christian home, but she was smart enough to know that living there didn't make her a Christian. There was no salvation by association. She just stared back at the pastor as he sat, waiting for an answer, but it was an answer that she was not ready to give.

Seeing how she struggled with this question, Pastor Allen quietly looked down and took a deep breath. He knew the answer. He had seen this response many times when confronted with the question of Jesus' place in their life.

"Sarah, God loves you. He wants to show you that love

through His Son Jesus Christ."

At that exact moment, a firecracker went off in Sarah's mind. A flash of white-hot light pierced her thoughts of her parents.

"How can there be a God that claims to love everyone and even sent His Son because He supposedly loves us, yet He constantly ignores our cries?" Unable to stop, she felt the flick of an unseen switch as her anger lashed out.

"And not just ignore us, but He takes people away from us that love us. The very thing He cannot give us, and He sees fit to take it away. That isn't loving at all … that's torture."

Years of repressed frustration and anger rushed to the surface like a balloon let loose underwater. Ripping through the layers until it reached the surface and then burst out in an explosion of violent intensity. The same force broke through her vain attempts to suppress her pain. Tears began to fall from Sarah's eyes as she dropped her head into her hands.

"He doesn't love me, and I don't love Him." She cried out even louder, "I am so angry at God!"

It was true, but she had not said it aloud in a very long time. Shortly after Sarah turned twenty-five, the life she had known came to a horrific halt. It was the July 4th weekend, and the entire town was in a buzz. Since Independence Day landed on a Sunday that year, Monday was the observed holiday. Moreover, since Phoenix had been hitting record-high temperatures, the three-day weekend gave everyone the excuse to escape the heat. Thousands of people crowded the few highways out of town to find respite in the high country's coolness and comfort. Mountain areas like Flagstaff and Payson became a beehive of activity as their respective populations practically doubled in size.

On that particular weekend, the same throngs of people that had fled the city at various times over the past few days all hit the road home at the same time. Invariably, the cars, trucks, and RVs would crush the few arteries that brought travelers back into the city, and Interstate 17 was no exception. What should have taken two hours was taking travelers well over three to four hours to get home. Once the motorists got past the last hang-up just before the city, it was like dropping the green flag. People took off and raced the last few miles home. That fateful day, however, not everyone was done partying.

As her parents were driving home from a late afternoon church prayer meeting, their car was struck broadside by a drunk driver. The police estimated that the driver was going over ninety miles per hour in a forty-five-mile-per-hour zone. Her father was killed instantly—the result of head trauma caused by the collision. The front of the drunken man's pick-up truck collapsed the driver's side door of her parents' older sedan. The force of the collision pushed their car up an embankment and into a concrete barrier. Sarah's mom was trapped inside the car with her body pinned between the immovable concrete titan and the body of her lifeless husband. Rescue workers spent over an hour prying her out, and finally, they were able to get her to a hospital.

Sarah had been over at a friend's house, enjoying the holiday when she got the news. The authorities tried to reach her multiple times, and each time, she ignored the call because she didn't recognize the number. It was only after the same number kept appearing on the screen that she finally answered it. When a police officer told her about the accident, she couldn't even move for a few moments. After she got her senses back, Jimmy drove her to the hospital, where doctors stopped her before entering her mother's room. They told her about what had happened to her dad and what her mother was dealing with. The diagnosis was not good.

Sarah's mind and body went numb. All of the sounds and lights were suddenly miles away, and her mind refused to accept the reality of what was really happening. Slowly, and by sheer force of will, Sarah moved each foot forward. Unseen forces pushed her body into the brightly lit hospital room. Everything was brilliantly white save for the lone figure in the bed. The variegated shades of purple strewn across her mother's face and arms cast a stark contrast to the white around her.

The sight of her mother lying there brought Sarah's motion to a sudden halt. Once she recognized this figure was indeed her mom, Sarah snapped to attention, and her body went into action. It would be a long time before she realized that her mind never truly came out of that dark, numb place.

She gently took hold of her mom's hand and softly kissed it. Sarah squeezed tighter—willing her mom to get better as she put her mom's hand against her cheek. Tears blurred her eyes as she watched her mom's chest rise and fall. Sarah heard the bells and sirens from the heart monitor for a second before realizing her mom's breathing stopped. The tightness in her mom's grip she had felt just a moment ago was gone. And now, so was her mom.

A torrid of tears were still falling across her stunned face as the doctors and nurses rushed in to help. They pushed Sarah out of the way as they tried to revive her mom. She stared in horror as she watched her mother's limp body dance under the voltage from the shock paddles. She didn't even feel it as someone took her by the shoulders and guided her out of the room. The remaining tears left wide tracks as they rolled down her face.

An hour later, Sarah found herself kneeling before the altar at the hospital chapel. She wasn't sure why she went or how she got there. She just remembered a lot of voices that echoed in her head. They kept telling her to go and have some time to pray. As if that would solve the problem. As if prayer would magically bring her parents back from the dead. She sat there before the plastic embodiment of Christ on a cross, and her blood boiled with anger. The tears had dried up, and her eyes were red. She wanted to cry more, but she couldn't. She wanted to scream at the top of her lungs, but she was empty. A hollow, vacant feeling crept through her psyche.

Maybe, just maybe, she hoped she would not be able to cry again. The swirl of emotions ripped at the fringes of her mind, and her soul darkened. Every minute she sat in that little sanctuary, the door to her heart sealed a little tighter. She did not want to pray. She wanted to lash out at God. To yell at Him for not being there. Or maybe there was no god at all. There couldn't be a god that would take her mom and dad from her. All those years her mom and dad had devoted to the church and God Himself, how could a loving God hurt them so tragically?

For a God that called himself pure love, how could a loving God leave her so alone? That was the first time she felt the Darkness come to her. Unlike the absent savior, the Darkness felt comforting. It felt peaceful. It was numbing, and that was the best part of it. She wrapped herself in the Darkness, and she could be free from the pain.

That was also the day she turned her back on God once and for all. As she left the chapel, she stopped and stared at the plastic Jesus. It almost looked as if He was looking back at her. A mix of false sadness and mocking pity in His eyes. Even if it was, she wanted Him to know how angry she was. Angry at Him. She knew that she wanted no part of a God that would do something like this to those that loved him.

Little by little, Sarah's life disintegrated for her over the next few years. Each time something difficult would happen, Sarah would relate it back to the feeling of how God was punishing her for not going to church or not believing in Him. She felt like she was being prosecuted in the courtroom of the universe, and each time she was found guilty as charged. The Darkness was always there though. To give her the peace that nothing else could. It washed over her like a cascade of warm water. It surrounded her and pulled her deeper.

And now, here was this simple man sitting in front of her. A typical puppet for God, declaring God's goodness and unending love, yet it was just like a bag of hot air. She hated God, and that included His cheerleaders.

Although he was not ready for her outburst, Pastor Ryan instinctively reached out and gently put a hand on Sarah's shoulder.

"I understand, Sarah. I really do." The tears and outbursts were not uncommon for Pastor Allen. Over his many years in ministry, he had seen many different levels of doubt, anger, and pain. Even though he had struggled with his uncertainty for a while, but now faith has allowed him to give his fears and doubts to God. He knew her reaction was not solely based on her question. There was something more than her curiosity about what to tell someone who was dying.

"I know you are hurting, and believe me, God knows you are hurting too. He doesn't want to see any of his children in pain."

"He took my parents in a terrible accident. They loved him, and they served him faithfully." Sarah raised her head and glared at Ryan. Her eyes were red and still wet from fresh tears.

"How did he show them love? By killing them horribly?" Unable to keep her gaze fixed on the man's face, she looked over at a small picture on his desk of the pastor's family. The volume of her voice rose higher than she expected.

"How did he show he loved me? By torturing me and leaving me to die inside?"

Silently, Ryan said a quick prayer to God and asked for His mercy to surround this poor woman. He also asked for wisdom about what to say to her.

"I know the death of your parents must have hurt you, and I know it was a tragedy that we cannot begin to understand. God was not the author of their death. He doesn't want us to suffer at the hands of bad things. He sent His Son here to save us from death. Not the kind of death as we know it, but the death that can separate us from Him forever."

Like a viper ready to strike out at his statement, Sarah's head snapped back to stare again at the pastor. He continued, hoping she would give him the chance to explain.

"Please believe me when I say that God still loves you, and He loved your parents dearly. His love does not stop just because bad things happen. His love is even more evident when they do happen. God is the creator of everything. Part of that *everything* was the option of free will for his children. People were given free will to make their own choices. Both good and bad choices, but ultimately all of the choices have consequences."

"So, my parents *chose* to die," Sarah quickly snipped. "They were killed by a jerk that drank too much and decided to drive! He made the decision, not them!"

"Your parents did not decide to die, Sarah," he offered in a soft voice. "The man that drank too much decided out of his own free will. A decision that had tragic consequences. His choices resulted in the loss of precious lives and it affected countless other lives still here on earth. God did not make the man drive drunk, nor did He kill your parents in the accident."

Cutting him off, "Well, He certainly didn't do anything to stop it from happening."

"That may seem true, but God loves us enough to allow our free will to run its course." Leaning back in his chair.

"Yes, God could have stopped your parents from getting in the car. He could have stopped the driver from drinking too much." Taking a deep breath, "And yes, He could have saved your parents from death. But where would the stopping of free will end? Should God have stopped your grandparents from having children so your parents would not have been hurt? God created mankind with free will, and we abuse that independence, even to a point where we reject the One that gave it to us."

The tension rose in the pastor's voice as he continued. "We

fight so hard to defend our independence. Then we get so angry at God when He gives it to us."

Pastor Allen caught his voice and knew he was coming off far sterner than he wanted or intended. Calming himself with a quick sigh, he continued, this time with a more soothing tone.

"Yes, some people abuse that freedom and turn to bad, while some turn to good. But all have the gift of choice."

"Why doesn't God stop just the bad ones?" Sarah felt like a boxer that was getting waylaid. Her opponent knew what he was talking about, and he was pounding her into an intellectual corner. She had always felt like her mind was her strongest asset. She was logical and relied on solid understanding, but his argument seemed logical and sound. Yet, her best asset was now turning against her. Despite the anger and desire for vengeance grinding away at her emotions, her mind was taking control and listening to his logic.

"Then who is the judge? Who'd be the one who would judge what is bad or good?" He steepled his fingers and pressed his fingers against his lips before he spoke again.

"The Bible says that all of our good deeds are like filthy rags to God. No matter how good an action is, it is still not good enough compared to God's full goodness. So, if our very best sense of goodness is not nearly good enough, how can we say what is good or bad? How can we even know? If someone knew Adolf Hitler when he was a little boy and knew what he would become, would it have been 'OK' to kill that little two-year-old boy?"

She thought about it for a moment. A flash of memory came to her mind of Kenny, the sweet, chubby-faced little boy from the café. His infectious smile and giggle made everyone's heart melt each time he came in. Could someone hurt that little boy because of something he might do much later in life? No! She couldn't hurt that little boy.

"Maybe someone that knew what he was going to do could have taken him aside and taught him differently. Maybe someone could have helped him. Saved him!" Her voice rose with each statement, hoping that her thoughts were correct. Her mind was racing as fast as her pulse as she tried to find a way to save this hypothetical boy. More than that, she wanted a way to refute his logic and shoot down his argument.

"Ah, but now you are involving choices and free will again. Maybe someone did see the anger in him early and tried to stop it. Maybe someone else saw it and even encouraged it. Somewhere along the way, you have to imagine there were many choices that could have been made differently. Each one would have changed the outcome, but none of them stopped what happened." He paused for a second as he collected his thoughts.

"God might have sent people to persuade Hitler from doing what he did, but it was up to those people He sent to complete the task that God gave them. If God just forced His will on someone, that would be contrary to the love that God wants from us. Forcing someone to comply or change is contrary to free will. If He wanted us to be mindless robots, then that is what He would have created. If He forced us to love Him, that would not be any form of love at all. Instead, He gave us free will and a choice to love Him and follow Him. People make poor decisions. People make mistakes. Not God."

Sarah's mind raced with confusion. Her mind was swirling. Her thoughts were battling her emotions in an all-out war for her sanity. She nervously cleared her throat and looked at her empty wrist.

"I really should get going. You have given me a lot to think about, and I need some time to wrap my brain around it." Standing up quickly, Sarah said her good-byes before the plump pastor could respond or add anything more to her swirling thoughts. She raced past Ginny as the young woman tried to be polite.

The weather was just as ominous as before when she went in. A peel of thunder rolled across the darkening sky as she closed the door behind her. Luckily for her, the bus pulled up moments after she got to the stop. As she settled into her seat, the rain began to fall and echoed the gloom in her thoughts.

Michael had to wait until after Noon before he got the approval for his surveillance request. It didn't come easy, and it was only after he showed the video and the transcript to his Lieutenant.

"Sir, I know this may sound strange, but she is definitely yelling at someone else," Detective Wolfe pleaded. "She doesn't even look at the driver of the vehicle as she is yelling. Then, to top things off—she just disappears. I spoke with guys from video and IT. They say there was no missing footage from the feed, and the video surveillance hardware is working perfectly. She just vanished!"

Handing his boss a yellow legal pad, the frantic Detective added, "And I had a tech from the second shift study the video. He can read lips, and he told me she was yelling angrily at someone just before she disappeared."

The overweight Lieutenant shifted uneasily and turned towards the Detective, "Well, I will agree with ya; this is pretty strange." The Lieutenant scratched the stubble on his chin. Even though it was only late morning, the man had a five o'clock shadow.

"I can give you one officer for surveillance. A street cop. He's young, but he's eager. I'll have him report to you tomorrow. You can have him for a week. If you can't find anything suspicious or more convincing, you're gonna have to let this one go."

Michael left his boss's office and gave himself a fist pump in the air. Score one for the home team, he said to himself. When he got back to his desk, he realized he left his cell phone there. Glancing at it, he saw he had a voice mail waiting. Tori wanted to know if he could get off work early and go shopping with her. Work had been crazy, but he felt the need to spend time with her. It wouldn't be too long before there was a third member of the family, and alone time with Tori would be a thing of the past. He called her back, and they set a time for him to come home and pick her up. After he hung up, he started to put together his notes for his case against Sarah Thompson.

A few hours later, Michael picked up his wife and they were set to find some final things they needed for the baby's room. He was thankful that he had brought the umbrella with them as they went out shopping. The weather looked pretty bad before they left the house. There were times when nothing but dust would come from even the most ominous dark clouds in Arizona. Most of the time, they just sailed on by without a single drop of rain. Not today. The weather change was usually a welcome sight, but Michael could have done without it right now. As they went from store to store, the rain got worse, and so did Tori's mood. If it wasn't for her stubbornness, Michael would have insisted they went home. She wanted to finish the list with him. She was grateful that he took the afternoon off to spend with her, so she wouldn't waste it sitting at home.

"OK, this is the last stop, right?" he asked as he parked the car as close to the entrance as possible. They had spent the last three hours looking for some last-minute items, but mostly they just needed a stroller and crib. Chiding himself for being a typical male, Michael was ready to buy the first one they looked at, but Tori wanted something unique.

"Yes, yes. Let's just take a look around and see what they have," she said as she got out of the car. She loved the fact the Michael still opened doors for her. He raced around and opened the large black umbrella. Keeping the cold rain from her, she thought to herself, 'he's such a gentleman.'

"Good, then we can go get some Chinese take-out food, then go home and start a nice fire."

"God, that sounds amazing," she exclaimed as they raced to the entrance of the baby supply superstore. "I hate shopping at these places, but maybe there is something in here we could find."

The aisles were filled with every conceivable item that a new mom could want for their new baby. Toys, bottles, clothing, and bedroom furniture, and they even had luggage and medical equipment in case a person wanted to make sure they had all of their bases covered.

"Oh!" Tori turned to him holding up the tiniest dress he had ever seen. "Wouldn't she look beautiful in this?"

"Well, yeah. Absolutely. I think it looks OK."

"Yeah, you're right. It is just OK." Tori put the dress back as quickly as she grabbed it. "Maybe something in lavender."

As Tori darted off down another aisle, Michael just took it all in and let her look through everything. He knew his role in today's events was to offer encouragement and help her with toting everything. And, of course, to pay for it all. He didn't mind that she made the decisions when it came to the baby. What was he going to say anyway? She was the one carrying their baby, and she was the one that would give birth to their little girl. All of that should at least earn her the right to decide what pattern she wanted on the changing table or what the baby's first blanket was made of.

They had been in the store for over forty-five minutes before they even made it to the cribs. Tori stopped and studied each one carefully. She touched and caressed the sides as if she was imagining their daughter lying in it. Michael found the rocking chair selection placed perfectly at the end of the aisle. If he was tired, he knew she had to be exhausted. He marveled at how conscious she was of everything that had to do with the baby. She was going to be a great mother.

Tori got to the end of the cribs and bassinettes without any success. Turning to look at Michael rocking back and forth in a large white chair, she felt instantly bushed.

"Comfortable?" she asked with a smirk.

"Actually, I am. These things are great." He noticed her looking at him with curiosity. "But the one your mom gave us is much better."

"Good, because she spent a lot of money on it when I was born." She punched his arm playfully. "It's practically a family heirloom."

He smiled and acted hurt by her punch. They had found a few outfits, so she grabbed him by the shoulder he was rubbing and drug him towards the front of the store.

"Come on, ya faker. Take me home, and I'll let you rub my feet."

When they got to the register, they noticed a small group of people in a corner. Quite a few employees were surrounding a young couple. By the looks on all of their faces, they had been crying. One of the young workers came over to the empty register. She unsuccessfully tried to put a smile on her face, but the red-stained eyes gave a different story.

"Is everything OK?" Michael asked in a hushed tone.

"Oh," the teenager said, startled as if she thought they might not have noticed. "Everything is fine." She glanced back at the group and leaned into Michael and Tori.

"That couple had been coming in here for months. They had just finished their baby's room when she miscarried. They just came in to see if they could return the stuff they bought."

Michael was stunned. He was used to hearing sob stories, but this one was too close to home. More than his reactions to it, was the way the news affected Tori. That is what hurt him the most. He felt her grip tighten around his arm as she stared over at the young couple. The redness appeared around her nose, and he knew she was about to start crying any second. He glared over at the insensitive clerk and wanted to stuff her brightly colored vest in her big mouth.

The clerk must have known she said something wrong because she sped up as she bagged the outfits. Michael had to practically drag Tori out of the store. Her body became rigid. The moment he closed her car door, he could hear her wailing. When he got to her side, she turned to him with tears in her eyes.

"Did you see them, Michael? Did you see how young they were? She was younger than me." She grabbed his arm again with the same unyielding strength. "What if that happens to us? What if we lose our baby girl," she blurted out in between sobs.

"Honey, the doctor just told you the other day that you and the baby are perfectly fine." He reached behind the seat and pulled out some old fast-food napkins.

"How do you know? Maybe their doctor told them the same thing?"

"I'm sure there were signs or warnings. Doctors don't just miss stuff, Hun." He was trying everything he could to calm her down.

"I want to go home. I'm not in the mood for Chinese food."

"Ya gotta eat, Hun. How about I call it in and have them deliver it to the house after we get there?"

"Fine," she said flatly as she stared out the windshield. Her mind thinking about the young couple they had just seen. Her hand reflexively went to her enlarged belly. She had not prayed in a very long time, but she found herself asking God to watch over her daughter.

CHAPTER FIFTEEN

When Sarah got to work, her mind was in overdrive. Still reeling from all the old feelings that were rushing back to her. Thoughts of her life before her parents died kept washing over her like the waves from a stormy ocean. Each one crashed against her resolve and weakened the wall she kept around her Darkness—her last line of defense.

There were memories of times when her parents would go out of their way to help her and teach her things about life. Things she hated at the time, but she understood them now. Then the sting of their funeral would rise up and strike at her fragile psyche like a viper. As she fought to keep her mind focused, she remembered a simple picture frame hung over the doorway in the house where she grew up. The dark wood frame enclosed a simple white sheet of paper with bold black lettering that read, '*Practice Random Acts of Kindness and Active Ways to Pay It Forward.*' Every day when she came home, she would look at the silly, old frame. Every day she would read the stupid phrases. She would roll her eyes or make snide remarks about it each time she passed. It wasn't until now that she fully understood what it meant. Her mom and dad were good people, and they were always looking for ways to be a blessing to others. Even if it meant that they had to sacrifice something of their own.

Sarah found herself standing in front of the small mirror attached to the outside of her locker in the employee breakroom. For a brief moment, she thought she saw her mother's face looking back at her. Then she blinked a few times and felt a small tear run down her cheek as the face in the mirror turned back to hers again. Oh, how she missed her mom and dad. She felt like she needed them now more than ever. God took them away, and now she was alone. Always alone.

The ghosts of the past were not the only things rolling around in her head. The words of Pastor Allen bubbled to the surface as well. Reminding her that God was not to blame for the loss of her parents. The man that killed them was to blame, not God. It was easy to blame God because He wasn't around to defend himself. She could just stay angry with Him and never try to resolve the pain she felt every day. Anger was her drug, her numbing agent. As long as she felt the anger, she was not required to feel anything else. With the comforting blanket of fury, she was practically indifferent to everything else. Now the fuel that kept her fire burning deep inside was dwindling. The waves of repressed emotions were coming back the same way the rays of the morning sun would burst forward to overtake the dark shadows of the night. Her logical mind was trying to stay in control—to continue to have full reign over her anger. Yet, the same part of her brain kept giving way to the logic that Pastor Allen spoke to her. The war of her sanity raged along the battlefront of her mind. She knew what the pastor said was right. God is, was, and always will be good. He was pure love. Among many other beautiful things her parents had taught her, she knew God was the purest expression of love to the point of sending his Son to die on the cross. Thoughts of her mom teaching Sunday school at their church burst forth from the deep recesses of her mind. These were the thoughts that she had kept locked away, along with every other happy memory. As if to remind her of what was taken, the precious thoughts were starting to rise to the surface.

Glancing back at the mirror again, she looked at her reflection. She had hoped to see her mom's face one more time. Even if only for a second and even if it was only in her imagination. She dried the remaining tears from her eyes, smoothed out her dark blue uniform, and started for the door. Luckily for her, she only had to work the short lunch shift. Work would be good for her. It would help take her mind off the onslaught of emotions. Another part of her, the sadness inside her, wanted to hide away from everyone and be alone. Wrapped within a cocoon of her own thoughts. The Darkness inside her longed to keep her frozen and lifeless. To let her past emotions wash over her, drowning her in a black sea of depression of her own creation.

The day itself progressed without much of a problem. A few angry customers, a few flirty customers, and a bunch of ordinary people going about their regular day. A few times, she found herself staring at a young child and remembered what Pastor Allen said. What would life hold in store for that little one? Would the free will he was given and the choices he will make be a blessing or a curse?

Just like her attitude, the weather took a change for the better as well. The daily grind of the workday did take her mind off the pain and allowed her to think about the good things that God had done for her. Now she needed some time alone and maybe a hot bath to think things over.

When she left the café, the sun felt warm on her skin as it danced in between the thick puffy clouds. The breeze was much warmer now and even felt refreshing. All things considered, it was a great day, so Sarah decided to walk for a while. Before she started, she dug into her purse and pulled out an old watch that her mother gave her. The next time she had to talk with someone for Azrael, she wanted to know how much time she had left. More importantly, how much time that person had left.

The streets were surprisingly busy for mid-day on Thursday. She scanned the faces of each person as they walked by her. Like any big city, Phoenix was the home of all types of people. Folks from all sorts of different races, religions, and backgrounds. Each one had a different story to tell. Each one had dreams and desires. She also knew that each one would die one day. She caught herself as she made the connection between the reality of life and death. When she used to think about death, painful thoughts of her parents would come rushing forward. Now, when she realized that she was thinking about death, she was anxious and nervous. Not so much about the thought of death itself, but at the fact that some of these people would be going to Heaven or hell based on their choices. This brought her to a terrifying halt. She stopped her brisk walk so suddenly that a man in a business suit almost knocked her over from behind. Standing in the shadow of a large office building, Sarah felt the chill of truth strike her. She would die one day too. She would be held responsible for her actions. Responsible for her sins. Would she go to Heaven? Would she see her parents again?

From across the street, Sarah heard a distant voice. When she looked, a man was standing there waving to her. He looked to be in his late forties with a wisp of salt-and-pepper markings around his temples. The man was modestly dressed in simple jeans and a t-shirt under a light tan jacket. He kept yelling something in her direction, but she couldn't make out what it was clearly. He cupped his hands to his mouth and yelled louder. She heard him calling to her, but it wasn't her name that he was yelling. As she listened closer, she could hear that he was calling for someone named Janet. Sarah instinctively looked around from side to side to see if there was someone else standing nearby. Clearly, there must be somebody else that this strange man was calling to.

"No," the calm, calculating voice came from deep inside her mind. "He is calling to you, Sarah. This is your next assignment, and he has you confused with someone else. Go speak to him. Time is ticking."

Oddly, Sarah did not feel angry or upset at the now familiar voice in her head telling her to talk with this stranger. For once, she felt like she had an idea of what to say to her next encounter. Azrael's voice even made her feel more assured that she was on the right track. She was more confident, knowing that this was what she was supposed to do. And as strange as it was, she was glad that the angel was with her, and she was not alone.

Darting out into the street, Sarah had to stop abruptly while a minivan raced past her. The driver was an older woman. She had her head partially turned and yelled at someone in the backseat. The van came so close to Sarah that the edge of the side mirror brushed past within inches of her body. Sarah thought it was ironic that she almost became one of the people that Azrael would take. She almost became a victim. As she felt the air blow past her from the rush of the van, she wondered if there was someone that was supposed to talk with her about the most important thing in her heart before she died.

Standing in the street, frozen by the thought, Sarah could see the man move quickly to the edge of the sidewalk. Breaking her sudden daze, she hurriedly walked over to the sidewalk and out of the traffic flow.

The man was about her height, with a slight belly that poked out from the front of his jacket. Up close, Sarah could see he had a friendly face with kind eyes. The man greeted her with a broad smile as he rushed over to stand abnormally close to her. He was definitely inside her personal comfort zone, and that was something she didn't like at all.

"Hi," he said quickly as he took her hand in his and shook it frantically. "You must be Janet," he said with a sense of excitement in his voice.

"I'm Barry. I certainly appreciate your help today!"

"Um, hold on a second, Barry," Sarah blurted out. Creasing her forehead as she backed away. "I'm not Janet. Sorry."

The man's mouth hung open as a look of pure confusion washed over him. In those few seconds, he was trying desperately to figure out what had just happened.

"You're not Janet?" His words were a mix of confusion and accusation.

"If you're not Janet, then why did you come over when I called you?" Leaning back and waving his hand towards the rush of traffic. "Heck, you almost got yourself killed just trying to get over to me."

He had a point there. Sarah may not have been who he was looking for, but he was definitely the one she was looking for.

"Sorry, I am actually not your friend Janet. My name is Sarah, and I came across the street because you were yelling at me. I couldn't hear what you were saying, but you seemed so excited that I thought it must be important." Sarah held her breath and hoped he bought it. There was a long pause, and she thought she might just have to try a new tactic.

"Well, I guess I'm the one that should be sorry." He continued to study her face with a sense of uneasiness. "I almost got you killed." His eyes darted back and forth between Sarah and the busy street. He paused for a moment as he tried to figure this woman out. Then as if a switch went off in his head, his face transformed from confusion to a look of disappointment.

"She's not my friend."

"Sorry, who's not your friend?"

"Janet. The woman that was supposed to meet me here this afternoon. The one that I thought you were." Glancing up and down the street, still looking for the other woman, he put his hands on his hips in frustration.

"Well," he paused, "She was supposed to come to help me at the food bank today. I help out there a few nights a week, and we're pretty short-handed. This lady, Janet, works with a friend of mine, and she said she was looking for a way to give back to the community." Rolling his eyes, he added, "I should've known that she wouldn't've shown up. She seemed too perfect. Volunteers don't just fall out of the sky, right?"

Sarah saw a way to get this guy to talk and spend time with her, so she quickly interjected. "Well, maybe I didn't fall from the sky, but I did just cross the street." Standing taller and pushing her shoulders back. "Forget Janet! I'll come help," she finished with a big smile. "What do you need me to do?"

Barry just stared at her. His face went back to the look of mixed confusion and excitement. He wanted her to be real. He needed her to help, but his instincts told him that she was too good to be true.

"Really, huh?" His tone was dripping with sarcasm. "So, you are just going to come along with me. Out of the clear blue and help me in the soup kitchen tonight?" When he closed his mouth, he pursed his thin lips while his eyes burned holes into Sarah with an accusatory stare.

"Yes," she responded confidently, even if it was only feigned. "I can help, but if you are not interested, I can go help someone else." She turned her hips and acted like she was going to walk away.

"No! No! Please don't go." His hands came up in a defensive surrender. "Sorry about that." His shoulders sank, "Ya see, not too many people want to help the less fortunate. They want to *think* they want to help. They tell everyone around them that they want to help, but when it comes time to actually make a difference, everyone seems to scatter."

Sarah knew exactly what he meant. She had always said she

would help out those around her, but she always seemed to stop just short of helping. Her parents would take her to a homeless shelter every year around Thanksgiving to volunteer. While she was there, she enjoyed herself, and she felt better after doing it, but the feeling was never strong enough to get her to do it any other time of the year. She would say that she wanted to help, but nothing came of it.

"OK, then. Let's get started. Time is too short." Sarah said it but almost winced at the statement. Time was short, and for Barry, it was even shorter.

As they walked, Barry told her about the food bank where they were going. St. Joseph's had been around since the '50s, but the economy and the lack of help had taken a toll on the place. Many of the people who would come in on a regular basis were just trying to get back on their feet. In years past, they were the people that had hit a bad stretch of luck and just needed a helping hand until things turned around for them.

Recently, most of the people that came were 'habitual homeless'. These were people that made it a choice to live on the streets. Some of them were good people who just needed to break away from the 'normal life', but there were some bad apples too. Barry told her stories of homeless thugs that would form gangs to harass and bully others. Sometimes for food, money, or alcohol, and sometimes even sex. Sarah felt sick to her stomach as she listened to him describe the violence among the homeless. First, it wasn't fair that the people were destitute and hungry, but now they were getting pushed around like children on a playground by a bully in the same boat as them. Senseless.

Glancing at her watch, Sarah knew that she had to get the conversation turned toward God pretty soon, or her time would run out. Well, to put it more accurately, his time would run out.

"So, where did the name St. Joseph's come from?" Trying desperately to change the subject to something lighter. "Is it a church or some other type of religious place?"

Barry's eyes widened, and his face lit up as he thought. "It *was* a long time ago. The place used to be a church way back in the day. The national parish that built it decided to shut down this location and move its congregation somewhere else. They said it was because of poor attendance or something like that. The church was having money problems."

Giving a little chuckle, he continued, "I guess the people needed to eat more than they needed God because St. Joseph's Food Bank took over the location from the city just before it was shut down. St. Joseph's kept the soup kitchen going and shut down the rest of the place."

Seizing the opportunity, Sarah interjected. "So, do you go for the food or for God?"

"Hmm, I guess that's a pretty good question, but I would be insane if I said I did it for the food itself. I mean, I guess the food is OK here. A bunch of us try really hard to make it taste good, but you can only do so much with canned tuna and vegetables. It's better than going hungry if I had nothing else to eat." He rubbed his chin for a minute and stared down at the concrete just in front of his brisk pace.

"Anyway, back to your question. In all honesty, I would have to say I do it for God. Ya know, serving others and all that."

Sarah nearly jumped out of her skin with excitement. The conversation was going exactly as she had hoped. "Do you believe in God?" she asked without trying to sound too eager.

"Wow, Sarah!" He turned his head to look at her. "Another great question!" He brought his chin up, and his chest seemed to inflate. "Yes, I do believe in God. I have ever since I was a little boy. I went to a church camp when I was just a kid, and I learned all about Him there. It was great!"

A few hurried paces went by before he shot back at her, "OK, your turn. Do you believe in God?"

"I did when I was young, but I wasn't so sure for a while,"

she said with a slight sigh. "Recently, you could say that I am looking for Him again and trying to learn more about Him."

"Well, you don't have to look far. God is always with us. He never leaves us or forsakes us. It says that in the Bible."

"I know, I know … I guess I know God exists. I'm just not sure if He is as good as everyone says He is. I was talking to a friend this morning, and he told me that God loves us." Waving her hands in the air as if to display something that was not there, "And He loved us so much that He sent his Son to earth to die for our sins. Is that real or are those just words in a book?"

"Yeah, I've read that too. When I first learned about God, they wanted me to 'give my heart to Jesus," he said as he used air quotes. "I figured I was OK with learning about God, but I really wasn't sure about the whole Jesus thing. I mean, I have nothing against those people that are 'born again,' but I didn't feel that I needed to commit to Jesus just so I could be saved," he finished with another set of air quotes. "You could say that I never 'accepted Jesus into my heart,' but I know I am going to Heaven when I die."

Startled, "Why do you say that? What makes you so sure?"

"Because the God that I know is a loving God. He is not going to send me to hell because of something so trivial. I have done things for Him and His church—His people. I have volunteered faithfully and given money to the church whenever they asked." The strength in his voice got a little deeper. "Overall, I think I am a good guy, and I know God will take me up when I am finished here. Besides, there cannot be just one way to get into Heaven. I can't imagine that it is such an exclusive place that only a select few can make it in."

Sarah slowed her step a little. Now she was baffled. She remembered Nadine telling her that Jesus was the most important thing. Also, she recalled her conversation with Pastor Allen was all about Jesus as the Savior.

"So, you don't believe in Jesus?"

"Oh, no. Quite the opposite. I do believe in Jesus. He is the Son of God. I just don't believe that He is the only way into Heaven. How could putting your faith in another man, even God's own Son get you into Eternity? He was just a man. How could He save you from sin?" Shaking his head incredulously, "He can't! No, I believe that God sent Jesus here to the earth as a model for us. To show us a way to live. He pissed off a bunch of people, and they killed Him for it. Plain and simple. Like I said, Sarah, God *is* good, and He knows that I'm not perfect. He will forgive me for all my sins when I die."

Sarah wasn't sure why her head was spinning, but she felt uneasy with the tone of the conversation. She knew Jesus was the reason that the entire New Testament was written, and He was supposed to be the most important person in history, but *was* He the only way to Heaven? Millions of people couldn't be wrong. God would not destroy millions of people because they didn't put their trust in a single person. God was bigger than that, wasn't He? He loved his children more than that. As her brain tried to wrap its intellectual arms around what Barry was saying, her stomach was tightening into knots. Everything sounded logical, but nothing seemed to make sense. Why did she feel so troubled about it?

"Here we go," Barry stated confidently, breaking Sarah's intellectual distraction.

She looked up to see a concrete building with only a few darkened windows. The original building was constructed in 1903 by a German Franciscan as an outpost for the Roman Catholic Diocese. He was charged with trying to get the English settlers and the Mexican communities to worship together under the banner of the Holy Roman Church. Over the years, the neighborhood around it grew and subsequently deteriorated over time, but the building itself had always been a place of refuge for the community.

Sarah noticed there were already a few men and women standing in a make-shift line near the front door. There was a wide range of ages, and most of them looked as disheveled as the building they were trying to enter.Both were covered in dirt and grime, and their exteriors were lined with cracks and creases that only years of neglect could produce.

Sarah's head was still spinning from the religious questions that she almost forgot why she was there in the first place. She felt a pang of panic as she looked at Barry again. Her self-consuming need for understanding nearly cost her the opportunity to talk with this man. Glancing at her watch again, she realized that it was getting close to the end of Barry's hour and, apparently, to the end of his life. Quickly, she turned her head from one side to the other, desperately looking to see if the angel of death had made his appearance yet. The only thing she saw was the throngs of people that seemingly appeared from out of nowhere. Drifting in from the edges of the alleys and surrounding buildings, their movement was like a silent processional of zombie-like stagger. They knew where to get food and help, and now was the time for both. She watched as people of all races and ages began to crowd the entrance to the small church building. Looking at their faces, Sarah noticed the glaring differences. Each set of eyes told a different story. Some, draped in ragged clothes, still had the undeniable sparkle of hope twinkling in their eyes. In contrast, others marched on with blank stares even though they were more moderately dressed. Some were alone while others walked closely together in small makeshift packs.

Not wanting to get stuck too far away from Barry, Sarah slipped her body in between some men as they started to gather in a larger group outside the building's front. Additional helpers came from inside the building, wearing white cooking aprons with some faded stains on them. Barry stopped and was talking with them as he pointed to the throng of people. The crowd seemed to undulate as it became a living mass of people.

Barry finished talking with the workers as they turned to go back into the dark doorway. He waved his hand for Sarah to come back over towards him. Trying to get through the crowd, she felt the mass move to one side as the thrust of people pressed against her like a moving wall. Just beyond the border of flesh, two men were shouting obscenities at each other. Each one blamed the other for trying to cut in line. When Sarah finally broke through the wall of bodies, she found herself standing in between two large men. Her sense of humor overpowered her body's desire to backup as she noticed these men were too heavy to be standing in line at a soup kitchen. Neither looked like they had missed a meal and were slightly out of place standing next to the others. One was bald with a beer belly pouring out of an undersized shirt, while the other was taller and ripped with muscles.

All of her wisecracks stopped when she saw the sudden flash of a metal blade. The fading sun reflected off the six-inch piece of steel that was gripped by the heavyset man. Beads of sweat dotted the man's bald head as his eyes flared with an animal-like ferocity. Sarah's body froze as she watched the blade whipping back and forth through the chilling air, making an eerie hissing sound. The echoes of people screaming faded into the background of her mind as the two men came into complete focus in front of her. Her trembling body was like a tiny child compared to the two men standing just a few feet away from her.

Just beyond the commotion, Sarah could see Barry on the other side of the quarrel. He was moving quickly toward the men. His eyes were fixed on the knife as well. Looking up at her, his face went pale with the realization of how close Sarah was to the fray. He yelled at the men to stop, but his cries were drowned out by the shouts of the crowd. With all of his strength, he grabbed each man by the shoulder, trying desperately to push them apart. Barry's grip on the man with the knife loosened as the man pulled his shoulder away from Barry, leaving his empty jacket in Barry's vain attempt to slow the man down. The bald man took a darting lunge at his larger adversary. The blade waved harmlessly in front of the stronger man as he dodged the fat man's clumsy attempt.

Barry continued to shout at the men, pleading with them to stop. "Come on, guys! There is plenty of food to go around," he cried.

"Ya wanna talk to me about cuttin' in line, then let me tell you about some cuttin'," shouted the heavyset man with the knife. He pushed Barry to the side and came at his opponent with a powerful stride.

Recovering his balance, Barry jumped back in between the men, begging them to stop. Sarah saw the gleam of the blade disappear from her sight. She wanted so badly for it to have been a trick of her eyes, but all she could do was watch as that metal shaft entered Barry's mid-section. With the shorter man's momentum, the two of them fell to the ground with Barry underneath. The crowd went eerily silent as reality struck everyone. The stronger man was gone before anyone could say a word, and the rest of the crowd started to disperse as if a bomb had just exploded. As the bald man lifted himself off of Barry, the handle of the knife was left sticking up like the mast of a ship, rising and falling with each of Barry's labored breaths.

Sarah stood frozen just a few feet away as she stared helplessly at the knife handle. A crimson outline formed on his white t-shirt. It grew with each breath he took. She knew he was hurt bad. His eyes stared blankly into the sky, the expression of shock and horror on his face. She never noticed the assailant as he disappeared into the thinning mob. Moving slowly as if in a dream, she knelt by his side and cried. Her whimpers muttered how sorry she was over and over again. Her head dropped into her hands as she wept.

"Sarah, it is not your fault." Azrael's voice was calm and gauging as ever. He appeared and stood over her. The sound of gurgled breathing stopped, and silence washed over the scene like a blanket. "It is time to go."

Sarah raised her head slowly and stared intently at the man in black. "At least he died knowing God, right?" She stood and waited for his response expectingly. "He is going to go to Heaven, right? He was a good man, and he was doing God's work here on earth, right? Right?" Her voice grew louder and louder as Azrael's face remained still.

"I know that he believed in God the Father, but he was wrong about what he said." The short pause between them seemed like an eternity before he spoke again.

"He believed that all roads lead to Heaven and that the Son of Man was not the one true way to God. He was mistaken. Jesus, the Messiah, is the only way to Heaven for those who wish to enter. Believing in the One True Savior is how to receive eternal life. Sadly, today, this man will not be going to Heaven."

"No," she screamed as the rage inside Sarah boiled over into tears. "That is not fair," she pushed through her sobs.

"I understand your concern for this man, and I can see the passion you have for what is right, but understand this: it should not be a surprise to those that do not follow the Son of Man. It was declared over 2,000 years ago, and it has not changed since. People have become so arrogant that they believe they are gods. They presume to tell the Almighty how to act or to treat His creation." His voice boomed in her head.

"Too many are lost on the singular notion that God is good, so they will be set free, yet they are only partly right. The Almighty Father is good, and in His goodness, He sent an atoning sacrifice for the sins of all mankind. They choose to ignore God's sacrifice and then have the audacity to blame Him for their failures and the judgment that comes from them. Yes, Sarah, there is a hell, and many souls make the eternal choice to go there. I have seen it with my own eyes."

His words trailed off, and silence once again took hold. The crowds of people were starting to push back in. Some moved around the edges of the widening circle, and some came rushing up to help the now-lifeless victim. Sarah was forced out of the way as a man rushed out of the doorway with a medical box.

"Come, it is time to go," Azrael said as he placed a hand on her shoulder. She felt the familiar weightlessness overtake her as everything faded to black.

CHAPTER SIXTEEN

Today was a new day and Detective Michael Wolfe sat at his desk, bright and early. He enjoyed coming in around this time of day—before the din of the masses that would rush in later. His mind relished the quiet, but his energy level could have used more of a jump start. His night's rest, if that's what it could be called, was fitful at best. His sleep, or lack thereof, was torn between his worry over his wife and the self-imposed frustration with the 'Thompson Deaths,' as he started calling them. He wanted to call the events the 'Thompson Murders,' but he felt like he was getting ahead of himself.

The previous night, after he and Tori got home from shopping at the baby store, they ate their Chinese food in relative silence. As usual, the food from Harold Lu's Palace was phenomenal, but Tori barely touched her plate. Michael made sure to order her favorite dishes, but he couldn't get her to eat much more than a few bites. In the end, he scarfed up all of his and even some of hers. He knew she was still processing what she saw in the eyes of the young woman that lost her baby. The unvoiced doubts brought wrinkles and worry lines to her face as she tossed her beef and broccoli from side to side, as if the arrangement of the food would bring her peace. Fear gripped her mind as she tried with all her might to hold it at bay. Michael had seen the look before. The look of sheer defiance mixed with an unhealthy dose of fear, set on a plate of worry. He would see it whenever there was an officer-involved shooting. Years back, a fellow officer had been gunned down at a routine traffic stop, and the press got wind of it before any of the families were notified. Every spouse that married a police officer held a certain dark place in their mind if their loved one's name would be called. Tori had the same look of panicked fear then that she was trying so desperately to hide now.

When they went to bed, she surprisingly fell asleep right away. Exhaustion and fatigue took their relentless toll on her body, and she allowed herself to sleep. Michael, on the other hand, lay awake and did some mental processing of his own. Sleep finally took him shortly after midnight, but his alarm clock broke the new day while it was still dark outside.

He woke quickly, showered, and dressed as quietly as he could. After leaving a note for Tori, he let her sleep and went to work. Thursday nights were supposed to be their pseudo date nights, and Tori was fiercely defensive of them, yet last night didn't feel like very much fun at all. It didn't take a detective to figure out that it was a disaster. Being a detective did, however, require a lot of odd hours. Michael tried his best to not let anything interfere with this sacred night, so he knew he would have to plan another date night very soon.

With his fresh dark roast coffee and a buttermilk donut from LaMar's, he was ready for the day. He laughed as he wondered why the beat cops kept bringing in donuts since it just reinforced the old cliché about cops and the excellent tasting pastry. Either way, his donut tasted exquisite this morning, and he didn't care what negative enigma it helped support.

The pile of case files on his desk was slowly getting

smaller. The harsh fluorescent tubes overhead washed the piles of tan manila folders in a surgically sterile light. The towers of files were, in fact, noticeably smaller, but it was not going nearly as fast as he, or his boss, would have liked. The wheels on his faux leather office chair squeaked as he rolled back and forth, putting folders into different filing cabinets. He had been trying to organize the cases into an organized system to get a better grip on them. Just as he pulled himself back to his desk, his computer dinged with an incoming email.

The rookie for the surveillance detail was on his way over. Lyle Walters, a recent graduate from the academy, was assigned to help him for a week. Typically, this kind of investigative and tailing work would be given to a detective. But given the low priority, Michael was thankful it was being done at all. This case had bugged him from the start, and he knew his window of opportunity to discover something was short. Whatever happened, he knew that it only took one little mistake by the perp to clinch the case.

If anything, it would be good to get another set of eyes on the case. The more he thought about the individual issues and the facts surrounding each one, the more he was convinced it was not just a simple case of random deaths. He kept bouncing ideas off his logical brain. How could this woman be at multiple, seemingly random deaths, yet she was not directly related to any of them? Not trying to hide her presence at any of the locations, she left obvious clues and evidence yet disappeared as if she were a ghost. He poured over the traffic video and re-read every eyewitness report. There was a second person at the scene, but she was nowhere to be found after the accident. And the car accident was just that: an accident. He talked with the officers on the scene and even had a written statement from the vehicle's driver. The driver admitted to being distracted and not seeing the victim until it was too late. Michael had to admit there was nothing suspicious on Sarah Thompson's part about the death, or any of the deaths for that matter. There was absolutely nothing suspicious about any of the deaths except for the same person being at each one. He was determined to find a link between them. Right now, Sarah Thompson was that link.

He was so lost in his thoughts that he barely noticed the officer standing next to his desk. The young man was well over six feet tall with tightly cropped black hair. He had a strong chin and a nose that had obviously been broken a few times before. This cadet looked like what a cop should look like. When Michael looked up, he was a bit startled to see the rookie officer standing at perfect attention with his right hand in a standard salute. Wow, this guy was fast and eager.

"Um, at ease, soldier. There is no need to salute in this office. If you did, you would be the only one. Have a seat," he said as he waved a hand toward the empty chair next to his desk.

"Thank you, sir."

"And you can cut that crap out too!" Michael said quickly. He couldn't help but laugh to himself. This rookie was fresh out of the academy, and he was already trying to impress everyone. He laughed harder when he realized that it was a lot like what he did when he came out of the academy.

"How can I help you?"

"Well, sir ... uh ... Detective, I received my assignment to keep surveillance on a Ms. Sarah Thompson, and I was reviewing her file. Not much on her in here, so I wanted to study her picture." His hands shook with nerves that the young police officer had hoped he could hide. There was a slight quiver in the manila folder as he brought it up to show the detective.

"I thought this was a test."

"You thought *what* was a test?" Michael asked with an edge of frustration. "Getting your first assignment to help with the detectives?"

"No, sir," he responded with enthusiasm. "I was studying the suspect's face from your case file, and I saw Ms. Thompson's face on a different file. One that wasn't in any of your paperwork." He opened up the folder, hands a little steadier, and handed it to Michael.

"Ya know … something to make sure that I was looking for the right person. The suspect was seen at another death." Pointing to the picture clipped to the inside flap of the folder.

"This picture was taken by a bystander during a stabbing at a Phoenix food pantry last night. Just off Central Avenue."

There it was—a rough, grainy picture of a woman standing over a body. Even with the low quality, Michael could see instantly that it was Sarah Thompson. His mouth hung open as he stared in disbelief. Things couldn't get any worse. There was no way this woman could have been seen at another death. It was statistically impossible. The sheer chances of this woman being around a single death were amazing. Now she was documented at four completely different and independent deaths. This was no longer a coincidence; this was now a murder investigation. She had to be involved in the deaths somehow.

"Did she kill the guy?" Michael asked, still with a stunned expression, not taking his eyes off the picture.

"Witnesses say that she was not involved at all. Two guys fought over some free food or something at the food pantry and one of them pulled a knife. The good news is there is a video of the fight."

Snapping his head up, "A video? Of what? What does it show?"

"Unknown at this point. It seems there was a security camera running in the entryway to the building. Detective Alexander told the people at the food pantry to make a copy of the video, and someone would pick it up today."

Michael sat still for a moment. The sounds of the busy office faded away as he processed the new evidence. He was excited that his hunch about this lady turned out to be real. Now they had another video to work from. Maybe it showed her disappearing again. Perhaps it showed how she was somehow killing the victims.

"Does the report say who is going to pick up the video or when it would be ready?" Michael was eager to learn as much as he could about this new piece of evidence.

Glancing down at the report, "Um ... No, sir. No one is listed."

Thinking quickly, "OK, thanks, Walters. I'll call the other detective to see if I can get it for him as early as I can today."

Leaning back in the creaking chair, "When are you going to start the surveillance on our suspect?"

"Well, I checked with her place of employment, and she left about two o'clock yesterday afternoon, and she is not in today, so I figured I would take a position outside her apartment to make an initial connection."

Walters was proud of his initial thought process, and he was excited to be working with experienced detectives. He quickly wiped away the beads of sweat that were trying to form on his nervous brow.

"Good job! Get on it right away and let me know if you see anything suspicious."

"Like a dead body or something," he said with a wry smile on his face, hoping to lighten the mood and make himself relax.

Without cracking a smile of his own, "Yeah. Or something like that," Michael said. He knew the rookie was only trying to be funny, and he might have even laughed, but he wanted to make sure that this kid knew his job. Michael's reputation counted on it.

"Uh, right. Yes, sir. I will contact you right away if I see something." The young man stood up anxiously, "Thank you, sir."

Michael watched the rookie leave and finally let out a small laugh. He wondered if he ever looked that uncomfortable when he was a new recruit. Michael turned his gaze back to the picture. *It might be time to pay Ms. Thompson another friendly visit.*

In the northeast part of the city, Tori sat in her living room, mindlessly watching TV. The furniture and décor gave the house a look of something you might find in a chic New York City apartment with its clean, simple contours. The black leather couch's creamy texture was a deep contrast to the faux snow-white fur rug underneath. The glass coffee table, which she kept meticulously clean, held a few fashion magazines and the remote to the large flat-screen TV typically hidden in the dark wood entertainment center.

Even though it was the middle of the day, Tori was still in her pajamas. She felt like a child sent home sick from school with no real reason to get dressed since she had no place to go. In essence, she was in prison. The doctor told her it was the best for the baby if she stayed off her feet as much as possible. So, her days consisted mostly of helping Michael get out the door in the morning and then sitting around all day, waiting for him to get home. Like a faithful Labrador Retriever waits for its master to return, she waited for her husband.

Since she had been given the doctor's orders, she had already watched each one of her favorite movies twice and her favorite, *The Princess Bride*, a dozen times. Although she did like to read, it was not something she could do all day. She enjoyed reading in bed at night to help her fall asleep. In recent weeks, the only thing that she needed to help her fall asleep was being horizontal. Being pregnant was exhausting. She always envied the women who were pregnant and had plenty of energy. She was the exact opposite: all the pregnancy and none of the energy.

Even though her body was a little tired, her mind was betraying her, racing from thought to thought. She kept thinking back to the young couple she saw the night before. Their image had been burned into her mind. Their pain and sadness were still palpable to her. She couldn't imagine the pain they must have been going through, but she felt a dark weight pulling at her every time she pictured them.

Tori sat fidgeting with the hand towel she was still carrying from doing the morning's breakfast dishes. She thought there was an unspeakable joy in having a child growing inside her womb and embracing the hope of giving birth to a new life. That was something she could relate to with the young mother, but then to have that innocent life snuffed out before it took its first breath was too much. Even as she tried to think about the depth of the pain, her mind put up blockades to prevent her from dwelling on it any longer. The thought was too hard. Their reality was too harsh. That poor couple was in a place that she could only know in her worst nightmares, but the fact that she could join them there is what scared her even more.

In her nervousness, she found and clutched a green throw-pillow. The anxiety gnawed at her psyche as she nearly wrung the stuffing out of the helpless pillow. Her fears of losing the baby entwined themselves with the ever-present fear of losing Michael. Being the wife of a police officer was tough. The department even encouraged the wives to attend counseling and support groups. She and Michael attended a few classes last year when a member of Michael's precinct was killed in the line of duty. The officer had three children. A young, beautiful family that will never get a chance to have daddy come home again.

"Oh, God!" Tori cried out to an empty room. *What if something happened to Michael?* Her fears mounted. One slice of darkness laid carefully on top of the other. Creating a tower of impenetrable gloom that could fall on her at any moment.

Tori knew these fears too well. They had been there before. Waiting in the back of her mind. Ready to spring forth whenever she was weak enough to let them in. Her grandmother died when Tori was just nine, and the loss of her Nana ripped a portion of her heart that never truly healed. The pain she felt, even at that early age, had scarred her for life. She feared not only the finality of death for the deceased but also the crippling pain left in the lives of those still living.

Her mind was spiraling around in the dance of distress when her ears caught the sound of something on the television. The person's voice on the show caused her to snap back into consciousness like a crack of lightning. She wasn't sure what it was, but something inside her told her to pay attention.

The image on the fifty-two-inch screen was that of a well-dressed man sitting in what looked like a reading room. He was middle-aged with chestnut brown hair, peppered with grey showing through. He gripped a large, gold-lined book in his hand as he spoke directly into the camera.

"My friends," he said earnestly. "I say again, we do not have to live in fear. We do not have to live in the shadow of death." Tori couldn't believe her ears. It was almost as if this man was talking straight to her. She stared at the face on the TV with her full attention now.

"God has already conquered death by the sacrifice of his Son, Jesus Christ," he continued as he flipped open the book on his lap and started reading from it.

"Jesus said in the book of John, chapter eight, '*If you hold to my teaching, you are truly my disciples. Then you will know the truth, and the truth will set you free.*'"

He snapped the book shut and stared intently at the camera. "Did you hear that, my brothers and sisters? Free!"

As if broken from a spell, Tori chuckled aloud. "Yeah … free to send you money." She reached for the remote when the voice continued. What he said next sent chills down her spine.

"I know some of you out there think that we only get on this television because we need money. Well, I am here to tell you, we don't need your money. This broadcast has been blessed and paid for by sponsors, so we are not going to ask for any money," the preacher said with a wry smile. "Our program is fully funded. My message is being sent to everyone that hears my voice as a gift. Free of charge, so to speak."

The preacher got serious again. "It is a free gift, not unlike the gift that God gave us through our redemption in Jesus Christ. And just as with any gift that is given, it is up to the receiver to take it and open the gift."

Tori's mouth was slightly open as she stared intently at the screen. The preacher finished as if on cue.

"Well, my friends? Are you going to take the free gift of God's love?"

The man on the television urged his viewers to contact the program for more information about receiving Jesus. She was stunned by the timing of the preacher's words. Something in them hit home with her. Something was still stirring in her heart as her mind recovered.

"OK," she said sarcastically, stretching the word out. "So, you are going to tell me to sell everything and give it to your program as soon as I call." She turned off the television and struggled to push herself up from the deep, leather couch.

"That's when they get all your information and start harassing you. Nope! They're not going to get this lady so easily!"

Sarah was still pretty upset when she woke up. Images of the knife sticking out of Barry's body flashed across the dark canvas of her memory every time she closed her eyes. She could not get the thought of his face out of her mind. It was as if there was a mental flashbulb that left a ghost resonance on the inside of her eyes every time she closed them. It's not like she hadn't seen dead bodies before. Heck, she helped bury her parents and even picked out their clothes, but the physical sight of death actually taking its victim away left her truly disturbed. Not so much the blood, but the finality. The sudden stoppage of something living. Death was an ugly thing, and she was tired of it already.

After making a cup of strong coffee, she curled up back in bed and tried to relax. Mindlessly, she turned on the television to try and take her mind off of Barry and the two men fighting. As she scrolled endless channels of nothing, her thoughts eventually drifted back to what Azrael had said about Heaven and hell. If both were real, then that would make our choices on Earth even more meaningful. If people knew that they would definitely be going to one of the two places based on their decisions on Earth, it might change the way they think. It was indeed beginning to change hers.

Sarah got up from her small bed and went to the closet. She silently stared at the blank door for a few minutes as if standing before a holy altar. It was an altar of sorts to Sarah since beyond this slim excuse for a barrier was the last domain for her depression. It was the playground for all the negativity in her life. The thoughts she kept physically and mentally locked away held sway when she thought about the things she buried. All of her memories were behind that closed door. Anything that triggered the Darkness to come back, she hid away. Packed behind a flimsy wooden door lay the personification of her pain. Despite the agony it had caused, her heart wouldn't allow her to throw the stuff out. But since she couldn't let them sit in plain sight and torment her every day, she had to create a shrine of sorts within her closet. Memories that manifested in pictures, books, and even paintings were locked away for their safety, as well as for hers. For a while, Sarah even started to hang her clothes on a rack outside the closet just so she could avoid any contact with the stuff inside. When she was weak, the draw was sometimes too strong.

Now, she wanted something from her Darkness. She wanted to take back something she would have to wrestle from her own internal demons just to hold again. To reach into the black and pull something from the fringes of her Darkness meant to confront it and overcome.

Standing at the open doorway, she shifted her weight from foot to foot like a boxer sizing up her opponent. Building up her inner courage; she knew she would need it to face her fears. The pile of boxes looked harmless and seemingly unimposing, but to Sarah they were like a roaring lion waiting to devour her. Each box held various pieces of her past. Each one had a painful memory. Things that would generally pose no real physical threat, created such a visceral reaction in her. Trying to ignore the call of the boxes, Sarah looked around, taking a mental inventory about where she might find what she needed. The past called to her like a siren's cry, begging her to open the boxes and fall back into her Darkness.

Stretching on her tippy-toes, Sarah reached up to the top shelf and found what she wanted. Her fingers wrapped around an old, dusty book. She pulled it down and wiped away the thick layer of dust. The black cover simply read *The Holy Bible*. She had put it there to keep it out of sight. The faded leather cover still had the stickers and writings she put on it so many years ago. Her parents had given it to her when she started high school, and she loved it at the time. But now it held too many good memories to be left out in the open, allowing her to be mocked by the Darkness. Sarah held the book close to her chest as she went into the kitchen and poured herself another cup of coffee.

She heard the bookbinding resist with audible groans as she opened the cover. Looking at the first page, she found the inscription her father wrote to her when she first got it.

All Scripture is God-breathed and useful for teaching, rebuking, correcting and training in righteousness, so that the man of God may be thoroughly equipped for every good work – 2 Timothy 3:16-17. Her dad had even crossed out the word "man" and had written "woman" underneath. Just below the Bible verse, her mom's handwritten note was beautifully written in purple ink. *'Be strong … for the fight never ends and be faithful … for it is not always our battle to fight.'* – Deuteronomy 31:6. Sarah knew she had probably read that verse from 2 Timothy a hundred times since she first got the Bible, but now the words truly made sense. Tears filled her eyes. This wasn't her battle to fight. For the past five years, she had been defensive and, even sometimes, aggressive with God. He hurt her, and she pushed Him away because of it. She had spent so many years fighting against something that was not even possible. Fighting and being angry at God got her nowhere except alone and exhausted. Just like a child that fights, kicks, and screams when the parent makes them do something that is best for them, Sarah forgot to see God's love, His never-ending love, through her own pain. She was the child, and He was the parent. Even though she didn't want to have her parents taken from her, it wasn't God that had been hurting her all these years. She was hurting herself. It shouldn't take a tragedy for a person to truly see the love that was right in front of them the whole time.

Smiling, Sarah took the Bible and the coffee into the living room. Curling up on the couch, she began to turn the pages without direction. Reaching for her cup, she sipped the warm, soothing liquid. The taste of the dark roast with just a hint of French Vanilla quieted her spirit as it relaxed her body. This was the most peace she had felt in an extremely long time. It wasn't long before her eyes closed, and she fell into a deep, restful sleep. Dreaming about her parents and their love.

She woke a few hours later to the bright sunlight shining through her blinds. The rain had stopped, and large white clouds slowly drifted across the sky. Some of the lights were still on from when she awoke the first time, and the empty coffee cup was sitting on the small table beside her. Sarah looked down to see that her arms were wrapped around the old, worn-out Bible.

Getting up and stretching, her body was a bit sore. She wasn't sure if it was the nap on the couch or from all the craziness going on. The stress took a toll on her body, and she hated it. Bringing the Bible into the kitchen, Sarah felt like she was finally hungry. Over the past few days, she hadn't had much of an appetite. It was fantastic for the scale but not great for her health and energy level. With a smile and lightness she hadn't felt in a while, she made herself her favorite breakfast dish, Mom's famous Eggy-in-the-Basket.

When she finished the delicious breakfast, she noticed a different kind of feeling, one she had not felt in a long, long time. It was a gnawing feeling in the pit of her stomach. It was a different kind of hunger. Not hunger for food, but the hunger that could only be satisfied with knowledge. A need to open the Bible and read it for all it was worth. To consume it and learn more. It was like being impatient as you reread your favorite book, knowing where all the good parts were. The kind of impatience that is only appeased when you get to that good part and allow the words to pour into your mind. She used to feel that way when she was young, but that was a time before her Darkness. A time when her parents were with her. A time when she thought she understood God's love.

After a few moments, her mind drifted to the thoughts of her parents. There was usually a flicker of joy that accompanied the warm memories of her parents. In years past, that flicker would succumb to a dark invisible weight that would move in on her mind like night reclaiming the dark after a match goes out. She felt the same familiar burden trying to pull her down again, dragging her into her waking nightmare. It was almost beautiful and inviting. It was comfortable and appealing, almost safe in its depth. It was something that she knew far too well. Her eyes began to well-up as she thought about the void that was left when her parents died. She was so close to the Darkness that she could feel its tendrils wrapping around her. It was then that she felt a new sensation. It was the peace that came from the feeling of God's love. It washed over her like the cascade of soothing water to dry bones. She opened her eyes quickly, and she knew she had to fight the Darkness. It wanted to take her back, but this time, she didn't want to go. God had given her the courage to resist. She knew this was her fight to fight!

Opening the large Bible again, she noticed a small bookmark sticking out of the pages' bottom. The paper was old, but she could have sworn that she had never seen it before. When she opened the book to where the marker was placed and looked at the paper better. It was a nice piece of stationery. As thick as card stock and about the size of an index card, it had an image of a sun rising over a beautiful beach on the top portion. The edges of the paper were frayed with a soft texture on the surface of the paper. Wherever it came from, this was expensive stationery.

There were a few verses written in black ink on the paper. Sarah didn't recognize the handwriting, but then again, if she didn't remember putting this paper in there, she wasn't going to actually remember who gave her the parchment. The first verse was from the Old Testament, 2nd Samuel 14:14. Scanning the Bible, it was open to the correct page. She found the verse and read through it – *Like water spilled on the ground, which cannot be recovered, so we must die. But God does not take away life; instead, He devises ways so that a banished person may not remain estranged from Him.*

Sarah read it and reread it. *Water that is poured on the ground is soaked in and cannot be brought back.* She thought for a minute about the quote from the movie *Braveheart*, "Every man dies, but not every man truly lives!"

"So, if everyone dies, then what is the point of God and knowing Jesus?" she thought aloud. She knew the second part of the verse was an answer to her question. If God does not take away life but found ways for people to come back to Him, they must live forever and never die. Suddenly, she remembered what Pastor Allen told her about the true meaning of John 3:16. God loved the world so much that He sent a way for everyone to come back to Him. He sent us a way for the world to live eternally with Him in Heaven!

Excited by the thoughts, she grabbed the piece of parchment again. There were two more verses written down —both from the book of John in the New Testament. Sarah surprised herself when she fanned the large book and remembered where the book of John was in the Bible. Her hands trembled as she turned the pages. Her breath was quick and shallow as she scanned the verses. The second one on the list was John 5:24. Finding it she read, *'I tell you the truth, whoever hears My word and believes Him who sent Me has eternal life and will not be condemned; he has crossed over from death to life.'* Looking a few verses up, she knew it was Jesus talking to his followers.

"This all fits together," she exclaimed, her voice much higher than usual.

She took the small piece of paper once more and found the last verse listed on it. Skimming forward a few pages, she came to John 6:40. Once again, the words were in red, so she knew it was Jesus speaking. *'For my Father's will is that everyone who looks to the Son and believes in Him shall have eternal life, and I will raise him up at the last day.'* She read it another time and then leaned back in her chair. As her mind raced through the words, her spirit was already at the conclusion. The corners of her lips broadened as she smiled brightly. Everything was beginning to make sense. God sent Jesus to Earth to restore a relationship with Him, our Creator. And everyone who believed in Jesus and believed in the One who sent Him will have everlasting life, eternal life in Heaven with God.

Sarah's eyes widened as she touched her fingertips to her forehead. "Of course," she exclaimed with delight.

"That's it! This is what would be the most important thing to a person that is about to die. *Everlasting life with God in Heaven!*", she squealed in delight.

Excited and full of energy, Sarah jumped up from the table and ran to her bedroom to get dressed. She knew she had to talk with Pastor Allen again. This time, she knew what she needed to ask him.

CHAPTER SEVENTEEN

Everything was completely different when she got off the bus this time. The sun was shining brightly, and the breeze was refreshingly warm. Sarah thought for a moment about how different the scene was from just twenty-four hours ago. Things did seem different, but then again, so was she.

Sarah nearly ran the entire walkway up to the church offices. The sounds of children playing floated in from a distance. She wondered for a moment if those same sounds were there yesterday. Did the children laugh before, and all the while, she was so caught up in her own problems that she just ignored them? Perhaps she pushed them away from her mind with the self-induced shield she would regularly put around herself whenever she stepped on to God's turf.

As Sarah reached the door, she was so excited about her new revelation that she didn't notice the black sedan pulling into the church parking lot just a few hundred feet from her. Even if she did take the time to look directly at the approaching vehicle, the tint was too dark to see any of its passengers. The car stopped and watched as Sarah entered the small office building.

Once inside, Sarah was greeted again by the bright smile of the receptionist. Although this time, Sarah's smile was grander than Ginny's.

"Hi," Sarah said in a voice that was quick and excited. "Me again. Is Pastor Allen in? I desperately need to talk with him."

"Oh, hi," Ginny responded with equal enthusiasm. She matched the perkiness and excitement of her guest. "He is here. Let me check to see if he is available," she said as she picked up a phone.

A few moments later, Sarah found herself sitting in the same chair as yesterday, but this time, her mind and heart were in a completely different place. Pastor Allen greeted her with his genuine warmth and offered to change his schedule so they could talk.

"I hate to ask you to do that, Pastor," she said with tempered enthusiasm, "… but yes. I could use some advice and want to talk about God some more."

"Well, I always have time for Him," he said with a smile. He picked up the phone and asked Ginny to clear his schedule and hold his calls.

Hanging up the receiver, he looked at Sarah, "OK. Let's talk!"

"The last twenty-four hours have been pretty crazy," she started, rolling her eyes, not even sure where to begin. "Let's just say, I am ready to talk about Jesus and where I am with Him."

The pastor started to open his mouth, but Sarah cut him off. "But first, let me ask you a question. Is it possible to be a good person, but not be good enough to make it to Heaven?"

Pastor Allen was taken aback by the change in the demeanor of this poor woman. Yesterday, she was in his office yelling at him about God, and now she was back, fervently asking more questions. *God was definitely working on this one*, he thought hopefully.

"Yes, most certainly," he declared with a slight sense of finality. "As a matter of fact, everyone that does get into Heaven started out as 'not good enough,' regardless of if they were truly a *good* person on Earth or not. The Bible says there is no one good, not even one person. Everyone has fallen in some way or the other. That's why we need Jesus. Sadly, there are many people who believe they are good enough to be accepted into Heaven when they die, but only the ones that have faith in Jesus will be saved."

"So, do you actually believe that Jesus is the only way to Heaven," she questioned as if still looking for a loophole.

"Yes!" he said confidently. Then he paused for a moment before explaining his conviction. "Ya see, Sarah, the Bible tells us a lot of things. All of them are true. It makes statements about things that could never have been known during the period of time they were written in. After many years, sometimes centuries, those facts and prophecies turn out to be true, every time!"

He watched her, waiting for her to say something. When she said nothing, he continued, "So if the Bible is 100% correct on those items, I have to believe that what Jesus said was correct too."

"But that is just using the Bible to support what it already says," she replied quickly.

"Ah, you are right," he said with a thrilled look on his face. Excited to have such a vibrant mind to talk to. "And if that was the only thing that told me about Jesus, then we could not use it. When you use something written in a book as the only proof that the book is real, it is called circular reasoning. The New Testament contains the details of the life, death, burial, and resurrection of Jesus, but those are not the only places that these things are mentioned. Those details give proof that Jesus fulfilled over three hundred different prophecies from the Old Testament."

He paused, "Do you know the difference between the Old and New Testaments?"

She nodded slowly. "I think so. The Old Testament was written before Jesus. It was written by the Jewish people to tell about their heritage. Then the New Testament came along and talked about the life of Jesus and the new church, right?"

"Right again," he said, getting more animated in his chair. "But the Old Testament held more than just the Jewish heritage. It contained the Jewish blueprint for their coming Messiah. There are hundreds of requirements and prophecies that this future king would have to fulfill. Not all of them were even in that person's direct control to accomplish, such as he would be born of a virgin as well as born in the town of Bethlehem. Jesus fulfilled each and every one of those prophecies down to the last 'T.'"

"Mathematically," Pastor Allen continued, "the chances of a single person even fulfilling a small portion of these prophesies would go beyond the mind's ability to comprehend. Years after Jesus was crucified, there were many other sources of proof that He was who He said He was. Even Jewish historians wrote about the existence and life of Jesus. A Jewish man named Josephus wrote that Jesus was a wise teacher that performed miracles and proclaimed himself to be the Christ. There have been many other separate and independent writings that cite Jesus' life and evidence for his resurrection. The Bible is just one of the documents about why we should believe in Jesus."

Relaxing in his chair, he added, "So, in answer to your question, I firmly believe that Jesus is the Messiah, and He is the only Savior we are ever going to get or need."

Sarah took a few moments to process the information she was just presented with. She knew Jesus was the Son of God, but she hadn't looked too much farther than that. She remembered most of her Sunday school class teachings, but she needed more information to connect the dots. "You seem pretty confident.

Are you willing to bet everything on all of this?"

Leaning back and thinking for a moment. "It's funny you should mention betting. Have you ever heard of a man named Blaise Pascal?"

"No. Was he in the Bible?"

"No, not at all. Actually, Pascal was a seventeenth-century mathematician that came to know God later in life. He specialized in probability, and he founded a thought process that is still in use today. It is called Pascal's Wager. Have you ever heard of it?"

"Nope."

"He declared it was a safer bet to live your life as if God existed, then to die and be proven right; than it was to live your life like there was no God and then be proven wrong. Does that make sense?"

"A little," she said hesitantly. Not wanting to seem ignorant, but this was some heavy stuff.

Pastor Allen saw the confusion on her face. "OK. Let's say the wager is that it is better to bet that the Bible is accurate, and Jesus is the only way to Heaven and then be proven right after we die than to go against the Bible and be proven wrong. Does that make better sense to what we are talking about?

"Yes, it does." Raising her hand up to him to stop it from going any further, "OK, so believing what Jesus says in the Bible is the safest bet, right?"

"Exactly! And Jesus also told us that He was the Way, the Truth, and the Life. He is the only way to Heaven!" He glanced at the picture of Jesus on the wall. "It is quite freeing if you ask me."

"Freeing? How so?"

"Well, many of the world's religions and philosophies believe a person must do certain rituals or meditate or pray a certain way to be eligible for an afterlife. This is what we would call Heaven. Christ did not come here because we loved God. He came to earth to save us because God loved us first. The only thing required of us," as he made air quotes around *required*, "is to accept the free gift of love and salvation. How great is that?" he finished with a broad smile.

"Pretty great, I think," she said as she reflected on his excitement.

"Yes, it is!" The smile suddenly vanished from his face, "But sadly, not everyone accepts this gift. Do you remember when we talked about John 3:16 yesterday?" Sarah nodded, and he continued. "When I quoted the words from the Scripture yesterday, I noticed your reaction to them. You seemed to have known them already, and that was great! A lot of people do, but not many people know the verse that comes shortly after it."

Once again, Pastor Allen grabbed the Bible that was sitting on his desk. Opening it, he quickly found what he was looking for.

"Just a couple of verses later, John 3:18 says '*whoever believes in Jesus is not condemned, but whoever does not believe in Jesus stands condemned already because they have not believed in the name of God's one and only Son.*'" Looking up at her, "Ya see, they are condemned already. It is up to us to tell them the truth about Jesus, and that truth will set them free. It is the truth that will help them believe!"

His words hit her like an anvil falling from the sky, like in those silly kids' cartoons. It wasn't enough just to be good. A person had to know Jesus before they died. That was what she needed to share with the people Azrael was bringing her to visit. Just like what she read in her Bible, Jesus was the answer.

Interrupting her thoughts, Pastor Allen said softly, "Are you ready to talk about if you believe in Jesus?"

This time the question was not met with an angry or closed reaction. Instead, Sarah felt as if a door was about to be opened, and she was excited to see what was on the other side. Far too long, she had kept Jesus at a distance, and now He was here again. Trying to show his love to her one more time. This time, she was not going to let herself get lost!

"Yes," she said confidently. "I want to accept His love and believe in Him as my Savior. I do."

"Good," he said with a nearly inaudible exhale as he praised God in silent prayer. "Sarah, I want you to pray with me."

Pastor Allen said the words to the sinner's prayer, and Sarah repeated them as if they were the deepest and truest words she had ever spoken.

"Dear Lord Jesus, I know that I am a sinner, and I ask for Your forgiveness."

She was hungry for the release from the anger. Her heart yearned for the love that she knew was so close. The same kind of love that her parents shared with their Lord and Savior.

"I believe you died for my sins and rose from the dead. I turn from my sins and invite you to come into my heart and life."

This was a way she could feel hope again. A way that she could connect with her mom and dad on something other than the pain of their death.

"I want to trust and follow You as my Lord and Savior. Amen."

Some people might describe the Holy Spirit coming into a person when they accept Christ, but Sarah felt a release. Years of self-inflicted pain and burden came pouring out of her. The shackles of guilt that she wore around her neck were lifted off, and she finally felt free. Tears of joy washed her cheeks as she said the words that every person needs to say.

"Heavenly Father, I know that I have broken your laws, and my sins have separated me from You. I am truly sorry, and now I want to turn away from my past sinful life and accept the gift of Your love. Please forgive me and help me avoid sinning again. I believe that Your Son, Jesus, died for my sins, was resurrected from the dead, is alive today, and hears my prayer. I invite Jesus to become my Lord and Savior, to rule and reign in my heart from this day forward. Please send your Holy Spirit to help me obey You and do Your will for the rest of my life. In Jesus' Name, I pray. Amen."

Pastor Allen wrapped his arms around the weeping woman and silently praised God for His mercy. The sounds of gentle sobs filled the quiet office.

Sarah wasn't sure of the time or how long she had been crying, but she felt so much better for having done it. She tried to rationalize how many tears it would take to cleanse her heart of all the pain she had. How long would she have to cry before the darkness would go away? But that was the odd thing; the heaviness that always came with the Darkness was gone too. When she tried to reach for the Darkness, she only felt the warm embrace of God's love. Her mind searched for the memory of the accident, the funeral, and her great loss. Each time she remembered, something in her mind whispered to her that it was OK. A gentle voice was telling her that she was loved, and everything would be fine. More tears came rushing out as she openly praised God over and over for His healing love.

When she opened her eyes, Sarah was looking right at Ginny. The young girl's eyes were red and glazed with tears. She explained that she heard Sarah crying, and she came in to see if the pastor needed anything. She knelt down beside Sarah as she was finishing the prayer. Together the women embraced and laughed at the tears. Mascara ran down Ginny's cheeks as she talked about the moment when she accepted Christ. This brought on another wave of tears.

"I'm very happy for you, Sarah," said Pastor Allen. "Today, you have become one of God's children."

"That's good because I feel like a child," she said as she

wiped her cheeks. Looking at the confused looks on both of them, she added, "No, I mean, I feel as free as a child."

"Oh. Got it," he chirped. "The Bible says we are to have faith like a child, but the mind of Christ."

Sarah smiled as she thought about what it meant to be a child of God. To have faith that everything would work out, even when the circumstances around her didn't show it. Her mom would talk about having "faith like a child" and how things would seemingly work out. 'God was in control' was what she would always say. She missed her parents terribly and wished she could have shared this moment with them. Oddly enough, a gentle feeling inside her made her feel closer to them now than she had been in a very long time.

Together, the three talked for a little while longer while Pastor Allen told her about baptism and what it meant to be a follower of Jesus. He encouraged her to come to church and let others know about her decision for Christ. Ginny offered to help find her a Bible study group to connect with. All the attention she was receiving made Sarah smile even bigger with joy. She felt loved.

Her smile soon diminished as she pictured Azrael's face. His ice-blue eyes stared at her intently. She thought about what he wanted from her. Was the seemingly simple fact of knowing God and accepting Jesus all that Azrael wanted her to talk to these people about? Was it that simple? Was that the answer he had been pushing for her to find all this time? If so, why didn't he just tell her in the first place? It didn't have to be such a secret. And what was Azrael getting out of all this craziness? Was he working for God? Why would it be important for the angel of death to be so concerned about where the souls of the dead were going to? Maybe he got some special perk for the souls he took to Heaven.

"Is everything OK?" Pastor Allen asked, seeing the change of expression on Sarah's face.

"Yes, I'm fine," she sighed weakly. "Probably better than I have ever been."

"But?" he questioned as he and Ginny waited for her to continue. The joy that was so apparent on her face a few seconds ago was replaced by a look of angst and fear.

"Pastor, does the Bible tell us anything about what is the most important thing that should be on a person's heart?"

"Wow," he laughed. "You do come up with some of the best questions!"

"Sorry, I guess. I just have some things going on, and I genuinely need to know about what should be on a person's heart."

He looked at her quizzically. "Funny, you should ask. I was just working on a sermon about the things that are in a person's heart. The most important thing is love. First, there should be a love for our Lord and Savior. And second, there needs to be a love for those around us. We are to love them as if they were family."

"I know this may sound odd, but may I see your notes?" she asked.

Pastor Allen noticed a glint of hope in her eye. Something that was not there yesterday. "Yeah, sure, but you could come by on Sunday to hear the live version."

"Oh, I will, don't worry. After all, I have my new family to meet, right?" she joked with a broad smile. "But I actually am interested in learning more about what you found. I'm not trying to be greedy or pushy, but I need to get my head around something the same way I got my heart around my new found hope."

"Perfect," he effused, clapping his hands together loudly. "Ginny, would you mind making a copy of my outline for Sarah?"

"Sure. My pleasure," Ginny said as she got up and practically bounced out of the room. Sarah watched her and realized that she needed to get home.

"Sorry to run, but I need to get going. I have something I need to take care of," she told him as she stood up.

"No problem. I want to thank you for coming into my office these past two days. I know God is pleased with the decision you made today," Pastor Allen said. "I know I am too."

"I want to thank you for all of your help and patience with me, Pastor Allen," Sarah said as she turned back to shake the man's hand. Walking down the hallway to the front part of the building, they found Ginny back behind the receptionist's desk.

"Sarah, it was my pleasure," he professed smiling. "I know God has something special planned for you. Sometimes people don't hear the call of God's voice on their heart until it is too late to do anything about it." He embraced her hand in both of his, "I'm just honored and thankful that you chose me to share this special time with."

"God had a plan for me to come here and meet you. It was exactly what I needed. You, quite literally, saved my life."

Smiling, "Not me ... God did. He just used me to do His work," he finished.

"Yes, He did!" she said excitedly, then added, "I think I know the feeling!"

"Take care, Sarah. I will have Ginny give you a call tomorrow to make arrangements for your baptism next week. So, can I save you a seat on Sunday?"

"Oh yes," she exclaimed with a joyful sigh. "I will be here. Thanks again." With that, Sarah smiled one last time and left. She was at the bottom step when a strong voice echoed in her head.

"I am glad that you made a decision based on your heart's conviction. It is important that you know what is on your heart and then tell it to others," Azrael said. His voice echoed in her mind.

"Yes, it is, and you have no idea how much I understand what you need me to do now," she said quietly to herself and nodded.

"Good because it is time to go. We have an appointment." The dark fog fell over Sarah, and she felt the weightlessness again. Somehow, things didn't seem so ominous this time.

Back inside the office, Pastor Allen took a few steps from the door. He was always amazed at how God worked in the lives of people. For some people, God would come to them in a moment of disaster. Others would find his mercy at the oddest times. He knew that God's timing was perfect, and he said another prayer of thankfulness for being a part of such a beautiful thing. When he opened his eyes, he saw Ginny holding out a paper to him and talking to him.

"Sorry, what? I was thinking about something else," he said with a startle.

"Pastor, you forgot to give Sarah the notes you promised her. You can still catch her. She took the bus yesterday, so she should be on her way to the bus stop."

"Oh, goodness!" He grabbed the papers and raced back to the door. He opened it with a rush of wind and called her name. He came to a stop at the top step, but she wasn't anywhere to be seen. The only response to his call came from some birds sitting on the edge of a nearby fence. There was no one in sight. A cool autumn breeze made some brown leaves dance across the vacant parking lot.

"Wow, she is fast!" Shrugging his shoulders, the confused pastor went back inside.

At the same moment, Officer Walters sat in his car just about a hundred yards from the church office's front door. He had been following the suspect from place to place for most of the day, and now he watched her exit the building just in front of him. Like a child on Christmas morning, Sarah Thompson practically danced down the stairs, her body language full of energy and genuine enthusiasm. As quickly as she was moving, she came to an abrupt stop at the bottom of the stairway. Like running into an invisible wall, Sarah Thompson stopped and began talking to herself. The officer assumed she was on the phone, accompanied by some sort of bluetooth device. Still, her mannerisms and body language acted like she was talking to someone standing directly in front of her. She smiled and raised her hand as if reaching for something or someone that didn't exist. Her head was tilted upward, looking up toward the sky. She nodded her head, and suddenly, she disappeared. The breeze blew leaves through the very spot where his suspect had been standing only a few seconds ago.

Officer Walters' heart pounded in his chest as his mouth dropped open with disbelief. Frantically, his mind tried desperately to come up with a rational explanation for what he just witnessed. Maybe she was quicker than he thought, and she went back into the office building. Determined to find out where she went, the young cadet opened his car door to investigate. Before he could get out of the unmarked police vehicle, the office door opened with a rush, and a man appeared in the entryway. The man stood, a confused look on his face, staring out into the nothingness of the parking lot. Whatever he was looking for, it was written on his face that he didn't find it. *Maybe he is looking for the same person*, thought Walters. Regardless, the bewildered look on the man's face told Walters that his suspect didn't go back into the office either.

After the man turned around and slowly went back into the building, the rookie police officer gazed out over the vacant parking lot. Part of him hoped the woman would magically reappear in any second the same way she magically disappeared. Beads of sweat formed on his brow as he thought of the different ways to explain this to Detective Wolfe. He swallowed hard as he grabbed his cell phone and slowly punched the numbers in.

CHAPTER EIGHTEEN

The shroud of black began to fade, and Sarah's eyes tried to focus on her surroundings. It was as if she was looking through a window that was covered in misty fog. Her eyesight was still a little hazy, but she could vaguely make out the outlines of dozens of small boxes lining the ground around her. The objects formed a pattern of rows and disjointed columns, dotting a lush green landscape. Once her feet felt the firm ground, she knew it would only be a matter of seconds before she was free of Azrael's transportation fog. Even though time seemed to stand still while she was in the haze, it always felt the longest during the last few seconds before she came out of the dark mist completely.

She heard the crunch of gravel under her feet as the fog finally disappeared. From a nearby tree, the sound of birds chirping was carried by a soft breeze blowing. The scent of the trees mingled with the fresh scent of fresh-cut grass. The smell was so far removed from the smells of the city, she stood frozen as she wondered where she was. She looked around from side to side, trying to assess where she was. *Am I still in Phoenix?*

Her disorientation was compounded by the revelation that

the boxes she had seen before were not boxes at all. They were headstones. Not just a few dozen of them, but hundreds, scattered over small rolling hills. Sarah found herself standing in the middle of a cemetery. Spinning around, she hoped to see Azrael standing close to her, but she saw nothing but more graves.

"Well," putting her hands on her hips. "You are definitely the 'love 'em and leave 'em' type," she said with a forced smirk. Spreading her hands out over the expanse of death in front of her, she continued, "Azrael, if this is where I am supposed to meet someone with only an hour to live, I have to give you points for atmosphere."

"First off. I never *leave them*, but I do *love them*." The deep voice came to Sarah in the air like an exchange of an old friend. She closed her eyes and had to smile when she heard Azrael's majestic voice try to mimic hers as he retorted. Moreover, she smiled because of the way his voice made her feel. It was the same voice she had heard all along, but her reaction to it was changing. At times, it held a comforting and warm resonance, but now it brought her a sense of peace and comfort. Either way, this was far removed from the feelings of dread and frustration she felt just a few short days ago. Somehow, when she heard his voice, she knew she was not alone, even if no one was there. Now his voice had a humorous tone to it as he tried to talk to her like normal, but she knew he was anything but normal.

"Secondly," the voice came again with an interrupting tone. "Death has no atmosphere. It comes when and where it pleases, despite the circumstances surrounding the person. All men must live as if death were coming for them that very day."

"And there is the Azrael that I know and try not to hate," she said sarcastically.

"You do not hate me. I foresee a day when you might even come to love me," he insisted dryly.

Sarah tried to ignore the boldness of his comment. She wondered how long she would be doing this little song and dance of talking to people before they died. It would only be a matter of time before the police started asking the right questions, and she would have all the wrong answers.

Looking around, she noticed the pea-sized gravel forming a small path through the headstones. She walked down the trail as it crested over a small embankment. The green grass shimmered against the sunlight as it swayed in the light breeze. There, on the other side, was a lone figure standing about a hundred feet away. For a moment, she thought it was Azrael by the size of this man. But by the way this man was swaying back and forth, she knew it must be her next conversation.

As she approached the man, a chill went up her spine, contrasted against the warmth of the midday sun. Even though she was walking right toward him, the man took no notice of her approach. He stood in front of what looked like a freshly placed headstone—still white and reflecting the sun among the newly engraved lettering. This one was not faded and tattered like most of the others. Fresh yellow carnations were sitting in a small vase next to the freshly turned soil. This was a new gravesite.

The man was a giant of a man. His massive body shook with the occasional convulsion. Each one preceded a small whimper. The large man stood well over six feet, with broad shoulders hidden under a dark raincoat. He had a tight set, squared jaw, and deep laugh lines around his eyes. She knew he was older than she was, but she wasn't sure just how old. There were wisps of bright white hair encircling the outside of his head that profoundly distinguished his dark skin.

The man didn't move when Sarah walked up next to him. He just continued to stare at the gravesite and cry openly, clutching a cloth hat he held in his big hands. When Sarah got close enough, she read the tombstone he was standing in front of:

Lillian Haynes
Beloved Wife, Mother, and Friend

Tears formed at the edges of Sarah's eyes as she fought back the waves of emotion. This dear man had just lost someone very special to him. She knew what it felt like, and she had both sympathy as well as empathy for this poor man. Gently, she placed her hand on his shoulder and squeezed it a little. Letting him know that she was there with him and sharing his time of sorrow.

He slowly turned toward her, wiping the palms of his large hands against his eyes. "Um … ah … sorry. I sometimes just can't control myself."

"There is no need to stop crying over a loved one," she said to him softly. "Sometimes, the tears are the only way to clean the wound." When she said it, she realized how true it was. Death creates a festering wound for the living. A terrible void is formed and feels like a part of your heart was taken away. The tears bring the healing salve that the heart needs to start rebuilding itself.

"Thank you, ma'am," he said as he attempted a smile. "Did you know my Lilly?"

"No. I'm sorry. I didn't," she replied softly. "I sure wish I did, though."

"Yeah … she was a good woman," he said, fighting through another wave of tears. "The best." Those words broke the dam that held back the cascade of tears as they flowed freely again.

"I am so sorry for your loss. I saw you here and thought no one should have to grieve alone. Besides, I wasn't sure if you needed anyone to talk with. My name is Sarah, by the way."

"I wasn't much of the talker. I'm Darren. Lilly was better at that than me. She used to do most of the talking for the both of us."

"How long were you married?"

"The Lord gave us thirty-six wonderful years together

before he took her home." He looked away, but Sarah caught the angry look on his face. "Or should I say cancer took her from me? Too damn soon."

"I'm so sorry," she said, moving a little closer. "I lost my parents when it was too soon. I know how unfair it can be."

"She was my best friend," he pushed out through heavy breaths. "We met when we were just kids." Turning to look at Sarah, "We even grew up in the same part of town back in Athens, Georgia. We were practically neighbors." Darren told her about how Lilly's dad got a new job in Nevada when they were just finishing grade school. When she left, they tried to write, but he wasn't much of a writer, so everything slowly faded away. Years passed, and Darren joined the Air Force and traveled over most of the United States. Eventually, he was stationed at Luke Air Force base just west of Phoenix. One fateful day in September, many years ago, he ran into Lilly while they were both shopping at a local grocery store.

"I was stunned. There she was again. Even more beautiful than the last time I saw her. I followed her around the store like a little puppy. I just kept staring at her. She probably thought I was some kinda stalker. It didn't stop me though. My heart knew who she was, but I couldn't get my mind to agree. It was like looking at a perfect picture," he said with a big smile. The tracks of his tears glistened in the sunshine. "She looked like an angel. Same lovely face as the girl I knew, but she was a grown woman."

Lilly grew up in Reno, Nevada, and then followed her parents to Arizona when they retired. Darren and Lilly rekindled their childhood romance and were married in less than a year later. When Darren got out of the Air Force, they moved into a small house in a suburb of Phoenix and raised three beautiful girls.

"She was an incredible woman. She always made the best of things. Even when times were tough, Lilly would always have a smile on her face. Even when the doctors told us that she had cancer, she took it like a champion. She was so strong." Fresh tears ran down familiar paths along his cheeks. "Oh, God, I miss her so much. I'd give anything to see her again."

Sarah hugged the man and squeezed him even tighter when she heard him call for God to help. "Darren, do you think that you might see her again? In Heaven maybe?" she asked, hoping that she could open the door to talking with him about Jesus.

"I know she is in Heaven. She told me that was where she was going just before she died." Turning towards Sarah again, "Lilly got real religious after she was told about the cancer. She would go to this little church near where we lived—nice enough people. The pastor would come over to the house and talk with her whenever she couldn't make it to church. Pastor Allen was his name. Ryan Allen."

Sarah was stunned when she heard Pastor Allen's name. "I know Pastor Allen."

"Well, then you know what I'm talking about. He is a good man. He got her to accept Jesus into her heart. That's why she knew she was going to Heaven."

A cool breeze came up and gave Sarah a chill against the warmth of the afternoon sun. "Do you think you will go to Heaven too?" she asked.

"Lilly tried to get me to go to church with her. She even had Pastor Allen talk to me a few times, but I didn't have time for any of that nonsense. If she was happier for having Jesus, then I was happy for her. I think it helped her deal with the pain."

Sarah could see the veins tighten in the large man's thick neck. "But that same Jesus took her from me. At first, I was so angry at God. Why her?" After he said it, his entire body relaxed and limped forward. "But over this past month, I just missed her so much. I was thankful that she wasn't in pain anymore, but I am so alone without her."

"Darren, I have to tell you. I was angry with God for a very long time too. He took my parents away, and I blamed him for everything. I have recently learned that God loves me, and now I understand how much he loved my parents. He doesn't want us to suffer in this fallen world. As angry as I was at him, he still loved me." She reached and turned the man's shoulders toward her. This was no easy task for the petite woman, but he moved slowly with her touch.

"And he loves you too," she paused. "He doesn't want you to be alone. He is with you. Just like he was with Lilly and gave her peace. God wants that kind of peace for you."

He looked deep into her eyes. Searching for a reason why this woman was being so nice. All he saw was love reflecting brightly against his pain. Darren always felt like he was a good judge of character, and he could tell when someone was lying to him. For whatever reason, this woman was sincere and believed what she was saying. He saw the same conviction in Lilly's eyes whenever she talked about God. He had to admit that what this strange lady was saying was exactly what he needed to hear. He was determined to listen and wished he had listened to Lilly when she told him about God's love.

"How do I find that peace?" he asked, almost pleading like a child with her.

"Jesus came to this earth to give us that peace. Through his sacrifice on the cross, He gave us the perfect relationship with God again." She took his strong hands in hers, feeling the callouses left there from years of hard labor. His hands engulfed her small ones as she held them.

"Darren, God wants to have that perfect relationship with you again. You just have to accept it. Accept Him."

His hands were nearly shaking as his body dropped to his knees. "I do. I do. Oh God, I do," he exclaimed as his eyes filled with tears again. This time from the release that only true love can bring.

Sarah knelt next to him and led him through a prayer. A soft, gentle, soul-shaking prayer like the one she had recited only a short time ago. Together, they praised God for Darren's life. They even praised God for taking the pain away from Lilly and hoping that they would be reunited one day. When Darren said the words about being reunited, Sarah stiffened as she remembered that this man's time was fleeting fast. She had no clue about how long they had been there talking and crying.

It was then that she realized the timing. She felt the large man's hands grow limp. Sarah watched as Darren's large body relaxed and softly collapsed on the ground near his wife's headstone. His massive body should have hit the ground hard, but it was as if he was gently laid down by unseen hands. His eyes were closed, and there was a noticeable smile on his face. Silently, Sarah praised God and thanked him for reuniting these two special people.

"It is time to return, Sarah," Azrael said from somewhere behind her.

Still looking at the man lying on the ground, she thought about how surreal it all was. She was just talking with him, and now he looked like he was just sleeping peacefully.

"Is he …," her words trailed off.

"Yes, his time on this earth has passed," he replied in a gentle voice. "Yet, I must tell you. Because of you, he went to a different place than the others."

Sarah stood quickly and turned around to face Azrael. Even in the bright sunlight and the lush green grass, this man still looked dark and ominous.

"Is he in Heaven?" she asked cautiously.

"Yes. He is in the understanding of Heaven as you know it to be," he answered.

Sarah felt absolute relief. Her muscles relaxed, and she would have collapsed from exhaustion if Azrael had not grabbed her. She welcomed the black fog as he took her home.

Detective Michael Wolfe was at the food bank when he received the call from Officer Walters. The weathered veteran swore as he told the young rookie that he needed to get his eyes checked and scolded him for losing the suspect.

"Get on the phone with her employer and find out when she is scheduled to work again," he barked into his phone. "If it is not any time soon, try to pick her up at her apartment again. Either way, get moving and find her!" He swore as he clicked his phone off. He knew that she had disappeared from plain sight before, so the rookie might not have been so far off. It was better to not let him off the hook too quickly though. Michael needed Walters to stay on top of his game and locate her. A little, healthy fear is never a bad thing.

Turning his attention back to the man behind the counter, "OK, sorry about that. So, you were saying about the fight and murder?"

"Yeah, I told the other detectives the same thing. I was just inside the doorway when I heard the shouting. By the time I got outside, Barry was lying on the ground with a huge blade sticking out of his body. Some heavyset guy was standing over him. I think the guy's name was Karl. He comes in here every once and a while, but he has never started any trouble. We don't keep records … we just try to feed them."

"I understand. I'm actually not here for them. Did you see this woman around at the time of the murder?" he asked as he pulled the picture of Sarah out of his jacket.

"Yeah, I saw her. She came rushing to Barry's side just after the other two jerks high-tailed it outta here." He handed the picture back to him. "I took notice of her 'cause Barry doesn't really hang out with too many pretty women. She seemed nice enough to try and help, but she just disappeared after our nurse arrived."

"What do you mean she just *disappeared*?" the Detective asked eagerly. "Like into thin air?"

"Well, not literally, of course, if that is what you're asking." He rolled his eyes at the thought. "She was standing next to Barry, but then she stepped into the crowd when we came to help. After then, I pretty much lost track of her. Pretty sure that was the first time I saw her around here. I am rather good with faces, ya know. Why, what's her story? Why's she important? Is she a suspect?"

"No, not at this time. Just a person of interest. We just need to speak to her about some things. If you see her, please contact me right away." Michael stood and debated whether he should warn this guy about Ms. Thompson's propensity to be around people that are about to die. If this guy saw her again, he might be the one with a knife in his stomach.

"So, do you have a copy of that security video?"

The man handed the Detective a black VHS tape. Wolfe thanked the man and raced out to his car. Before he brought it back to Detective Alexander, he had to find a place where he could watch the video and see exactly what was on it. Where in the world would he find a VHS cassette player? Everything today is on digital. As he was on his way back to the station, he had a revelation. Wolfe remembered an associate that ran a little electronics store not too far out of his way.

JG's TV Emporium was a hole-in-the-wall shop that sold new and used televisions, DVD players, and stereos. The store had been open for a few years, but all the signs and displays looked like they were bought straight out of the 1980s. The neon sign buzzed as he walked in. Detective Wolfe had met the owner, JG, just after he opened the store. A few people said that their house had been robbed, and JG's store mysteriously had the stolen electronics for sale shortly after. When Michael investigated, he found a few suspicious dealings but no hard evidence about stolen merchandise. JG got probation for possession of stolen merchandise, but nothing much came of it. Since then, Michael had kept tabs on JG, and they developed a mutual understanding. JG will get Michael information from the streets, and in turn, Michael wouldn't ask where any of his *"used"* merchandise came from. Michael always felt it was better not to ask, and he always appreciated the info.

"Oh man," JG whined. Spinning in his chair, "Here comes the big, bad cop man. Am I in trouble again?" He smiled wide, letting the fluorescent light gleam off his gold front tooth. He got it with the money from the sale of his first batch of stolen TVs. He stood up and waited for Detective Wolfe to get to the back of the store. It was best not to let anyone outside see them talking.

"Wow," Michael called sarcastically. "Ya got some new OLED TVs in." He eyed the eighty-five-inch screens and then looked suspiciously at JG. "They look pretty expensive for this part of town."

"Hey man," he raised his arms open wide. "Only the best for my customers, right?" Small beads of sweat formed on JG's lined forehead.

"Relax, Jesus. I'm just busting your chops," Michael said with a grin. "I need to borrow a VCR." Flashing him the tape, "I gotta take a look at something."

"Alright, amigo, but do me a favor," he said as he straightened up his white vest that covered his purple dress shirt. "Don't call me by that name. Keep it to 'JG' around here, man." He looked up to the ceiling and made the sign of the cross on his chest. "Mi Madre gave me that name. She wanted me to be a preacher or some kind of crap like that."

"Sorry JG. Look, I'm in a hurry. Do you have a VCR?"

"Yeah, man. That stuff is a little low-tech for my shop, but I think I have one in the back. Come on."

"Thanks." Detective Wolfe followed him down a short hallway to a white door marked with dirty handprints. The door opened to a small ten-by-ten office with a bank of video monitors along the wall, each showing a different angle of the store's merchandise. The VCR was stacked among five DVD recorders on a table that ran the length of the room. A few folding metal chairs sat open and in disarray around the room. JG walked into the room and started moving some newspapers around the table, covering up ashtrays filled with roach clips and burnt ends from some recently smoked joints. Some other paraphernalia was strewn about, but JG didn't have enough newspaper to hide it all. Michael knew what the obese man was trying to do, but he didn't care about that stuff right now. Instead, he chose to ignore it and focus on the security tape.

JG looked back at the Detective, not sure about what to say. He quietly took the tape from him and put it in the VCR. Snow filled the center television console for a moment until it clicked over to a scene of the food bank entrance. Michael took the remote and fast-forwarded it to the time of the murder. Together, both sets of eyes watched the video feed. They saw the same thing that the old man at the food bank described. Two men got into an argument and a fight broke out with the victim getting in the middle—the wrong place at the wrong time. On the fringe of the crowd, Michael stared intently at a woman that looked just like Sarah. She was watching the fight, but she wasn't yelling like the rest of the crowd. She just stared at the victim while everyone else seemed to be watching the two men fighting.

"Damn, man," JG jumped when he saw the heavy-set man plunge the large Bowie into the other guy's body. "Homey got stuck!"

Michael just watched as Sarah broke off from the crowd and moved in close to the victim as he died. When the rush of people came out of the food bank, Sarah backed up and let the crowd envelop her. Michael thought he saw her deep brown hair visible among the crowd for one second, but then it blinked out of the scene. People moved into the space where she would have been standing. He rewound the tape and watched it again and again. Each time, JG would make a snide comment about the man getting stabbed, even on how the assailant was a punk because he didn't do it right. Michael just ignored him and concentrated on getting his head around what he was seeing.

Yes! She definitely disappeared from the scene, he shouted to himself. Once again, his suspect was present at a murder scene and then vanished, literally, before anyone could talk to her.

CHAPTER NINETEEN

Sarah was drained—both physically and emotionally. Her mind wrestled with thoughts of the people she had met over these past few days. Moreover, she grieved over the people she didn't help. Azrael had brought her to them, but she did nothing to help them. She wondered how much of a difference she could have made in their lives. Instead, the real question that bugged her the most was how much of a difference she could have made in their deaths. Though she was drained after Azrael brought her back to her apartment, she still felt the desire to pray. Her body moaned as she dug deep to find the strength to kneel beside her bed. The thin carpet offered little comfort to her knees, but her mind was on higher things.

"Dear God," she started. "Thank You for all of Your gifts. Thank You for giving me the ability and wisdom to speak Your truth to Darren. I ask that You give his family peace as they accept his death and help them rejoice that their parents are together again." Sarah paused, took a deep breath, and smiled. "Jesus … thank you for loving me and helping me to live again."

Sarah felt a sense of peace wash over her. She climbed into

bed and fell asleep quickly—knowing that she was loved.

It only felt like a few moments had passed, but Sarah felt the sudden urge to get out of bed. Reflexively, she sat up and looked around the room. Still foggy from exhaustion, she felt like she was looking for something, but her eyes couldn't focus on what it was. The faint light from the alarm clock bathed the room in a gentle green hue. She wasn't sure why she was awake, but she knew something wasn't right.

She stared blankly around the room until her eyes settled on something strange. A small circle of light appeared on her closet door. It started out the size of a quarter but grew wider and wider until it consumed the entirety of the door frame and some of the surrounding wall. The more she stared, the brighter the light got until she had to shield her eyes from the intensity. That was when she saw what was on the other side of the light. She found herself looking through some sort of gateway.

Tall reeds of grass swayed in a breeze that she almost thought she could feel. The leaves on the lush green trees moved in time with the grass in an invisible dance. Large, billowy white clouds floated effortlessly across a beautiful liquid blue sky. The image before her was perfect. The more she stared at it, the more she felt drawn to the vision. The loveliness of the scene pulled at her like a magnet. Sarah moved to the side of the bed, hesitant to stand up. Not fully understanding or believing what she was seeing.

The hairs on her arm tickled as a cool breeze brushed past her. The smell of the forest also washed over her. She could smell the grass and the flowers that were just beyond what used to be her wall a minute ago. She could hear the wind rushing through the trees, and there was another faint sound—the sound of voices and laughter.

Sarah stood up quickly and watched as two figures, a man and a woman, walked out from behind the massive oak trees. They strolled, hand in hand, as they followed a path that seemed to appear from nowhere. Sarah tried everything she could, but she couldn't quite make out who these people were. Even without knowing them, she felt an instant peace about seeing them. Slowly Sarah walked closer to the large circle of light, trying to get a better view.

As if someone refocused a camera lens, Sarah could see the two people clearly now. Even though the couple was walking away from her, their heads were turned just enough for Sarah to recognize who they were. Her hand came up to her gaping mouth, and tears burst from her eyes when she realized that she was watching her parents.

They looked just the same way as she remembered them. The same smiles, the same laughter, even the same way their bodies would walk in unison as they looked at each other. This was her mom and dad.

"Mom! Dad!" Sarah's hand shot forward, reaching for them as her shouts filled the meadow. She called to them over and over again, but they would not turn around. Their unheard conversation continued uninterrupted as if they couldn't hear their only daughter. Sarah looked down at the grass floor that lay just beyond the portal of light. Desperately, Sarah tried to climb inside the gateway and enter this new world where her parents were still alive. The more she tried to move forward, the more she struggled against it. The circle wasn't a portal or a gateway at all. It was merely a vision. Like watching a movie on a big-screen television, Sarah watched as her parents walked away from her.

Tears poured down Sarah's cheeks as she called out to them over and over. Each time, her voice came out a little quieter. Her words were now just above a whisper, but they kept coming, not wanting to give up altogether. She continued to watch them, not wanting to miss a moment of this gift. Her parents were happier than she ever saw them. Slowly, they started to disappear as the path took them over the crest of the hill. Sarah stood glued to the scene until she could see them no more. She stared at the hill, hoping that they would somehow come running back over the top. Somehow rushing back to her. She didn't even notice that the circle of light was slowly closing.

When it finally winked out, Sarah's bedroom was dark again. She stood there, staring at the stark white door. Blinking through the flow of tears that blurred her vision. Only the memory of the scene remained.

Sarah's body and mind felt drained. Too tired to cry anymore and too tired to even stand. She collapsed into the bed and clutched her pillow for moral support. Little rivulets of tears led a trail down her cheek. She saw her parents again, and they were happy. They looked like they were filled with joy. Not knowing if she was dreaming or delirious, she felt the urge to thank God for the vision anyway. A sense of joy overtook her as she quickly fell asleep.

In the morning, she woke up rested and ready. Her heart was lighter than she had ever remembered it. Thoughts of her dream or vision filled her heart with such a profound joy. Sunlight bathed her living room with a refreshing brightness and blanketed it in a warm glow. Even though she had seen this same humble apartment for years, she felt like today was the first time she appreciated it. Her regular routine would be to make coffee, then sit on the couch to watch the morning news, but today she felt inspired.

She made her coffee without changing routine, but this time she decided to sit and read the Bible while she ate her breakfast. She flipped through the New Testament and settled on Matthew 12, where she read, 'Come to Me, all you who are weary and burdened, and I will give you rest. Take My yoke upon you and learn from Me, for I am gentle and humble in heart, and you will find rest for your souls. For My yoke is easy, and My burden is light.'

"What in the heck is a *yoke*?" she laughed to herself as she went to go dig out an old dictionary from the small bookshelf in her living room. She found it among some random books she had collected over the years. They weren't set up in any real order, but she did note that they were covered in a thin layer of dust. There were times when she would lock herself away from the world and get lost in a good mystery or a romance novel. It was her way of escaping the mundane life she had been living. Over these last few days, her life had become anything but mundane.

She found the dictionary buried under some other reference books that she bought just to say she had them in the house. Blowing off the dust, she looked up the word, *yoke*, to discover that the first listing was the description of a wooden frame that kept two animals together. Sarah sat, confused for a moment. She wasn't so sure that she liked the idea of being considered an animal in this Biblical scenario. Wishing to continue and hoping the listings got better, she looked more in-depth at the definitions. A little further down, she read that a yoke was also a bond or tie that kept people together. This must be what the Bible was referring to—a bond. Jesus was offering a bond that would help her through life. A connection to her Savior. This she liked.

Grabbing a second cup of her favorite breakfast blend, Sarah flipped through the Bible some more. She found another highlighted passage further along. It was from the Book of John, chapter three. In it, Jesus was talking to a religious man named Nicodemus. They met at night to avoid the loss of reputation for the religious man. Jesus told him that a person must be born again before they can enter the kingdom of Heaven. Sarah read the passage a few times. Wanting to make sure she was reading it right. So many things she remembered reading as a kid, but the Bible seemed so much deeper now. One of the lines that struck her was verse six, *"Flesh gives birth to flesh, but the Spirit gives birth to spirit." Very deep*, she thought.

She looked up haphazardly and realized that she was going to be late for work if she didn't get a move on. Saturday mornings were always busy at the café, and Gerardo hated it when people were late. He would tell the employees, "Coming to work should be like going to church. You come, and you show reverence and respect ... and you are *not* late." She could just imagine his heavy accent and see his hands waving in the air as he shouted. In the past, those were just words, but now she understood the relevance of going to church with those same qualities.

She showered and raced to the bus stop just before it was due to arrive. While she was waiting, she noticed a brown Ford sedan as it pulled up and parked across the street. The windows were so dark that she couldn't see who was driving, but she had a feeling that they were there for her. No one got out of the car. There was no movement whatsoever. She started to get nervous. She watched it suspiciously, as she did from years of living in the city. When she saw the driver get out of the car, she wished it had only been a mugger or a flasher.

Detective Michael Wolfe jogged across the street and took a seat next to Sarah on the bus stop bench. He never looked her in the eye, but he knew she was watching him.

"Havin' a good day, Miss Thompson?" he asked as he watched the cars cruise past.

"Actually, I am," she said with enthusiasm. "And good morning to you too. How is your day going so far?" She knew she was rattling his cage by not being afraid, and she wasn't even sure where the courage was coming from, but she liked it.

"Well," turning his head slowly to her as he replied, "No one has died today yet." Returning his gaze to the traffic, he finished, "But I figured that if I hang around you long enough, I might just find another dead body somewhere."

"Sure, you can come to the restaurant with me, but I don't think the cooking is that bad. Maybe my boss could hire you. Can you cook or do dishes?" she said with a sarcastic tone that she used to cover the slight quiver in her voice.

"That's funny. I happen to know that two other people have died with you around." He shifted his body so he could face her head-on. His face was red, and she could see a small vein in his neck pulse with every beat of his heart.

"How many people are going to die today, Miss Thompson?"

She paused. Just staring at him. Trying to read his face. She felt the words come to her mouth before she even had a chance to think about what she was saying. "People die all the time, Detective." She stood up just as the bus pulled up. She felt him watch her as she approached the doorway.

Turning back to face him, "But what truly matters is if they understand why they are living in the first place."

Sarah watched him stare at the door as the bus pulled away. He shook his head and crossed the street to his car. She knew this wouldn't be the last time she would run into him, but she prayed that God would continue to give her the courage to face him head-on.

The day went quickly for Sarah, and she was thankful for that. Her attitude was bright and cheerful, a stark contrast to what she was like throughout most of the week. Even Gerardo and Javier commented on how happy she was. She knew what was different. She finally understood how valuable her relationship to Jesus was and grateful to God she was for it. Oddly, she didn't want to tell them about it. She held that joy to herself, like her own little piece of treasure. Would they think she was some kind of nut case if she told them about loving Jesus despite the craziness around her? Telling total strangers about Christ was the one and only thing that mattered. It didn't matter what they thought about her. After all, they didn't know her. She didn't have to work with them or see them every day. Besides, she was quite sure Gerardo had a rule about sharing personal religious beliefs at work. She remembered a busboy a few years ago that talked to everyone about his Democratic point of view, even going so far as to challenge a customer to a debate about politics. Gerardo didn't care for that too much, so the busboy was let go. Religion was too close to politics for Sarah to lose her job over, so she decided to keep her mouth shut.

Towards the end of the day, Sarah worried that she might run into the Detective again if she took the bus. She felt like she got away with frustrating him earlier, but she also knew it wasn't too wise to poke an angry bear again. The more she paced back and forth through the kitchen, the more she thought that walking was out of the question. If she did, and he was following her, she would be an easy target. When she realized that Javier was getting off work around the same time, she asked him for a ride home.

"Sure," he replied. "My car is a little low on gas. Do you think you could help me out?"

Relieved to have a ride home, Sarah quickly agreed to give him some gas money. Despite her fears about mixing work and religion, she felt the urge to ask Javier about God. When he stopped into the QuikTrip for gas, she got out of the car too. The loud squeaking sound from the old, rusty door echoed under the shaded metal canopy.

"Javier," she said calmly, "do you believe in God?"

"Oh, yeah," he said with a big smile. "My family and I go to the Spanish-speaking church just off the freeway over on Indian School. They are great!" He looked up at her as he put the handle back on the gas pump. "Why? Do you wanna come to a service? I can translate for you."

Excited to hear his response, a broad smile spread across her face as well. "No, it is nothing like that, but thank you." Seeing the dejected look on his face, she replied, "I mean, I would like to see your church one day. I think it would be pretty neat." Looking for the right words, "I guess I'm just curious if you believe in God."

"Oh," he exclaimed. "You want to know if I believe in God

even though you know I go to church. I get it," he said with a smirk on his face. He waved his finger in the air.

"That is a great question. I have known a lot of people that go to church but don't really know God. I used to be one."

"Really? How so?" she asked as they got back in the car.

"Growing up, my mom and dad would make us go to church. It was almost every day that we would end up there somehow. For years, I would just sit in the back and goof around with my friends. I didn't truly know God, so it was easy to act like he didn't exist."

"But you believe in God now?"

"Yeah. Not too long ago, one of my good friends got shot. He was in the wrong place at the wrong time. Some jerk was robbing a 7-11, and the guy shot my friend as he was trying to run away." Javier glanced out the driver's side window a few times, trying to keep the tears inside.

"It tore us all up. Some of my friends went to the dark side and turned to the streets. Seeking vengeance or some crazy stuff like that. My dad made me come to church even more. I'm really glad he did because it probably saved my life. I found God. He was just waiting for me the whole time. Like He knew I would be coming back somehow."

He paused, and then a smile grew like something more profound was there. "He is good that way."

"Yes, He is," she said as she turned her gaze to the scenes flying by outside the window. Watching people on the street and driving in their cars, mentally clueless about how fragile life can be.

"Ok, so now you tell me something." He paused a moment before he questioned, "Why do you want to know?"

"Well," she searched for her words. "Let's just say that I found God waiting for me too."

"That's real good, Sarah. Real good," he said as he was pulling into her apartment complex. "You don't want Him to wait too long. It don't end well for the ones that do."

"You are far more right than you realize, Javier," she said with a smile on her face. "Thanks for the ride. I'll see ya tomorrow." As she watched Javier drive away, her eyes focused on the black sedan parked across the street. She knew right away that it was an unmarked police car. It had the same blacked-out windows that she would expect from someone that didn't want to get noticed. Plus, they had just a few too many antennas sticking out of the trunk to be a random vehicle. She thought about going over to the car and pounding on the glass to see if it was Detective Wolfe, but she didn't want to rile him up too much. She was in too good of a mood to deal with his negativity. Instead, she just smiled at the mysterious vehicle and turned to walk up to her entryway.

When she knew she was out of sight of the parked car, she began to sprint. Sarah was filled with a mix of excitement and nervousness. It was a youth-filled, inebriated feeling of an unknown anticipation. Sarah felt freer than she had ever felt. Her body was on fire with exhilaration. It was like the thrill of Chrismas morning, when a child races to the tree, eager to discover the presents waiting for them. Sarah passed the elevators as she ran gleefully to the stairs. Her spirit flew faster than her body, and she reached the stairwell in a flash. Ascending the stairs two at a time, barely touching them as she went, she got to her fourth-floor apartment in a matter of seconds. Once inside, she locked the door and ran to the window. Staring down at the black car, she just smiled again. She knew she was obeying the right laws this time.

"Yes," Azrael said from the shadows behind her. "You are making the right choices. That man downstairs cannot and will not harm you."

"Good," she said with a startled yet noticeably happy tone

to her voice. "I was wondering if I was going to see you today." She spun around and found nothing. She glanced from side to side, seeing she was alone. She knew he was there somewhere.

"What makes you so sure that you want to see me again?"

Sarah tried to follow the source of the voice, but it echoed from corner to corner. "I didn't say I *wanted* to see you again … I was just wondering if I *would* see you again. There's a difference. Moreover, I was wondering if you were finished with me yet."

"Not yet, Sarah Thompson," he said with an upbeat tone.

"Good because I finally know what you want me to tell people, so I guess I am a little excited to see the next person." She wandered aimlessly around the room, running her hand along the back of the old tan couch.

"But you do know that the next person is still going to die, correct?" he asked coolly, still invisible from her gaze.

"Yes, but I think I can help them."

"If you are so willing and eager to help the ones that are dying, what about the ones that may be living longer? Are you willing and eager to help the ones that are still living? There are people in your life that you will see for more than one hour."

Conviction fell upon her like a stone. Her smile faded as anxiety crept up from the pit of her stomach. She knew right away what he was talking about. He knew about her apprehension of talking to the people she knew best—the people that knew her the best.

Timidly she spoke, her words barely audible. "I hope so. I am still learning," she said as she swallowed hard. "It is not easy, ya know."

"No. With that issue, I cannot relate with you," he lamented as he materialized from out of the growing shadows left by the fading sunlight.

"I do not see it to be a problem when you talk with

someone about the most important thing in life. The death of the body is a tragic loss. It is sad, but it is inevitable. The death of the soul, however, is a far more dreadful forfeiture. It is the result of a wrong decision. A choice that is made, oftentimes, with erroneous information, yet it is a decision that will echo through all of eternity."

Sarah stood still as he approached. She watched his ice blue eyes as they stared unwaveringly at her.

"These ill-informed people are neither good nor bad. They are just ignorant of the truth." He moved closer and closer to where Sarah stood. "The truth that you have so recently learned." Azrael towered over her as he looked down at her. "A truth that has recently set you free."

Seconds seemed like hours as Azrael just stared at her. She could hear the clock tick away the time, but nothing else moved except her heart racing. It pounded inside her chest and her blood pulsed in a thunderous rhythm.

"Do you feel free, Sarah?" he asked flatly.

All she could do was stare at him as she felt her head nod up and down. Again, the minutes dragged on until finally, he broke the stare with a sudden movement. He turned toward her front door as his long black jacket fanned out behind him.

"Come," he said as he tilted his head back to her. "We have an appointment to attend to."

Sarah felt more than just relief in the dark fog. She was thankful that it clouded her vision of him. It stopped Azrael from staring at her. Though the more she thought about it, the more she knew he was right. The truth about Jesus did set her free, and now she was withholding that freedom from so many others. It was her friends and coworkers that were dying. They were still trapped by the curse of the fallen world. She held the key.

Inside the car parked outside Sarah's apartment, Officer Lance Walters stared back at her. He wondered if she could see him through the tinted windows and was angry at himself for being so obvious about where he parked. He hated to admit it to himself, but he was a little afraid that the woman would approach the car. The woman had looked like she was about to come closer, but she just sneered and turned on her heel to leave. Even though he was sitting in an air-conditioned car, Officer Walters felt the perspiration form on the back of his collar. He waited a few minutes before he made the call to the detective.

CHAPTER TWENTY

Sarah came out of the fog with a renewed sense of conviction. There was a fresh confidence that came from every fiber of her being. She was blessed to be a blessing to those that did not recognize the redeeming grace of knowing Jesus.

The sounds of the city came to her ears. Distant wailing of sirens mingled with the gentle thrum of a freeway. From what she could make out, Sarah was standing on a sidewalk that looked to be somewhere south of downtown. Across the street from her was an old junkyard with a sign over the main entrance. "Hector and Sons Auto Salvage."

The air was thick with the smell of rusted metal and dust mixed with the slight overarching scent of motor oil. It was a good smell. It reminded Sarah of her grandfather's garage. She would visit him with her parents, and she liked hanging out there. She and her grandfather would talk for hours while he worked on old cars.

Although the scents weren't the only thing lingering in the air tonight. The breeze also carried the faint sound of an argument. Maybe not so much an argument, as it sounded like one person yelling at another.

"Is this right?" Sarah asked out loud to no one. Even though she was alone, she knew Azrael was close by.

"Is this where I'm supposed to be?"

"Yes, Sarah," the ominous voice came from inside her head. "The older man is the one who you are to speak with. Go to him. He needs to hear what you have on your heart."

Sarah crossed the street toward the junkyard entrance. The shouts emanated from a small wooden building with a faded office sign hanging above the door. As she walked closer to the yelling, she could make out some of the words.

"Damn it all to hell, Oscar. I'm tired of covering for you!"

Just as she got within a few feet, the shouting suddenly got louder as the door whipped open. A man came barreling out. It took her mind only a second to recognize the man's face, but it took longer to accept the reality of it being there.

This was the face that haunted her dreams for years. It was the face of the man that killed her parents.

The panicked look on the man's face made Sarah realize that he knew who she was as well. He quickly reached back and grabbed the doorknob to pull it shut behind him.

"We're not done here. You owe me some more work. Your life here isn't cheap," came the voice from inside.

Oscar McKinney was a middle-aged man whose life had sprinted past him. The bar he set for his life was pretty low, yet he still failed to reach it. Repeated run-ins with the law and three failed marriages gave him lousy track records on all accounts.

Now the one person who hated him the most was standing directly in front of him. He moved quickly to the side as he made his way down the sloped walkway. In an almost comical run-walk pace, he tried to make it around the corner of the building before she could reach him. Maybe she wasn't there for him. Perhaps she just needed some spare car parts.

Sarah stood frozen with her mouth wide open. Here was the man that destroyed her life. Just walking past her like she was a beggar on the street. No big deal. This couldn't be the man that she was supposed to talk to, was it? It must be the man in the trailer.

"No, Sarah. This is the one," Azrael said calmly. "I know this is difficult, but the road to salvation is never easy or convenient."

"I can't do this," Sarah thought to herself. "Not him. Anyone but him."

"I understand. But are you back to playing God again? Judging who is or is not worthy of saving grace?" His words were cold, and they stung her deeply.

"If there is a person who is in desperate need of your words right now, this is he."

Sarah watched as the man darted around the corner and out of sight. She stood glued to the ground. Unable, or unwilling, to chase after him.

"Go, Sarah. Time is against him."

She closed her eyes and prayed that God would give her the strength to do what she knew needed to be done. The Gospel of Jesus Christ was to be shared with all. Not just the ones that are easy to reach or the ones that deserve it. Jesus came to this earth for the sick, not the healthy.

Breathing deeply, she collected as much conviction as she could muster. Putting her head down, she rushed to the corner where she last saw Oscar. He must have been moving pretty fast himself because he had already put some distance between them. His dirty jeans sagged and billowed as he quickly moved his way past the wrecked cars. The Harley Davidson shirt, which had once been black, had seen better, if not cleaner, days.

Oscar looked back at her as he made his way around a pile of old Buick frames, picking up his pace. She called out to him, but he disappeared from sight before she could catch him. Sarah knew he heard her because he turned his head right at her.

"Ugh! This is ridiculous. I don't even want to talk with this jerk, and he's making me chase him." As she made her way closer, she turned the bend in the path to reveal an old, dilapidated single-wide trailer up on blocks. The ancient travel trailer was caked in dust with a small living area stretched just outside the only door. The door hung open, and Sarah knew Oscar must be inside from the slight rocking of the trailer.

"Oscar? I'm pretty sure you recognized me," Sarah called out to the emptiness. "I'd like to talk if that's OK."

"We ain't got nothing to talk about." The voice came from the open door.

"Oscar, I'm just here to see how you're doing."

"Well, you can see how I'm doing. I'm just fine. Now would you please leave me alone?"

Sarah knew this was Oscar, but the voice didn't match what she remembered. She thought back to the voice that echoed in the courtroom so many years ago. Strong and defiant. The voice she now heard sounded hollow and broken.

Slowly, Sarah walked toward the door, stopping long enough to hear the sound of crying coming from inside the trailer.

"Oscar? May I come in," she asked in a tentative voice. "I really just wanted to make sure that you're OK."

"Well, that's fine, seein's how no one's going to have to care about me anymore." The man's voice cracked through the stifled sobs.

Sarah knew something wasn't right, so she pushed the door open fully. The hinges fought with audible resistance. As her eyes adjusted to the darkness inside, she could barely make out the source of the sobbing. Oscar was leaned back on a dirty couch—a pill bottle in one hand and a whisky bottle in the other. It only took an instant for her to know what was happening.

"Hey, Oscar! What are you doing with those pills, huh?" She moved in closer, climbing the two small steps into the trailer.

"Never you mind," he snapped in a slightly firmer tone. "Besides, this is what you want, isn't it?" He raised both hands to mockingly show her what he intended to do.

"No, not at all," she blurted in a lower tone, trying not to sound too nervous. Part of her wanted to keep him calm, and the other tried to hide the tense eagerness in her own voice. For whatever reason, his words hurt her like a slap in the face. How ironic that she had fantasized about this man's death all those years ago. Now she could watch him die just like he watched her parents die. Sarah knew in her heart what she needed to do. She made it all the way inside and stood just a few feet from him.

"It's Sarah, right? Isn't that your name?" His voice was wavering between conviction and pure despair.

"Yes, Oscar. It is."

"I have to tell you," he mumbled. "I am so sorry for your loss."

Sarah heard the words, but they rang empty. She had listened to the same story from this man before. She remembered clearly how he shouted those same words to her in the courtroom as he was being taken away. Then she saw them again in the newspaper when he was interviewed after pleading down to a sentence of involuntary manslaughter.

"I never meant to hurt anyone. I was running from my own demons, trying to free myself of the pain, but I ended up causing even more pain. I know it was my fault, and I am so sorry. I killed your beautiful parents."

Sarah could not move. She just looked at him. Unsure of

exactly how she felt. How was she supposed to feel? What was she supposed to do—grab this man and hug him and tell him everything was OK? It wasn't OK.

He hung his head with his chin to his chest and put his hands on his temples. "I am a terrible, terrible man. I'm a disease. I cause pain to everyone around me wherever I go. I just want to die."

The shock of those words hit Sarah and woke her up from her pity-induced trance. She reached out and took his grease-stained hand.

"Oscar, I forgive you," she blurted out unexpectedly. She couldn't believe the words that were coming out of her mouth. It was like she was having an out of body experience—someone else was talking, and it wasn't her.

"I forgive you," she whispered again. The words were so delicate that Sarah wondered if she had even spoken them out loud. The world seemed to come to a completed halt. Oscar's mouth opened as his eyes stared at her without blinking.

"What did you say?"

Sarah's throat was suddenly scratchy as she swallowed hard against the dryness. Trying to make sure she was louder this time.

"I forgive you," she declared more confidently.

As the words hung in the air, and the realization of their meaning hit home on Oscar's face, Sarah knew they were the right words to say, whether she felt she meant them or not. The words that needed to be said—for both of them. Tears ran down his cheeks, which became a stark contrast as his face contorted in sudden anger mixed with disbelief.

"I don't need any of your pity. I can't never be forgiven," he shouted.

"I'm not offering you my pity—I'm offering you my

forgiveness." Her temper started to rise up within her, but it was met with an overwhelming feeling of peace. Sarah didn't understand it, but she knew she couldn't fight it either.

"And why would that be," he said condescendingly.

"I have forgiven you because I have been forgiven. I was lost and crushed by sin. I was destined for a life of pain and bitterness. I hated you for what you did, but I have learned that God's love is more important than harboring resentment. Only recently did I come to understand the power that comes from forgiveness and acceptance of Jesus as my Lord and Savior."

Oscar's tears flowed as he wailed in agony. Looking up to an unseen sky, he forced himself to speak through his pain.

"I know God is real." His voice cracked as he continued. "I have had people talk with me about Him. But then I would always start to think about your parents looking down on me. Reminding me that I'm not worthy of God's love. Or your forgiveness for that matter."

"You're right, Oscar," Sarah reassured him as she squeezed his hand even tighter. "No one is worthy. The Bible tells us that very thing. But God loves us so much that He was willing to send His only Son to die for us so we could become worthy of His love."

Oscar stopped crying and looked at Sarah. Tentative and childlike fear radiated from his face. "Do you think He could forgive me? God, I mean."

"Yes! Yes, I do," Sarah exclaimed. "I believe that with my whole heart. Why else would I be here?" Sarah knew she had not spoken words that rang more real than to know it would have taken God's love to bring her to sit beside this man.

"It says in the Bible that if we confess our sins, God is faithful and just and will forgive us of our sins," Sarah reassured. "Would you like to pray for God to forgive you?"

His lips moved, but no words came out. Only the

whimpering sounds of someone holding back a wall of emotion. He could only nod in response to her question.

"OK, but you have to say the words after me."

"OK," he faltered as he nodded again.

"Dear Lord Jesus, I know that I am a sinner, and I ask for Your forgiveness. I believe You died for my sins and rose from the dead. I turn from my sins and invite You to come into my heart and life. I want to trust and follow You as my Lord and Savior."

When Sarah was done leading him through the prayer, tears began to flow from both of them. She openly hugged him —surprising her at first, but she knew this was not the same man that killed her parents anymore.This was a new brother in Christ. His sins were gone, just like hers.

Slowly, Sarah felt Oscar's embrace weaken. It was like he was melting into the couch. Suddenly, she remembered the pills and the empty bottle. Pulling back, she held Oscar's limp body in her arms as she guided him back against the cushions. His face was peaceful as if he were sleeping. Sarah lifted his feet up on the couch, then made her way to the door. She turned to look at Oscar one more time. A gentle snore came from the man. A mixture of emotions came over her as she looked at him. She knew he would be dead soon, and she wasn't sure how she felt about that simple fact. Her mind kept reeling from the roller coaster she'd just been on, but a deep sense of peace settled over her—a feeling she hadn't felt in a very long time.

As Sarah left, the jumble of emotions continued to pulsate in the back of her mind as a sudden feeling of dread gripped her. Memories of her mom and dad appeared in her mind. Walking down the long dirt path toward the main street entrance, Sarah kept wringing her hands. Did she just dishonor the memory of her parents? Shouldn't she have avenged her parents by killing the man herself?

"No, Sarah," a voice answered. "Quite the contrary. You

have brought great honor to your parents' memory by acting with forgiveness. You held tight to the teachings and the example they set for you. I know they are smiling on you for the choices you made today." Azrael appeared next to her, walking by her side.

"Due to you acting as you did, that man will go on to live a long life. Very much changed from the one he knew prior."

"What do you mean, 'long life,'" she challenged. "I knew we went over the hour, but aren't you going to take him away? Is he dead?"

"No, Sarah," Azrael protested. "He is merely sleeping. You helped to change his life dramatically, and subsequently, his timeline. He was going to die by his own hand. Within the hour of when you first arrived, I was slated to take him away."

"I thought you said I could do nothing to stop a person's inevitable death," sputtered Sarah.

"My dear child," he said in a fatherly tone. "It wasn't you that saved Oscar, but the power of Jesus Christ that changed his life. You were the vessel that brought him the life-changing news."

They walked in silence as the sun set around them. Shadows filled the junkyard as he put his arm around Sarah.

"Come. You need your rest," he instructed. "You have a big day tomorrow."

Just as Sarah started to question, she felt the fog lift her. Quicker this time. When everything cleared up, she found she was sitting on the side of her bed. A cup of tea was steaming on the nightstand, and her Bible was next to it. She picked it up, and her eyes instantly went to an underlined verse.

'And you shall love the Lord your God with all your heart and with all your soul and with all your mind and with all your strength.' The second is this: 'You shall love your neighbor as yourself.' There is

no other commandment greater than these.' – Mark 12.

"I love You, Jesus," Sarah whispered as she sipped her tea. "I love You with my whole heart." That night she slept better than she had in a very long time.

The morning brought sunshine. The joy she felt the previous night still lingered in her mind. She knew she was doing God's work, and He was using her to reach the lost. She hummed the old hymn, *"For once I was lost, and now I'm found. Once blind, but now I see."*

"Yes, you are correct," Azrael's voice called from the living room. Sarah let her head fall forward as she sighed. Thinking to herself that it was too early.

"I am sorry for the early hour, but we have a crucial meeting, and the clock is ticking."

Sarah rose slowly from the bed, then remembered that she could make a difference in a person's life by sharing the love of Christ. This new revelation brought with it a wave of energy as she got dressed and raced out to the living room.

"OK," she conceded. "Let's go save someone's life!"

CHAPTER TWENTY–ONE

Sarah could vaguely see her surroundings as she settled into consciousness. The wind rustled through some trees close by, carrying with it the sweet smell of autumn. Nearby, someone was burning a wood fire. The romantic aroma combined with the distinct smell of desert trees after the rain yesterday created an intoxicating fragrance. She loved Phoenix during this time of year.

When the fog fully cleared, she found herself standing on a street corner. The lush trees and beautiful houses made her wonder if she was still in Phoenix.

"So," she questioned, "how far does your power stretch?" She knew that just because she couldn't see Azrael didn't mean that he wasn't around.

"My power is limitless," he answered. "But yes, you are still in the immediate area."

"Hey, does that mean you can take me to the beach in Hawaii?" she asked. "Or maybe to a penthouse overlooking Central Park."

"If those were places that I needed you to be, you would be there." His tone was cold. His voice was tinged with a hint of frustration.

"Sorry. I was just curious."

"Fear not. I would take you to greater places than those if the need arose, but your task lies here."

Just as he finished his statement, Sarah saw a woman walking toward her from around the street corner. She walked next to a beautiful Chocolate Labrador Retriever. *Walking* could be a loose term since the large dog was pulling the petite woman along. Sarah could see the woman struggling with the leash as the excited animal pulled it tight. Her awkwardness was compounded by the enlarged belly protruding from under the light grey sweatshirt. Her auburn hair was matted against her forehead from the exertion as she struggled to keep up.

Sarah tried to act naturally as the woman approached where she was standing. This was not an easy task for her since she was about to meet someone she knew would die very soon.

"Just be yourself," came a calming reply in her head.

"OK, you're the boss," she sighed. Sarah steeled herself, smiled, and turned to walk towards to woman and the dog. Before she even walked more than a few feet away, the tip of her sneaker caught a crack in the uneven sidewalk. The ground came up quickly, and Sarah fell like a punch-drunk fighter that was left in the ring a bit too long. She put her hands out to brace for impact. The fall was cushioned by the meaty part of her palms as she felt the flesh tear away. The white-hot burning sensation raced up her arms and flooded her mind just as the equally painful feeling radiated from her right knee. Sarah held her breath as she waited for the pain to subside. When she finally caught her breath, she found herself on all fours. Tears filled her eyes and she thought to herself, *it couldn't get any worse*. It was something she should not have expressed, but she couldn't help it.

It was then that she felt a wet nose rustling through her hair. The dog that was pulling the woman was now very interested in her. The playful dog's hot panting was a bitter contrast to the cool evening air and reminded her that things can always get worse.

"Lady," the woman yelled, obviously upset. "Lady! Get off!"

"Get off what? I'm not on anything," Sarah replied in a frustrated voice. "Unless you consider the fact that I am already on my knees."

"I am so sorry. Not you," the woman pleaded. "My dog's name is Lady. My husband says she is still just a puppy, but I can't imagine how big she'll be when she's fully grown. I'm so, so sorry about her. Please let me help you." The woman extended her small hand down and helped Sarah up. As most young Labs are prone to do, the dog continued to prance around the two women as if one of them was going to suddenly turn into a tennis ball.

Sarah stood up and stared at her hands. There were deep gashes on both. A slight trickle of blood pushed out past the pieces of dirt and concrete embedded in her skin. Sarah typically had a high pain tolerance, but these cuts gave her a run for her money. There were times when she would burn her fingers on a hot plate or hit her hip on the corner of a table at the café, but the quadruple hit on all four extremities was too much. She felt like all of the blood in her body was running out of her head and into her hands.

"Oh, wow," exclaimed the woman as she pulled her free hand through her red hair. "You're bleeding pretty good. It looks like you are turning a little pale too." Leaning down and taking a closer look at Sarah.

"Hey, do I know you?" Tori puzzled as she continued to study Sarah's face.

"No, I don't think so," Sarah replied quickly as she took her eyes off of her wounds to look the woman straight in the face.

"I'm not really from around here."

"Here, let me see your hands," the woman commented as she took Sarah's bloodied hands into hers. "My sister is a nurse, and she showed me a few things." After a slight pause, she added in a tentative voice as she pulled pieces of gravel out of Sarah's palm.

"So what brings you around these parts then?"

"Well," she thought quickly. "I got turned around on the buses, and I guess I got off at the wrong stop."

"Oh," the woman said, still holding Sarah's hands in hers. "That has happened to me before." Looking back at the wounds.

"Hey, these look pretty bad. I live right here." She nodded in the direction of a white house a few doors down. "Please let me help you. It is the least I can do since my dog practically mauled you."

"Well..."

"Perfect! Right this way," the woman said as she led Sarah down the street. "My name is Tori, by the way. And I know you already met Lady here."

"Thanks, Tori," she replied with a grateful look. "I'm Sarah, and yes, we've met," gesturing to the spirited pup as the dog stared up at them after hearing her name.

Tori led the three of them around to the back door and into the kitchen. Lady pranced off to get some water and probably find some other person to pester. Sarah wiggled out of her coat, careful not to get any blood on her clothes; she rinsed her hands in the kitchen sink.

As she looked for a paper towel to dry her hands, she glanced around at the modest furnishings in the small kitchen. The countertops were in a disarray of dirty dishes and piles of unopened mail. She smiled at the normalcy of the quaint little house. The pain in her hands, however, quickly took that smile away. Even though she was frustrated and embarrassed by her fall, she remembered why she was here with this woman. Sarah didn't know how, but she knew that Tori was going to die soon, and she needed to tell her about the love of Christ.

"Sorry about the mess," Tori said self-consciously. She returned with a small first aid kit and sat it on the table. "The cleaning lady is seven-months pregnant and gets in trouble when she stays on her feet too much. My husband would be furious if he knew I was walking Lady. I just needed to get some air."

"No, not a problem," Sarah said with a reassuring smile. "And your secret is safe with me. Anyway, my place is the same way. Except I'm not pregnant, so what's my excuse?"

The room filled with Tori's nervous laughter, but Sarah noticed that she was more relaxed after letting it out. She took out some gauze bandages and gently wrapped her hands. Looking up at a sunflower-shaped clock on the wall, Sarah realized she only had about forty minutes left with this woman. In forty-one minutes, her hostess would be dead. She was thankful that she was inside this stranger's house, and they had already started to talk. Whatever the conversation, Sarah knew she had to get this woman talking about God, and she had to do it soon.

"When are you due?" she asked as she smiled towards Tori's protruding stomach.

"I am being told I could have a Christmas baby," Tori said as she held her belly.

"Perfect," Sarah perked up. "Then you wouldn't have to worry about missing any presents, right?"

Tori's nervous laughter filled the air again, light and child-like. "Yes," she smiled. "And the birthday would be easy to remember. Her and Jesus, right?"

Stunned by the name of Jesus, Sarah replied questioningly.

"Yes, it is the birthday of Jesus, huh." She paused for a moment, "Do you believe in Jesus?"

Now it was Tori's turn to be stunned by the bluntness of this woman. She stared at Sarah for a few moments. Shifting her eyes up and down as she sized her up to see if Sarah was some religious freak.

"I'm not sure," she replied tentatively. "I mean, that's why we have Christmas, right?" She smiled, trying desperately to deflect the conversation she accidentally started.

"Yeah, you're right," Sarah replied with a reassuring smile. "I didn't think about Jesus too much and I even doubted he existed for a long time too. Even though my parents took me to church all of the time, I didn't understand anything more about Jesus other than what you learn from Easter and Christmas movies."

Sarah gingerly pulled out a chair, "Sorry, do you mind if I sit down a minute? My knees are killing me."

"Oh my gosh," Tori exclaimed. "I'm such a terrible hostess. Yes, please sit down. Can I get you a drink? Hot tea? Maybe some water, or I think we have some soda?"

"Tea would be wonderful," Sarah said as she collapsed into a low-back padded chair at the kitchen table, instantly taking some of the pain away from her knees.

Tori darted quickly around the small kitchen. Well, as quick as an eight-month pregnant woman could move anyway. Her nervous movements were highlighted by her pregnant body. She quickly poured some water in the kettle and put the tea bags in the cups. While she was waiting, she took a seat at the table.

Sarah didn't want the momentum of their fledgling conversation to slip away, so she tried a slightly different tactic. "Have you thought of a name for your baby?"

Tori studied the stranger for a moment, then sighed begrudgingly. "Yes, we are going to name her after my husband's mom." Her face changed from concern to pride. "Her name is going to be Abigail."

"Oh, I love that name. Simply gorgeous," Sarah responded with equaled enthusiasm. "Is your husband excited?"

"I know he is, but he doesn't always show it." She looked down at her protruding tummy and rubbed it lovingly.

"He's worried about my health and the finances," she added with a small laugh. "The doctor says everything is OK with the baby," Tori said, looking back at Sarah.

"I'm having a few problems that have forced me on bed rest." She smiled and leaned in closer to her guest. "If he knew I was out walking the dog, he would kill me." Leaning back, "Actually, I think he would kill the dog first. She may be man's best friend, but my husband wouldn't hesitate to throw Lady out if she caused a problem with the baby."

Sarah laughed to herself a little, but only after Tori did it first. Her hands and knees were throbbing so badly that she almost couldn't pay attention. The wounds pulsed in her brain like the ticking of a clock. A clock that was winding down for both of them.

"Well," Sarah finally offered. "Worry can be a good thing. It lets you know he cares. And besides, it isn't anything too serious for you, right?"

"Right," Tori replied encouragingly. "It isn't anything life-threatening or anything like that. I'm sure I'll be fine."

Sarah noticed the look on the woman's face was anything but fine. Lines of freckles on her forehead crinkled in small rows of tension as her eyes welled up.

"But?" Sarah said, letting the word hang in the air, begging the question that was hovering between them like a fog waiting to be cleared.

"But," she said in a matching tone. "I have been thinking

about some pretty dark things lately," she responded without lifting her head. "I have just been worried and thinking about life and death a little too much." Finally, looking up at Sarah with a forced smile.

"Maybe I've been cooped up in this house too long. I am going a little stir crazy."

"You are not crazy, Tori," Sarah said as she tried comforting her. "These are things that everyone must think about at some point. You have a new life growing inside of you. So yeah, I think it is a perfect time to think about life and the hope that comes from it."

Sarah waved her wrapped hand in the air, "And some of us should think about our own mortality a little more often too." Trying to make her hostess smile, she added, "Ya know ... I heard a wild statistic. They say that five out of every five people die sometime in their life."

Tori tried to stop the tears by laughing, but everything came out at once. Her feigned chuckle forced its way out, along with a few tears. She reflexively grabbed some tissues from a box on the table.

"Sorry," Tori said as she wiped her eyes. "I'm just a little overwhelmed about death right now. I keep thinking that I'm going to lose my baby."

"Oh, Tori," Sarah said softly as she leaned closer to her new friend. "I'm the one that should be apologizing. My big mouth says some of the stupidest things sometimes." She knew it was better to not say anything right now. She had said enough already.

Detective Michael Wolfe had spent most of the day doing paperwork, locked to his desk. After his encounter with Sarah

Thompson earlier this morning, he wanted to make sure he cleared his caseload just so he could spend more time focusing on how she was killing people and then disappearing without a trace.

He had taken some time to re-write the final draft of the Councilman Wingfield report, careful to interject Miss Thompson's name in it a few more times. He wanted to lay the groundwork for a search warrant on her residence when the time came. He knew she was hiding something about the murders, and he knew he would find evidence linking them all together somewhere. He had already snooped around the locker room at Gerardo's Café but came up empty. He slipped in early one morning just after they opened and picked the lock on the locker with Sarah's name on it. Not exactly very challenging police work, and definitely not very legal. He knew that he would need hard proof if he was going to convince Lieutenant Bradder. His boss was already taking a chance on Michael by assigning an officer to follow the suspect. If Michael couldn't get something concrete fast, he would lose that help as well.

The freshly brewed cup of black coffee offered him little relief from the stress he was feeling. He had already been in touch with Officer Walters a few times. Miss Thompson had gone straight home after work and had not come out since.

The phone on the detective's desk rang, and the sound made him flinch a little bit. *Funny,* he thought to himself. He could sit tight in a gunfight, but a ringing phone spooked him. The voice on the other end of the call belonged to Detective Dwayne Alexander. When Michael had taken the food pantry's surveillance tape over to Detective Alexander's office, he confided in him about the Thompson killings. Michael wasn't sure why he told the veteran detective at the time, but he knew he wanted a second opinion about his accusations. Alexander told him it was all too suspicious. 'Nothing added up, and it stunk to high heaven,' were the exact terms he used to describe Michael's growing case file. This was all the confirmation he needed to confront Sarah face to face.

"Mike," Detective Alexander asked in a grizzled voice. "Are you still following that woman about all those so-called natural deaths?"

"Yeah, I am," he responded cautiously. "Why? What's up?"

"Well, I was just over here at 40th Street and Shea, and I swear I saw that woman from your photos. She was walking along with some other lady. They were just strolling down the street together."

Michael sat straight up knowing that was his neighborhood. His instincts were tingling as the hair on the back of his neck went rigid. He swallowed through his dry throat and asked the other detective if the woman the suspect was walking next to was pregnant. When the old veteran confirmed it and added that they were out walking a dog, Michael got to his feet in nervous anticipation. He then asked him to describe the dog. After a few curse words about why he would want to know about the dog, Detective Alexander told him it was some kind of brown dog, maybe a Labrador. That was all Michael needed to hear.

"Hey, Dwayne," he asked as the panic set in. "How long ago was that?"

"'bout fifteen or twenty minutes ago. Was that her?"

"I hope not, but I'll let you know." Michael thanked his peer as he slammed the receiver down. He picked it back up again and quickly called Walters. He was supposed to be watching the suspect and report in if she went anywhere. Michael needed to make sure his instincts were wrong this time.

"Walters," he said in a forcibly controlled voice. "Can you confirm that the suspect is still at her apartment?"

"Yes, sir. She hasn't left since she got home from work."

"Can you confirm she is there?"

"Well, I can go check if ya need me to, sir."

The calmness was now gone, and he shouted at the rookie to get his butt up to her apartment and make sure she was still there. Meanwhile, he was going to head over towards where the suspect was seen. Michael knew the area had to be close to his house. He knew the brown-colored dog, and he knew the pregnant woman that was with his suspect. This was too much of a coincidence!

The women had sat silently in the kitchen for a few minutes as Tori composed herself. She had smeared mascara just underneath each eye from the tears she was trying to hide.

"Do you mind if we talk in the living room?" Tori said as she reached her hand around and pressed on her lower back. "These chairs are wreaking havoc on my body."

"Sure," Sarah said, standing up. "You lead the way, and I'll bring the tea."

They went down a short hallway that opened up to a nicely furnished front room. Tori settled into one end of the deep sofa, and Sarah took a seat at the other end. She turned her body to face Tori.

"So, tell me, Tori," she said softly. "What do you think about the whole religion thing?"

"Well, I can tell you that I'm not too keen on the whole idea." Tori saw the question on Sarah's face before she asked it, so she beat her to the punch.

"OK. See, I grew up in a house where you were taught to take care of yourself. My dad was a good man. He was a Marine Drill Sergeant, and he always told us that religion was for the weak people that could not survive on their own. He did whatever it took to take care of us."

Sarah shifted on the sofa. She knew the familiar view of religion that she held so close for so many wasted years.

"I know what he meant, but it's not really like that." She thought for a moment and added, "It sounds like you love your dad."

"Yes, I love him dearly," she said, a bit startled by the change in conversation. "He's retired now and lives in Florida with my mom."

"So, he's a military man," Sarah said with a genuine smile. "That's great! None of my family was ever in a war unless you consider when they started talking about the feud between the Cowboys and the Steelers." The women rolled their eyes and chuckled.

"Seriously though, was your dad ever in a war?"

Tori thought about it for a moment. "Yeah, he was. He told me that he spent some time in the Vietnam War. Terrible stuff," she added as she shook her head, thinking of some horrible memory.

"I guess there is some truth to the term, war is hell, right? Was he injured?" Sarah asked, trying not to be too obvious that she was leading the conversation.

"As a matter of fact, I think he was." Tori looked as if she was looking at a point somewhere in the far-off distance. "Yes, he received a purple heart for fighting off an attack." Her face lit up with a big smile. "He even received a commendation for valor."

"Wow," Sarah said with pure enthusiasm. "He sounds like an amazing man." She paused for a minute. "Did he need a medic or someone to fix him up when he got hurt?"

"Oh yeah. My mom would tell me stories about all that," she said, still smiling. "He spent some time at an Army hospital, and that's where he met my mom. She was a nurse."

"That's so beautiful! A true love story. I love it." She paused again, thinking about exactly how she wanted to phrase the next statement.

"Does he ever think that the doctors were a crutch to help him get better?" Before Tori could answer, Sarah added more to her line of questioning.

"They were vitally needed, right? Without the doctors' help, your dad might have been injured more, or worse."

"Well, sure. I guess so," Tori finally responded with a quizzical look on her face.

"That kind of leads me to think about how we need help sometimes. Too often people get hurt spiritually, and they need help." Sarah paused again. This time it was to let her last comment have some time to find home. "They are wounded by life, like a tragic loss, or a divorce, or death, or any one of life's terrible tragedies. And without Jesus, those people will die spiritually. Just like your dad needed the doctor to heal him, people need Jesus to heal them, or else they will never find Heaven."

Tori shifted uneasily. Being as pregnant as she was, nothing looked easy when she moved. Sarah wasn't sure if her words were landing somewhere in the woman's psyche, or if she had already put up her mental shield. Repelling her words without giving them a second thought. Either way, she knew she needed to reach this woman, for her and her unborn baby. Sarah watched as her new friend grabbed a small green pillow and started to twist it mercilessly between her fingers.

"Tori," Sarah said as she reached over to touch Tori's hands gently. "Has anyone ever talked with you about Jesus?"

"No, not really, I guess," she replied nonchalantly. "I mean, people have talked about Jesus around me. I'm not entirely ignorant of religion or anything, but if you mean has anyone come knocking on my door and wanted to talk about where I would go after I die, then I would say the answer is no."

CHAPTER TWENTY-TWO

Michael had a cell phone in one hand and the steering wheel in the other. He gripped both like his life depended on them. He had raced out of the precinct parking lot so fast that he didn't even bother to check out with dispatch about his location. If he was right, his boss would understand. If he was wrong, then he would have some explaining to do when he got back. Weaving his way through traffic like a race car driver, his mind kept fighting against the logic that could not be real.

Moreover, he would have to explain why he thought it was prudent to race across town solely on a hunch. If his instincts were right, he knew Sarah was guilty of multiple homicides. Now the killer could be out having a leisurely stroll with his wife.

"Walters? Well, is she there?" he screamed into the phone.

The young officer had gone up and knocked a few times on Sarah's door, but got no response. He even used a line that he had practiced since he was a little boy playing cops and robbers.

"Open up! This is the police!" When he still got no answer,

he reluctantly called Detective Wolfe back. He was not ready for what came next.

"Knock the door down, Walters," Detective Wolfe shouted.

"What? Are you serious?" the rookie asked. He knew he shouldn't have said it as soon as it left his mouth. The words just came out when he thought about crashing through this woman's door without a warrant.

"Yes, I am absolutely serious," the detective barked. "If you know for a fact that she didn't come out of her apartment and she is not answering the door, then she is obstructing justice." Michael knew he was lying and treading on thin ice, but he had to find out if she was there. He had no legal ground to ask Walters to break the door down, but his instincts were going wild, and they were never wrong. He just hoped he could convince the young officer into doing it.

"Sir, you are telling me that I don't need a warrant to enter her home?" he asked with a noticed waver in his voice.

"What I am telling you is that the suspect you have been observing is known to be in that apartment, but she is not responding," he shouted into the phone, trying to maintain a feigned calmness to his voice.

"For all you know, she could be hurt or worse in there. Heck, son, you might just be saving her life." Now he knew he was grasping at straws.

"That sounds like pretty shaky ground, sir. Do you think someone would believe that I am entering for her safety?" he asked in a hopeful voice. Looking for some sense of truth as to why he was about to illegally break into a suspect's apartment.

"Rookie, need I remind you?" Michael asked in a now commanding voice. "You told me you saw this woman vanish into thin air. Should I put that in my report about your first assignment? That you were seeing people disappear." He knew the suspect could somehow vanish into thin air. He had seen it for himself. She would be in one frame of video, and then less than a second later, she would be gone from sight. He also knew what he was doing to the young officer was wrong, but he still needed answers.

"No, sir," Officer Walters replied with a nervous, defeated tone. "Hold the phone. I'll try the door."

Michael could hear the young officer call to Sarah one more time. Calling out to her to open the door for the police. There was a short silence before the booming sound of the young man's voice came through as he shouted to let anyone inside know he was going to enter the property. After a short pause, he heard the loud thump followed by an audible grunt. The sound of splintering wood filled the phone's receiver. Michael pictured the rookie slamming through the thin door and charging in. He hoped that he would find the suspect sitting quietly in her apartment. Frightened and alone in her living room and not anywhere near his wife.

Detective Wolfe heard Officer Walters' words, but they didn't register. His fears had already told him what the rookie would find. The apartment was empty, and his prime suspect was gone. If his instincts were right, then his murder suspect was dangerously close to his family.

Sarah thought for a moment as she sipped her tea. The chamomile flavor was great, but the opportunity to pause the conversation was even better. It gave her a quick second to collect her thoughts. And to her surprise, it gave her a chance to pray. *God, please give me the words and wisdom to reach this woman. Amen.* It was still odd that she felt so natural to pray at a time like this. Although, it was amazing how much she had changed in the past few days.

"I appreciate your honesty, Tori," Sarah said as she set

her cup down on the table. Her palms still throbbed from the deep cuts, but they were getting better with the medicine and bandages. "Sometimes, we find God in the strangest places. Most of the time, we find Him because we are looking for Him. Jesus said that all who search for Him will find Him."

"But I'm not sure that I am actually searching for Him," Tori interrupted defensively. "I will admit that I am curious about death and about what happens after we die, but I wouldn't say I'm *looking* for Jesus."

"But death could be considered a good reason for seeking Jesus," Sarah replied quickly. "Finding Him is the only way to save us from a life of eternal hell."

Tori's eye widened at the words. "Hell? Oh, I never said anything about hell." She nervously brushed her hands along her pants. "I don't believe I'm going to hell when I die. I think I'm a good person, and I don't think God would send a good person to hell."

"Oh Tori," Sarah pleaded. "Being good in life isn't good enough in death. Think of it this way. What if a person hurt you deeply," she paused for a second. "Say, this person hurt your baby." She watched Tori squirm at the thought.

"Now say this person is brought before a judge. How would you feel if that judge let the person go because that person was nice to everyone else and was good in every other way?"

"I would be angry," Tori said sharply. Her face reddened. "Very angry!"

"Exactly. We want justice for the wrongs committed against us. A perfect judge would hold that person accountable for their actions. Regardless of how good they were with everything else in their life. Right?"

"Yes! Definitely."

"Well, God is that perfect judge," Sarah said lovingly. "He will hold us accountable for the things we have done wrong. It's called sin."

"OK, so now we're screwed," Tori interrupted. Her bottom lip quivered with raw emotion.

Without trying to hide her growing frustration, she quipped, "If we can't be good enough to go to Heaven and God is going to send us to hell anyway, what's the point of living?"

Sarah slid a little closer across the couch as she reached out and took Tori's trembling hands in hers. The pain she felt in her hands was nothing compared to the pain in her soul. She wanted this woman to hear what she was about to tell her.

"That's the thing. God loves us so much that He doesn't want us to die and go to hell." Tori's face wrinkled with evident frustration and disagreement.

"Hear me out," Sarah said as she raised her hands defensively. "The Bible tells us that God loved us so much that he sent his only son to earth. To die at the hands of evil men." She paused and finished in a voice just above a whisper.

"He loved us even before we loved Him. He is the perfect judge, but He is an even better Father."

The sound of Detective Wolfe's police siren was only momentarily overpowered by the sound of his car's squealing wheels as he rounded the corner and turned onto Greenway Road. He was pushing the car harder than he had ever done before, and he was more than a little worried about causing an accident.

Michael called the house again but still got no answer. He even tried to call Mrs. Kelly, a stay-at-home mom up the street, but her line just rang through to voicemail. Something wasn't right, and it was making the hairs on his neck tingle, and that was not a good thing.

He kept running the scenario through his head. Sarah Thompson was a normal, average woman on paper. She didn't show up on any police radar, so technically she was not even a suspect outside of his infatuation with her. But all the pieces didn't fit together. How was it possible that she could be at the scene of multiple deaths? According to the numbers and timelines that he compiled, Miss Thompson was at the scene of each death within an hour or so of the victim's demise. If this woman was with Tori, and he knew it had to be her, then it gave him less than an hour to save her. His foot pressed the gas pedal to the floor, pushing the car to go even faster, even if by sheer willpower.

The thought of God being a loving father was precisely what Tori needed to hear. Her father wasn't a loving sort, and she had always sought that affection from him. As she grew up and understood him more, she knew that he wasn't that kind of man. She also knew that he could never be the kind of father she needed. It was one of the reasons why she married Michael. He was a loving man that was excited about showing her the love she looked for. She knew he would love their daughter the same way. The tears started to wash her face as she tried to turn away from Sarah.

"Sorry," she said as she wiped her tears away. "I'm just a mess. Hormones and all."

"No," Sarah said reassuringly. "You're perfect."

A slight smile broke through the tears. Tori patted Sarah's hand that was still holding one of hers. "I guess I'm just all messed up in the head. What you said about God being a loving father really hit home for me. My dad wasn't always the kind of dad that you would run to if you needed a shoulder to cry on." A short laugh came to her.

"On the contrary, he was the kind of dad that you would call on if you needed to talk sports or politics. Or if I had an ex-boyfriend that had to be reminded to stay away."

Tori turned her puffy eyes to Sarah. "I guess that's why I act the way I do sometimes."

"I understand and trust me ... I know all about having problems," she reassured her with a smile. "When someone is sick physically, they need a doctor, right?" Sarah remembered something that Pastor Ryan told her.

"Jesus even said that He didn't come to the earth to heal the healthy, but He came to heal the sick. We are all sick spiritually and need His help to get healthy."

"Well, I feel fine ... physically," Tori said. Sarah could see the anguish on the young woman's face. She could read the tension that sat just below Tori's words. There was something that she was not telling her.

"But?"

"But I'm not sure about all of this," Tori said with a wave of her hand.

"OK ... all of *what* stuff?" Sarah pressed. She knew she had the woman thinking about God, and that was the hardest part. If Tori had any questions and problems, at least Sarah knew she could hit those head-on. Still, if she genuinely wanted Tori to accept Christ as her Savior, she would need to get her talking about those problems.

"Well," Tori started sheepishly. "Don't get me wrong. I believe in God and know that Jesus came to Earth." She paused for a moment.

"I'm just not sure if I am ready to give my life to Jesus. I understand what you're saying, and I appreciate that you care, but I'm not ready to give him control."

"Control?" Sarah asked quizzically. "Is that what this is

about?"

Tori looked at her and slowly nodded in agreement but didn't have the conviction of someone that had thought her answer through.

"Oh, Tori," Sarah said in a caring tone. "I have learned over the years that control is just an illusion. Even before I came to Christ, I knew I didn't have control. As much as I wanted my parents not to die, I couldn't control it. When I watched my mom pass away right in front of me, I realized I had no control over the things around me." Sarah's eyes were jeweled with tears.

"Then, I went into a spiral of depression after the funeral. It was only just recently that I truly came to God and realized just how little control I had. God is in control, whether we believe in him or not." Sarah perked up and sat back.

"Like as if I wanted to have my boss's job. If I had control, then I could go take it without any problems, but I don't have true control over my life. I think I am in control of so many factors in the real world that I forget just how powerless I am in life." She paused, staring out the window.

"That is until I understood that God was my power. I am at my freest when I give Him 100% control," she said confidently. To her surprise, it was the most trustworthy statement she had made in a long time, and the power of it struck her. This was the first time she actually admitted it. Over the past few days, there were times when she would tell God that He needed to be in control because what she was doing was too crazy. Yet, she never really looked at it from the spectrum of her entire life. She didn't have control, and that was OK. At this exact moment, she genuinely understood what Pastor Ryan had meant when he said following Jesus would bring freedom. It is the sheer fact that a believer is not in control of their own life, nor are they capable of earning eternal life and *that* makes all this so freeing.

"Wow," Tori said. She stared at some unseen spot far away.

"I guess I never really looked at it that way." She sighed, "I don't know, maybe you're right."

Sarah could see her new friend's face contort as she continued to wrestle with her emotions. A fierce war erupting before her very eyes between this woman's logical desire for a false impression of control and the grace-soaked free gift that comes through submission to a Savior could not see yet. Sarah didn't want to say anything more. She knew God was working on this woman's heart, and it was best to just let her think.

Tori's face did indeed reflect the storm of thoughts and emotions boiling just underneath the surface. She had hoped that it would be easier to say yes or no to the notion of accepting Jesus. In theory, it seemed so easy when people got down on their knees and prayed for God to come into their lives. She had seen it in movies and even at a few funerals. It's funny how death brings the thought of life into better focus. Tori knew death was what opened the door to this conversation in the first place, and she found herself strangely thankful for it.

"Oh, Sarah," she said with a deep exhale. "I'm just so confused. I think I know what is right, but my mind won't let my heart do what it wants to."

CHAPTER TWENTY-THREE

Detective Wolfe could have driven to his house with his eyes closed. His muscle memory had controlled his movements countless times when he would come home too tired to think straight. There were times after long stakeouts when he didn't even remember driving home, but he would find himself sitting in his driveway with the car idling. He was thankful that he knew where to go even though his mind wasn't actively telling him where to turn. Today was one of those days. His mind was so distracted that he surprised himself when he turned sharply onto his street.

White smoke floated up from his tires as he screeched the car to a stop just inches from his wife's Highlander SUV. At first, nothing seemed out of the ordinary, but his eyes started to take stock of his surroundings. Not only was nothing out of the ordinary. As a matter of fact, there was nothing. Period. Nothing or no one moved on the street. It had always been a quiet neighborhood, but there were constantly kids playing or somebody out for a jog during any time of the day or night. As he quickly glanced up and down the street, the detective instincts kicked in, and Michael felt the hair on the back of his neck stand up again. Something was wrong. This place was too quiet. The only movement he could see was the gentle rustling of the leaves, but even those looked like they were moving in slow motion.

The sun sank quickly, and the shadows were already growing thick across the front door of his house. Just shy of running, he took the ten-foot walkway leading up to the front in three massive strides. He would have made it to the door in only a few seconds, if not for the scene that stopped him cold. He felt the air sucked out of his lungs as he looked into the front bay window.

◆ ◆ ◆

Sarah sat on the edge of this woman's couch, trying frantically to think of how to get her to give her life to Christ. Just thinking about that thought sounded funny. For human beings to have a loving relationship with Jesus, they have to surrender themselves. They have to submit or surrender their minds and their wills to His. For years she thought surrender meant failure. She saw it as the world saw it. When one person surrenders to someone or something, they become a slave to that person or thing. They instantly move to a lower class of citizen. It was then that Sarah remembered what Pastor Ryan told her about Paul becoming a slave to his calling. It was a fantastic example of how a strong and dominant person like Paul actively and knowingly submitted himself to Christ. It is encouraging to see how that relationship works for someone that had already given their heart to Christ, but how does someone convince a non-Christian to believe this illogical fallacy?

Sarah felt a chill come through the house as the alarm on her watch started to beep. It was as if someone opened the door to a winter's morning. The air seemed to grow colder with every beep from her wristwatch. When she looked around, she felt the coldness grow even tighter like a hand gripping at her. A thousand icy fingers clawed at her spine when she saw him. She looked up and there was the dark, shadowy outline of Azrael standing just behind Tori.

"It is time," he said with the same coldness he'd used every other time someone's life was about to end. It must have been the same coldness that came from his heart when he took the people in the prime of their life.

Sarah stared blankly at Tori. Waiting for the woman to turn around in horror to notice the strange man standing in her living room. Instead, Tori just sat there. Still as a statue. Her eyes were open, but they were devoid of any movement at all. She looked like a zombie just frozen in time. Sarah suddenly remembered where she had seen that look before.

"You froze time again?" she asked sarcastically. Staring at the hard lines in Azrael's face. Were those lines there before, or did he grow more callous looking with every death. She wondered if these deaths took a toll on him. *Do they hurt him in some way?*

"I thought it would be easier this way," he said, again devoid of any emotions that would tell her what was going on in his head.

"Easier?" she scoffed. "How can any of this be made easier?" she said as she shook her head. "You can't have her yet. I need more time." She stopped to look back at Tori. "She needs more time!" she said, raising her voice.

"She has had her whole life to know what she needed to know. You even presented it to her, and she still refused," he said with a slight hint of gentleness in his voice.

"Others have tried, and yet, she has continued to remain defiant. You are not the first person that has talked with her about her salvation, but you will be the last."

"But she is so close," she said frantically. "I know in my heart that she is close to accepting Jesus. She is close to making the right decision. I just need more time!"

"How close is close, Sarah?" he asked in an accusatory tone. "How much time do you think these people should get? People have opportunities to listen to the truth. No one passes from this earth without the chance to make a choice. Thankfully, some of the lost sheep come home and give their hearts to Him, who sits on the Throne. Others listen and harden their hearts to the truth. They are the truly lost ones because they know the truth, yet they refuse to believe in it."

Azrael's blue eyes bore into Sarah. "Then, there are others that flatly ignore even the existence of Heaven or hell and in their ignorance, forego the ability to decide, but their indifference makes the choice for nothing at all."

His body seemed to grow in size with each word he spoke. The shadows filled the room behind him, darkening the corners and blocking the fading sunlight that came in from the windows. Suddenly, and with a speed the stunned Sarah, the large man moved around from behind the frozen pregnant woman and directly in front of Sarah, separating her from her new friend.

"Either way, Tori Belle Wolfe has had enough time in this life to decide as to where she will spend the rest of eternity!" he boomed.

Detective Michael Fitzpatrick Wolfe stood frozen in mid-stride. The concrete sidewalk that led to his front door seemed to grab the bottoms of his shoes with incredible strength. The blank expression on his face told the story of his mind's inability to process what he was seeing. Through the large bay window in the front of his house, the same place he would come home to every day and see his wife, he saw the one person he had been tailing for weeks. This woman that he was sure was involved in at least three murders was now standing right in the middle of his living room. This time, he noticed, she wasn't alone. Now a man was standing in the living room with her. *This must be her accomplice,* he thought. *This must be how she was able to kill people without actually moving or even touching them directly.* Michael could see these two were having some sort of argument by their actions and body language. The female suspect was red-faced and yelling up at the taller man. He looked to be average-sized; dressed in all black with jet black hair. His stoic face showed he was taking all the abuse he could handle from this woman.

Watching with amazement at the strange circus that unfolded in front of him, Michael had almost forgotten about his wife. His eyes darted around the room. He hoped that maybe she wasn't even there. Perhaps she had gone out before these two got there. His stomach sank when his vision finally came to rest on his wife seated on one end of the couch, nearly blocked from his sight by the man's flowing jacket. His wife had an odd look on her face, almost mannequin-like. She didn't move or react to anything that was going on just a few feet in front of her. Michael knew right away that something was very wrong with her.

"Tori!" he shouted with fear in his voice. The deep voice that had commanded so many people to do what he wanted just simply bounced off the window and echoed in his head. No one in the room paid him any attention. Then Michael moved like someone had put a lightning bolt through him. He raced to the front door and grabbed the handle. It was locked. Fumbling for his keys, he listened to the voices coming from just inside the house. The keys clumsily fell to the ground when he heard his wife's full name being shouted by the male suspect. Grabbing for them again, he found his house key and tried to push it in the lock. Something was stopping the key from sliding into the hole. He had heard of burglars using crazy glue to prevent homeowners from coming into the house before they were finished, but there was nothing on the lock. The key would not slide into the tumblers.

"Open this door!" he shouted wildly. "This is the police!" Grabbing the door handle again, he gave the door a shove with his shoulder. Michael was not a big man, but years of experience taught him how to break through a locked door. When it didn't budge from the force of his shoulder, Michael reared back and slammed his foot into the door just next to the handle.

Azrael's voice still hung in the air. Sarah dropped her head, but she could still feel his cold eyes fixed on her downcast face. Her shoulders slipped slowly to the sides as she came to grips with the fact that he was right. Tori did have time. She spent the last hour giving this woman a chance to reconcile her sins with Jesus, but even after all her ploys and arguments, Sarah still had no effect. If Azrael was right, others had tried to talk with her as well. Sarah was not the only person who had talked with Tori about her salvation. It didn't matter what Sarah's emotions told her; her mind was right. Azrael *was* right, but her heart knew that it was wrong. This was all wrong, and something had to be done.

Sarah stared past the powerful-looking man. He nearly blocked the small pregnant woman that was still sitting perfectly motionless on the couch. Azrael kept staring at Sarah with his judgmental eyes. She tried not to look back, fearing that he would pierce into her soul. Finally, she had to turn her head to force herself from making eye contact. As she looked around, her eyes came to rest on a small piece of pink cloth. It was sitting on the back of the couch. Folded neatly along with some other clothing. When her mind registered what the fabric actually was, Sarah felt like her world just got tilted on its side. It was a small pink baby blanket.

"What about the baby?" she shouted at Azrael as her head snapped back to face him. She was stunned to see he was still staring at her intently. As if he was trying to read her mind or to get her to read his. Whatever his reason for the glaring stare, she wasn't going to let him win.

"You can't take Tori. The baby will die!" she shouted again.

"The child will pass with the mother," he said in a voice that was way too calm for the situation.

"What? That is ridiculous!" she said passionately. She raised her bruised and torn hand up to point her finger at him. "What choice did that baby have?"

"None," he said flatly. "This child, like all children up to a certain age, is the true innocence of this world. They are taken to Heaven without a thought or a choice. Unlike their adult counterparts, they have not been given that chance to decide either way. Even if they were told the circumstances around such a decision, they would not have had the depth of understanding or cognizance to believe firmly in a choice one way or the other. To an innocent child, they do not understand anything more than today. Tomorrow is a fantasy wrapped in an illusion."

"Damn you, Azrael!" she shouted again. "That's not fair!" Her anger was building inside her. She could feel the adrenaline rushing through her body. She knew she was going to start crying if she didn't calm down. If she lost control, then she would lose this fight. The lives of Tori and the baby were too important. They deserved to live!

"My dear Sarah," Azrael said in an incredibly loving tone. "Have we not been over this before? Life in this world is *not* fair. This is a fallen world filled with sin and unrepentant hearts. Truly, it is not fair when an innocent person gets hurt by someone else, but it does not change the fact that the pain happened. Fairness is too relative to be fully understood. It is like being happy or grateful. One could see fairness in the lion eating the antelope, while others will say it was unfair for the lesser creature." Azrael's eyes were shimmering like deep pools of crystal blue water. There was a sincere depth behind them.

She was slowly losing this fight, but she refused to give in. "Don't give me that line about the natural order of things!" she cried. The wetness was starting to well up in the corners of her eyes. She didn't want to cry. She didn't want to give him the satisfaction of seeing what he was doing to her.

"You enjoy doing this, you monster!" The tears came streaming down her cheeks. "You're not even sorry about it!"

The force of Michael's kick should have shattered the door frame. Instead, it just sent waves of pain back through his leg. The door didn't budge. Panicked at his lack of success, Michael ran back to the front of the house to see if he could get his wife to open the door.

The scene was much the same. The woman was still yelling, and the man was still standing between her and Tori. Quickly Michael tried to make eye contact with his wife, but instead of getting her attention, Michael was stunned by what he heard. He found himself listening to the entire conversation in the room directly in front of him.

A few years ago, Tori and Michael had installed double-paned glass windows in the house. The kind that would keep the heat and the noise outside—a smart investment in Arizona. They had always enjoyed the quiet that the windows gave them even though their house was just off of a busy roadway. With all the sound-suppression built into the windows, Michael still heard the two people talking as if he was standing in the room with them. He reflexively put his hand to his ears, but the sound didn't change. He wasn't even sure what was happening, but he knew that he shouldn't be able to hear the conversation with this kind of clarity.

Still staring at the strange scene, he heard the man in black say that his baby must go with the mother. *Was he talking about Tori and his unborn child*, he thought as panic gripped him again. He found himself transfixed by the conversation. He wanted to run inside and stop the madness, but his body just froze in abandoned voyeurism. All he could do was watch helplessly.

◆ ◆ ◆

"Sarah, I will not say I am sorry about taking these souls to their final destination. By doing so would mean this event is somehow wrong. Death is not something a person has control over, so why would a person say sorry for it." His voice was noticeably agitated. She was getting to him, and she liked it.

"To your former point. I have told you before. Death is not something I am happy about, nor do I enjoy taking these souls away." He looked at Sarah with soft eyes. "I am no monster, Sarah. The monsters are pride and selfishness that harden the hearts of these people. Regardless of their decision here on this earth, their departure leaves sadness, grief, anger, and loneliness."

His voice dropped to a whisper. "I do not envy or desire any of those feelings. I do not wish them on anyone. I am sorry for your frustration, but one thing is for certain ... I am taking a soul back with me today."

His words hit her like a punch to her stomach. Her body grew weak, and she dropped to her knees in front of him. The pain from the cuts on her knees flared up and reminded her of the deep wounds. She just ignored the problem on the outside. Trying desperately to suppress her pain on the inside—the ever-growing feeling that death brings. Her tears were still coming as they formed tiny trails and dropped silently to the floor. She closed her eyes and took a deep breath. To her own amazement, she prayed a quiet prayer. Taking another deep breath, she opened her eyes and stared up at the dark figure.

"Then take mine," she said in just above a whisper.

There was a surprising curiosity in the dark man's blue eyes. Stunned by her command, Azrael reached down and helped Sarah back up.

"Sarah Thompson, that is not how it works," he said quickly, trying to refute her wish.

Wiping the tears away with her hands, "You once told me that if I did anything wrong when I spoke to the people, you would take my soul instead." She lifted her head to meet him eye to eye as best she could.

"Now, I want to do something right. The rules should still stand."

Azrael watched her for a full minute. Watching her as she straightened her back. Trying in vain to reach his level, but here she was giving him an ultimatum. He could see her veil of strength slipping. And yet, through the fading illusion of her facade, he could see the fire that burned brightly inside of her. The edges of his lips curled slightly. He had to admit that he admired that fire.

"Do you truly understand what you are asking?" he questioned her sternly.

"Yes, I do," she said confidently. "I will go instead of them. Leave Tori and the baby here. To live and to love." She paused. "And hopefully have enough time to make the right decision when you come back for them."

"Sarah, this would mean you would go to the place where they were going." He stepped aside so she could see the pregnant woman again. "At least the place where the woman is going."

She swallowed hard against the sudden dryness in her throat. "I know," she forced out in a whisper.

"Are you ready to die for this person?" he asked accusingly. "This woman whom you just met a little over an hour ago? Do you care for this woman enough to sacrifice your life for hers?"

"Yes," Sarah quivered with as much conviction as she could muster. "And the baby."

"Then you must say it out loud. You must declare it," his voice grew in volume. "You need to own it!"

She took a deep breath. "I wish to give my soul in exchange for the lives of Tori and her unborn baby." Her voice betrayed her confidence as she tried to sound in control.

"I understand that by doing this, I will be ..." her voice cracked. "... taken to hell as a substitute for Tori. I just pray that someone will talk to them about making the right decision for Christ."

He placed his hand on her shoulder. "You know you cannot confirm whether this sacrifice will ever bring them closer to salvation or not. Free will makes that impossible to foresee. She may still end up in eternity apart from God."

"I know," she said as she looked at the ground. "I just want to have faith that God will not give up on her."

"Believe me," he said lovingly. "He never will."

Sarah flinched back when Azrael moved toward her. Fresh tears filled her eyes.

"Relax, my child," Azrael said like a loving father talking to a daughter. He raised his hand slowly and touched Sarah's forehead with his fingertips. His bright blue eyes wrapped in tears as well.

"It is finished now."

The room began to fill with a light as strong as the brightest Arizona noon-day sun. Sarah instinctively raised her hand to shield her eyes, but she was surprised to see that the light was coming from her. She stared at the back of her hand as it glowed with an unearthly radiance. The rest of the room started to fade into brightness. Sarah's eyes lifted up from her hand to see Azrael was glowing too. His once dark outline was now shining with a similar illumination.

It wasn't the sudden light that surprised Sarah. It wasn't even the familiar floating feeling she usually experienced whenever Azrael would take her to each appointment. It was what she saw right before her eyes. Azrael began to transform. The person that she feared and sometimes hated slowly started to change into something completely different. His dark hair reflected a lighter color. A soft brown, or maybe it was from the light shining around him. The dark clothes were falling away, as well, the black leather duster, the black slacks and shirt ... everything.

In its place, Azrael was adorned in a white flowing robe, shimmering as if it had a million stars sewn into the fabric. It reminded her of the kind of robe a monk might wear. It was made of pure white cloth. The light seemed to reflect off it like it was glass. The soft fabric swayed and shimmered lightly around him.

When Sarah looked up from his captivating new attire, she was equally startled by the smile that greeted her. Azrael was still there, or at least the eyes and face looked like him, but his features were changed. His face was somehow softer. His clean-shaven face was replaced by a light brown beard and mustache. Each one perfectly trimmed, so it framed his face. His once short black hair was now golden brown and flowed down past his shoulders.

As the glow intensified, the image of Azrael changed. Everything about him was different, yet it all felt very familiar to her. Everything about him screamed at her as if she saw something that she knew she should recognize. Every fiber of her being wanted to call this man exactly what he looked like. He looked just like …

"Yes, Sarah," came a voice inside her head. It was Azrael's voice, but it was so deep and filled with compassion. "I am He."

"Jesus?" she whispered.

"Yes, my child," He said as He put both hands on her shoulders. "I am as you see Me."

"How? Why?" she exclaimed.

Jesus gently smiled. "My daughter, the spark in you was there long before My time with you. It just needed to be fanned into the flame burning brightly in your heart now. If I came as a mighty wind and told you who I truly was from the beginning, the spark would have been blown out."

"Long ago, I spoke in parables so the ones that earnestly wanted to find Me, would seek Me with their whole heart. Some heard what they wanted to hear, and they were not able to advance My Kingdom. But to those that heard My true message and sought Me with all they had—those were the ones that were fit to be called the Children of God."

"Today, Sarah, you have learned how to love someone so much that you are willing to die so that they may live. Even if they do not understand or even want your sacrifice. Even if they do not even know the truth about My love for them, you are still willing to lay your life down for theirs." A soft smile crossed His lips as He looked at her straight in the eyes. Even though Azrael, or now Jesus, was a full head taller than Sarah, they were both looking eye to eye. He held her there—suspended in mid-air as the world around them faded away.

"Now you know what it takes to be My disciple," He raised His hand to her eyes and gently shut her eyelids. "And now it is your turn."

CHAPTER TWENTY-FOUR

Sarah felt the hand of Jesus leave her face. She wanted to open her eyes and look around so badly, but the weightlessness lifted her body like a feather in a soft wind. She knew right away; this was different from any of her other trips. This was not another trip to see any of the appointments that Azrael, or Jesus, sent her to. Through her eyelids, she could see it was so bright. The darkness never came over her like in the past. Finally, forcing her eyes open, she was stunned as the air around her shone with the light of million tiny suns. Each one filling its own little area with a powerful light. The glow was intense and filled the room. There were no shadows that could stand against this fierce radiance. Sarah brought her hand up to shield her eyes, but it was no use. The light formed all around her. Every inch of her skin glowed as if she were covered in tiny mirrors. The radiance wrapped itself entirely around her, coming to her and from her at the same time.

So … this was the end, she thought. It was everything that people said it would be. The white light. The weightlessness. Seeing Jesus. She remembered hearing about all those people that would describe death. Most of them were written off as being crazy. She wondered if what people might think about her stories—would they even listen to her. She'll never get that chance now, but she was OK with it.

Her new friend, Tori, carried a life inside her. She had that chance to make a difference. One life is no better or worse than another, but when one life was about to give birth to a new generation, it held a greater magnitude. It held hope. People needed hope. Hope brought them to a place where they could rise above the mess of life. It provided the strength to raise a child despite the earthly circumstances.

Hope led people to seek something more significant than themselves. Something that would take them somewhere they couldn't get to on their own. Hope led to faith, and faith led to Jesus. Sarah was OK with it. Surprisingly, she was OK with the idea of dying. She hoped that the people at the café would be OK too. She hoped that Gerardo and Robyn, and the other servers would take care of her customers—the special ones that came into her section just to share time with her. She wished she could see them again. She would tell them about Jesus and about how precious time is.

With each second, the light started to fade away as the powerful glow grew dim. Sarah still felt the weightlessness, but nothing was moving or happening. Everything was just growing darker. Small tendrils of inky black fog pressed in against the fading light. Even though she hoped her sacrifice would be enough to save her, Sarah knew Azrael needed to take a soul. Since she took the place of Tori, Sarah was heading to an eternal place apart of her Savior.

The more she watched the encroaching darkness, the more she realized the little light that was left was radiating from her. A faint luster outlined her body. The luminescent surface of her skin pushed back the increasing darkness. She tried forcing her body to make the light stronger, but the light slowly surrendered its hold on her world. Finally, the darkness made its way to her and wrapped around her body, engulfing her in its shadowy cocoon.

Yet Sarah wasn't afraid—she was filled with a sense of comfort and peace. She no longer feared the darkness anymore or what it could do to her. She had the Light of God within her, and nothing could take that away again.

Minutes seemed like hours, but nothing happened. The murkiness of the black fog stayed around her like an unending blanket. She patiently waited for the end. She longed to see the glorious face of Jesus again.

She wasn't sure how long this transition would take. Time had no bearing or purpose here. None of the people that described death ever spoke of this kind of darkness. Maybe once the light faded, there was no going back. Once they stepped past this point, there was no return.

That is when she heard a voice. A muffled sound at first, but it was definitely a voice. It sounded like someone talking far away. The voice was resonant and deep. The kind that echoed throughout her mind. She strained to hear it again. Was it talking to her? It was definitely a voice. A male voice. She could hear the bass coming from the sound, but the words were still too distant to hear.

Sarah's heart raced when she heard the words get clearer. It was as if she was coming up out of the water when someone was trying to talk to her. As each moment passed, she fought to listen, straining with everything she had on the words as if they would save her from the darkness. When she finally heard the words and understood what they were saying to her, her body went rigid and listened with a laser-like focus on the voice.

"Sarah, it is time to wake up from your slumber," came the now clear voice. "Time to wake up."

In an instant, Sarah felt her body press against something.

The weightlessness was gone, and she was lying down on something soft. Her mind raced, trying to make sense of everything.

What kind of slumber was she in, she thought. How could someone wake up from death? This isn't at all how she imagined it would be. As the voice faded, a variety of new sounds welled up—each one rushing to her awareness like tiny explosions flashing in the darkness. The sounds were vaguely familiar. She thought she knew the sounds, but these shouldn't be with her in Heaven. There were the sounds of nearby traffic. The high-pitched honking of a car horn broke through the darkness like a shaft of light. Then there was the whining sound of a distant police siren, followed clearly by the sound of a barking dog. This must not be Heaven. This couldn't be Heaven. If not Heaven, then where? Maybe she was in hell, and this was her punishment.

She felt her pulse start to race as her breathing became shallow. Not even understanding why she would have a heartbeat or need to breathe in the afterlife, she listened closer. Wait, she thought as panic gripped her tightly. That is not just any dog. That was the sound of Mrs. Shapiro's dog. Sarah would have known that blasted Pomeranian's bark anywhere. It was then that she opened her eyes as if someone had flipped a switch.

Instead of seeing Heaven or the pearly gates, Sarah found herself staring up at the drab white ceiling in her bedroom. She was lying in her own bed. The cottony sheets felt cool against her skin, and the pillow was perfectly soft. She wasn't dead after all—or if she was, this better not be Heaven. If this was indeed Heaven, she was highly disappointed. Sarah knew enough about the Bible to understand what Heaven was supposed to be like, and she knew that there were no barking dogs or wailing sirens.

Sun poured into the room and filled the small bedroom with the bright rays of the morning sunrise. She was wearing the same clothes that she had on when she went to meet Tori.

Sarah rolled over and pushed herself up on her elbow. Sitting on the nightstand was a steaming cup of black coffee. The smell washed over her and brought her fully awake. Looking closer at her nightstand, she noticed her Bible was resting next to the cup. It was opened to a page as if it were calling to her.

Sarah grabbed the open Bible and eagerly pulled it to her. It was open to the Book of John. A passage was highlighted with a bright neon-colored green ink. Reading it out loud, her voice filled the quiet in her bedroom.

John 21:17 - *The third time Jesus said to him, "Simon son of John, do you love me?" Peter was hurt because Jesus asked him the third time, "Do you love me?" He said, "Lord, you know all things; you know that I love you." Jesus said, "Then feed my sheep."*

Underneath the passage was a small yellow sticky note. The handwriting on it was in perfect penmanship. It read,

My Dearest Sarah,

You have discovered what are the most important things in a person's heart—to love God and to love others. With this knowledge, you now know what it takes to love and save the lost.

As I told Simon Peter long ago—now go and feed my sheep.

–Jesus.

Sarah sat, staring at the page. Her eyes dancing from the note to the Bible verse and back again. Letting her eyes read and re-read each word. After a long while, she smiled a broad grin and closed the old book. Reaching for the cup of hot coffee, she settled back against her pillows, knowing what she had to do now. Taking a sip of the delicious brew, she knew what God had wanted her to do all along.

This time … she was ready.

The End

AFTERWORD

Thank you for walking with me (and Sarah) on this incredible journey of forgiveness, faith discovery, and redemption. As we know, life is fragile, and tomorrow is never guaranteed—not even the very next hour for that matter. Each moment we have is a gift, and with it comes an opportunity to make decisions that have eternal significance. As the book comes to a close, I hope it has touched your heart in a profound way. The journey of our characters is a reflection of the greater journey we are all on—a journey that points to the love and redemption found in Jesus Christ.

If you felt a stirring in your heart as you read, that's not by chance. God is reaching out to you, inviting you into a relationship with Him. His love is unconditional, His grace boundless, and His arms are open wide to welcome you just as you are.

The Bible says, *"For God so loved the world that He gave His one and only Son, that whoever believes in Him shall not perish but have eternal life"* (John 3:16). This promise is for you. It's not about what you've done or where you've been. It's about what Jesus has done for you on the cross. He died for your sins, and He rose again, conquering death so that you can have eternal life.

If you're ready to begin this life-changing relationship with Jesus, you can do so right now. All it takes is a simple prayer, spoken from your heart:

The Sinner's Prayer

Lord Jesus, I acknowledge that I am a sinner in need of Your grace. I believe that You died for my sins and rose again to give me eternal life. I confess my sins and ask for Your forgiveness. Come into my heart, Lord, and be my Lord and Savior. Help me to live for You from this day forward. Thank You for loving me and saving me. Amen.

If you prayed that prayer, welcome to the family of God! The Bible tells us that there is great rejoicing in heaven over one sinner who repents (Luke 15:7). Your decision is the most important one you will ever make.

Now that you've taken this step, it's essential to grow in your faith. I encourage you to find a Bible-based church where you can connect with other believers, learn more about God's Word, and walk this journey of faith together. Surround yourself with people who will encourage and support you as you grow in your relationship with Christ.

Also, spend time each day reading the Bible and praying. God's Word is a lamp to our feet and a light to our path (Psalm 119:105), guiding us in truth and righteousness. Prayer is your lifeline to God—a way to share your heart with Him and to hear His voice in return.

Thank you for taking the time to read this story. My prayer is that it has drawn you closer to the heart of God and inspired you to live out your faith boldly. May the grace of our Lord Jesus Christ, the love of God, and the fellowship of the Holy Spirit be with you always.

With humble gratitude and love,

Andy